THREE
BODIES

THREE BODIES

A Reshma Patel and Ian Jack thriller

NR Brodie

MACMILLAN

First published in 2020
by Pan Macmillan South Africa
Private Bag X19
Northlands
Johannesburg
2116

www.panmacmillan.co.za

ISBN 978-1-77010-702-1
e-ISBN 978-1-77010-703-8

Editing by Helen Moffett
Proofreading by Kelly Norwood-Young
Design and typesetting by Triple M Design, Johannesburg
Cover design by publicide

Printed by **novus print**, a division of Novus Holdings

ALSO BY NR BRODIE

Knucklebone (2018)
A Reshma Patel and Ian Jack thriller

'A cracking novel. Brilliant original writing.
The pace is insane – in a good way.'
– SARAH LOTZ, bestselling author of *Missing Person*,
The White Road, *Day Four* and *The Three*

'There are many fantasy thrillers out there but none as uniquely
South African as *Knucklebone*. Every story I was told as a child
about abathakathi and tokoloshes came to life and it was
nothing short of electrifying.'
– PAM MAGWAZA, *Drum* magazine

'Brodie's crisp writing, her short chapters, which often end in nail-biting
cliffhangers and a great plotline drive the narrative along.
She brings all its strands together in a stunning magical finale which
I found highly satisfying ... *Knucklebone's* pace and imaginative prowess is
invigorating. A sequel is something to be wished for.'
– KARINA M SZCZUREK, *Cape Times*

ARCHIPELAGO

Jonas Jiyane stood at the edge of the Hartbeespoort Dam, gumboot soles gripping onto the part of the lawn where the grass turned muddy, and he would slip if he wasn't careful.

The land flowed almost seamlessly into the water, an illusion facilitated by an algal bloom that had been killing off the fish for weeks. The surface of the dam near the lock was covered with floating scum one shade off the rich green of the lawns. The water looked like thick soup and smelled like bad things. Jonas could taste it even when he breathed through his mouth; a slight rot that permeated the air.

A few metres out from the shore, an island of hyacinth floated above the algae, unbothered by the transient invaders, two predators leaving each other alone. Some of the hyacinth plants were in flower, pale lilac preening in the green. It was these that Jonas was after.

Jonas dangled his long pool scoop out over the water and dipped the net, slowly, working his way under and through the growth until he could separate a clump of hyacinth from its neighbours before lifting it and pulling it back to shore.

Behind him was a pile of plants already harvested, perhaps two or three wheelbarrows' worth. By the end of the morning there would be enough to fill the back of a trailer. And when Jonas came again next week, it would be as if he'd never touched the alien mat at all.

1

Jonas didn't complain about the futility of the task. The occasional cropping was enough to keep the hyacinth from clogging the estate's canals, and, if he was honest, he liked being at the water's edge where it was mostly pleasant, algae notwithstanding, and almost always quiet.

On one of his previous hauls Jonas had accidentally netted a fish, dead from the algae. Other gardeners had found plenty more, the yellow-olive ones – Kurpers – and even a few waterfowl. The green water was poisoning the animals, but the golfers remained undisturbed.

Jonas harvested golf balls, too, when they washed up in the silt, or got trapped among the hyacinth clusters. There were at least four golf estates along the dam's perimeter, not including the one at La Gondola.

Jonas didn't get the apparent pleasure of repeatedly hitting a tiny ball into a giant human-made water feature, but he passed no judgement on those who did. One or other of the club members would always give him a few notes for a bucket of balls in good-enough condition. He already had a small haul of dimpled chestnuts stacked in their own pile next to the draining plants. He would need to wash them off before he sold them again – they were all looking decidedly more green than white.

Nobody was sure what had caused the algae to go crazy. Jonas had read a report in the local *Kormorant* that it was because of the sewage coming in from the Jukskei and entering the Crocodile River. Some people at the estate whispered that it was because of chemicals from the nuclear chemical facility at Pelindaba. Jonas and the other gardeners took extra care to wash their hands after working lakeside, but they didn't stop working.

The only thing the algae didn't seem to affect was the hyacinth.

Reach, scoop, lift, repeat. Jonas carried on with his work. He started humming a tune he'd heard on the radio. He wasn't sure what it was called.

By 10 am, Jonas thought he only needed to add a few more nets to his harvest before calling it a morning. The waterline was unobstructed for a few metres along the entire stretch of the lock, where the water from the dam entered the canals that gave the estate its fancy-sounding name.

Jonas stepped closer to the edge, and then almost into the water – he could feel the cold and wet enter his right boot through a tiny hole. He didn't really mind. He wouldn't have to feel it for long, and he could change his shoes back at the staff quarters.

He took another step forward and held out the long metal handle of the net, dipping it under the surface again, aiming for a clump of plants just outside his reach. The hyacinth floated on its own buoyant bulbs hidden beneath the leaves. The roots gradually connected to each other, forming ever-larger networks that would cover the entire surface of the dam, given half the chance. After a moment's calculation, Jonas thought that if he could pull this particular patch of plants a little closer, he'd be able to scoop all of them out easily.

He reversed his approach. He placed the net over one of the plants near the centre and let the plastic lip flop over the sides so it made a laager around the leaves and stems. He pulled, hard enough to yank the plant away from subterranean neighbours, but not so hard as to dislodge the net attached to the pole with a jury-rigged piece of wire.

After a couple of drags, the hyacinth gave way and started bobbing in his direction. Jonas stepped closer, ignoring the water that now filled up his other boot. He pulled the pole towards him, guiding the

3

plant with the net as he did, until he was ready to turn, scoop, and drop.

The net and its cargo carved a wake through the green sludge. Jonas turned the net around and lifted his haul.

As he did so, something in the water caught Jonas's eye. A long black strand, thick as a man's thumb, twisting along the surface as if it was caught in an invisible current. For a moment, Jonas thought that it was a snake and he nearly dropped the pool net in shock. Caution helped him catch his breath and realise that, whatever it was, it was not alive. Just a piece of rubbish, he thought. An old power cable or something someone had chucked off a boat, something that had gotten stuck in the webs of hyacinth, and which had now come ashore.

Jonas reached into the water and pulled on the black strand with his bare hand. The rope felt spongey beneath his fingers. As he pulled, he felt movement on the other end, as if it was attached to something. Something big.

A second later, the water around him filled with more black shapes, more snakes, writhing in the water, reaching for his rubber feet where he stood. He had to stop himself from screaming out loud.

It took Jonas another second to realise that what he was holding in his hand was a length of human hair. And at the other end of the hair was a body.

BRIDGES

The golf cart crawled along the brick causeway in almost complete silence. Only a very faint whirr gave Ian Jack any indication that it was switched on at all. Myburgh had told him it was electric. There were plug stations for the carts all over the estate.

'Do we have to drive in this thing?' Ian asked, feeling stupid, a grown man bundled up inside a toy mobile. 'We could have taken my car.'

Myburgh didn't turn his head. 'None of the roads go straight in this place, and it's further than it looks on the map. You got to cross water, go over canal bridges,' he said, pointing as he steered with the other hand. 'And the bridges are only big enough for the carts.'

Ian thought Myburgh was secretly enjoying the drive.

The older man was wearing mirrored shades that, together with his blue slacks and pale blue shirt, made him look more like an ex-cop than he might have realised. Or, Ian thought, maybe Myburgh knew exactly what he was trying to look like.

It was a perfect autumn day out at the dam. The last of the rains had come over Easter, six weeks ago, clearing some of the sludge from the water. While the rest of the province was slowly turning brown at the edges, the greens at La Gondola were a uniform shade of emerald.

Ian took in a deep breath of almost-country air as Myburgh navigated. There were few street signs in the estate – those that Ian could make out all had Italian names, which Myburgh said were named after bridges – and even fewer house markings. To add to the confusion, all the houses looked more or less the same to Ian's eye: two-storey replicants, rendered in either off-white or off-pink. Ian guessed that in the brochures the colours had proper names, like Tuscan Cloud and Tuscan Sunset. He wondered to himself how visitors knew which of the 150 houses to go to. 'It's the third Tuscan Cloud house on the second block after the corner of Ponto Pugni and Ponto Paglia.'

'What did you say the houses went for here?' he asked.

'The two-bedroomed ones start at five-and-a-half,' Myburgh said. 'Million.'

Ian gave a low whistle. 'Are they nice at least?'

Myburgh paused, and offered an awkward smile. 'It's not so bad. My handicap's down,' he said, looking briefly embarrassed before turning his attention back to the miniature road.

Myburgh's wife had passed away the previous year, finally defeated by the cancer she had fought for so long. Two months after her death, one of Myburgh's old mates had offered him a job as head of security for a group of housing estates on the edge of the Hartbeespoort Dam, an hour north-west of Johannesburg. Myburgh had sold his house and almost everything in it, and had moved out to start a new life in the country. He had been asking Ian to come and visit for months, and Ian felt a twinge of guilt at putting off the trip until now.

He wondered if that was why Myburgh had called him and asked him for help.

'I'm sorry I haven't come sooner, Oom,' Ian said, offering a small apology. 'I meant to, it's just ...' He trailed off.

Myburgh gave a small smile. 'It's fine, Cousin,' he said, the nick-name sliding easily off his lips. 'You needed time, anyway,' the older man said, diplomatically avoiding mentioning Ian's injury. 'You alright now?' Myburgh asked without looking, his concession to personal conversation. Ian knew it wasn't that Myburgh didn't care; it was just that he didn't know how to get into it. Which was fine with Ian, who didn't particularly want to talk about physiotherapy and how his arm still hurt in certain positions two years after he'd been shot. He was mostly fine. It wasn't bad enough to feel justified complaining about any more. He could still type, still drive, still shoot. Ian shrugged, and hoped that was enough of a response for his father's old friend.

'And work's alright? Your degree?' Myburgh asked, moving the conversation along so neither of them had to feel stuck in an uncomfortable moment.

Ian grinned. 'Ja, Oom. I'm finished now. The graduation ceremony will be in July. You should come. If you want to, I mean,' he said, covering up the momentary lapse into spaces that might be too personal. But Myburgh smiled.

'I've never been to one of those fancy-ass things. Maybe I'll come through. Dress up in my old uniform. Scare the shit out of some of your classmates,' he cackled.

Ian tried not to react outwardly, but his jaw clenched. He knew Myburgh hadn't approved of the student fee protests the previous year. Ian had even considered muting the old man's rants on Facebook during the demonstrations. All the while Ian had been on campus, helping his undergrad students deal with beatings from security guards and police, and the tear gas. He was about to say something when Myburgh burst out laughing.

'I'm just pulling your leg, Cousin. Didn't realise it would make you turn purple,' he said, evidently enjoying his own joke. Ian was about to feign his own laugh in response when Myburgh announced that they had arrived.

The merriment disappeared the moment they stepped off the silly golf cart and onto the bare patch of land between the canal and the dam. The water lapped at the lock's edge. About a hundred metres off the shore, just past a clump of moored boats, Ian could make out a few islands of green. 'I thought the plants came all the way up to the shore,' he said. 'You said the gardener found her?'

Myburgh nodded.

'We had one of those ... boat things, those harvesters, come through after they found the girl,' Myburgh said. 'Cleared out a couple hundred metres. But it's still covered on the other side. They usually die back a bit in winter. The cold's supposed to make them grow slower. And then they spread again as soon as it gets warm. Just in time for the boat owners to complain,' he said, nodding out at the bobbing craft. Ian wondered if they counted as yachts.

From somewhere across the dam, he couldn't see where, they could hear what sounded like children screaming – the pitch was just on the right side of play, rather than panic, but the dislocated noise still made Ian feel uneasy.

'You hear strange shit from across the dam,' Myburgh said. 'Water carries noise. Come, I'll show you photos of the dead woman,' he said, walking over to the golf cart and reaching into a small cubbyhole to retrieve an oblong black item almost the size of a small book. Myburgh took off his shiny silver shades and replaced them with a pair of reading glasses from inside his shirt pocket. 'Now let me just try find them,' he said, holding the tablet-sized phone at arm's length and peering down his nose as if the phone screen were a crossword puzzle.

Ian could just see the screen from where he stood, although there was a slight glare coming off the glass. He watched as Myburgh flipped through photo thumbnails, selecting one that suddenly came up large. It was a bad picture of a set of golf clubs. Myburgh scrolled through eight almost identical golfing still-lifes before changing to another set: Myburgh at a restaurant, with a woman somewhere in the general region of his age. Myburgh with the same woman, holding hands above a serviette sculpted in the shape of a heart. They both looked very happy. Myburgh blushed and scrolled past the images without saying anything. Ian kept equally quiet.

'Here we are,' Myburgh said, still blushing, as he eventually found the right album. He handed the phone over to Ian. 'Those are the photos I took that morning. Right before the police came.'

Myburgh stood back to give Ian a chance to look at the photographs of the body that Jonas Jiyane had pulled to shore.

The victim was a black woman, somewhere in her twenties, Ian guessed. Medium build. Skinny-ish, or athletic. There were no photos on the phone that captured her body in full, so Ian had to make her up from pieces, a montage of her head, torso, arms and legs, wreathed in ropes of water hyacinth.

The body's time in the dam made it hard to tell, from the photos at least, what was an original feature belonging to the woman herself and what had been imposed on her underwater. Her eyes were closed, the face very slightly swollen, all of which rendered the corpse expressionless, neither calm nor angry in death.

The woman's skin appeared dark in some photos, almost purple against the green of the grass and the hyacinth leaves. In others – where Ian suspected Myburgh had tried to use his flash – the skin looked lighter, and there were areas where the flesh appeared marbled, with some spots of grey. Ian knew these things could be used to estimate the time of death, but he made no comment as he browsed through the gallery.

In the pictures, the dead woman's long black locks spiralled out against the lawn. In among the strands Ian could make out green, brown, detritus that must have been dredged from the lake. Most other features were indistinct, in part because Myburgh's photographs were terrible and often out of focus.

'Do they know how long she'd been dead?' he asked, as he scrolled back to the first photos of the woman's body sprawled on the dam embankment.

'They say two months. It's hard to tell from looking at the corpse because most of the dam is completely ... something. Toxic. No. *Anoxic*,' Myburgh said, locating the right word. 'There's no oxygen. Because of those fucking lilies, and the ... algae. The whole lake was covered in it, for weeks. It slows down the soft tissue damage.'

'How come they said they were so sure of the timeline then?' Ian asked.

'I'll explain that in a moment,' Myburgh said, the tone of his voice shifting. Ian caught a bitter note, but decided to wait to dig for what lay behind it.

Ian returned to the photographs. In some, Myburgh had tried to take closer shots. There was what appeared to be mud across the victim's face and throat, which could have come from when her body was dragged ashore. She was wearing a pink T-shirt with a circular, surfer-type logo, and a pair of cut-off denim shorts. No shoes. A blue plastic bag was tangled around one of her ankles and lay, deflated, to the side.

Ian scrolled further, wishing that Myburgh had at least asked someone who knew how to use a mobile phone camera to take the pictures. He flicked past blurry close-ups of hands and feet, saw that the skin on one hand had started to slip off, like a thin pair of finger gloves. Something else caught his eye, and he went back to the picture. 'What's that?' he asked, pointing at a line visible around the woman's wrist, even though the picture itself was out of focus.

Myburgh got grumpier. 'Your guess as good as mine. She had them on both sides. Like tattoos. But I didn't want to touch her before the investigators came, you know?'

Myburgh looked like he was chewing on what to say next, so Ian waited.

'The cops came, they spoke to Jonas, they spoke to me, and a couple of the other people on the estate. And then they took the body off to Ga-Rankuwa in a van. To the mortuary. They, uh, opened the docket, and they said she drowned.'

Myburgh had put his hands in his pockets, which made him look like he was trying to hide something.

Ian frowned. 'So, it was an accidental death. What's the problem then?' he asked.

Myburgh gave a sigh and took his hands out of his pockets so that he could reach over and retrieve his phone. He stared at the screen and then tapped on it a few times before handing it back to Ian.

'You asked me how they knew when the girl died. That's from the security camera at the entrance to the estate. Start of January. Eight weeks before the body washed up,' he said.

Ian looked down at the screen and saw what looked like a still from a security camera. There was a tiny date and time stamp in the bottom corner. Behind that, the scene clearly showed the booms at the entrance to the La Gondola estate, and a small sedan car on the roadside.

'You can't see much on the phone, but I've got the video file. I can send it to you,' Myburgh said. 'Anyway, Tuesday afternoon, that car drives in,' Myburgh said, pointing at the screen. 'Three women inside. Driver, two passengers. And there's my security guard,' he said, pointing to a figure about two metres away from the vehicle.

He took the phone back and used his fingers to zoom in on the image before handing the device back to Ian.

'You see that,' the older man said, as Ian looked. Despite the poor picture quality, Ian could make out what looked like a woman's face above a pink-coloured shirt. And silhouetted against the sunlight, ropes of braids all about her head.

'Three women came in. Then, ten hours later, early Wednesday morning, just two of them came out.'

Myburgh swiped to another image on his phone again, showing the same car, only this time leaving the estate.

'You're sure that was the dead woman in the front?' Ian asked.

Myburgh's face remained in its slight scowl. 'They found, what you call it, a slip. A voucher, in the pocket of the dead girl's shorts. It was in one of those plastic bankies – you remember those?' he asked. Ian nodded. 'Anyway, the airtime voucher in her pocket, it was bought the morning that they came in, from one of the shops around here,' Myburgh said. 'And before you go thinking I've completely lost my touch, I already went in and asked the okes behind the counter, and they couldn't remember shit. They sell hundreds of vouchers a day.'

The old man wasn't done yet. 'To make matters worse, nobody else on this goddamn estate claims to have seen any of these women after the time they came in. Not at the clubhouse, not at the boats, nothing. Which tells me that somebody somewhere here is lying, only I don't know who. We don't have cameras inside the estate, for "privacy",' Myburgh said, making quote marks in the air as he said the last word.

'So what does your guy say – your guard,' Ian asked. 'Did he identify her? Who did the women say they were coming to visit?'

Myburgh shook his head in annoyance. 'No. That's the whole problem. Nobody can ask him anything. Zebulon's disappeared.' Myburgh paused for a moment. 'That's why I called you,' he said, slowly, as if Ian was being particularly daft. 'I need you to help me find him.'

AS ABOVE

Seventy-four kilometres away, Captain Reshma Patel stood in a tunnel underneath Johannesburg's Park Station and tried not to gag.

She used the thin fabric of her scarf to cover her nose while she tried as best as she could to breathe in and out through her mouth. There was a thick stench of something like sewage, cut through with rotten egg. And, underneath all of that, a foul aftertaste of blood and iron.

She held her torch out in front of her, the light shining on an underground channel that was filled with unpleasant-looking brown water, the source of some of the smell. The sides of the drain (or whatever it was) were caked in thick yellow grime, making the entire scene look like something out of a science-fiction movie.

'Where does the water come from?' she asked the woman standing behind her.

Reshma's escort was the bored railway company official who had accompanied her and two other officers down the tunnel an hour ago. Six hours before that, four separate witnesses at Park Station claimed to have seen two men drag a woman into an alcove and then disappear. The tunnels were a possible route of concealment, or worse. But by the time Reshma and her team had arrived, there was nothing to be found. Even the security cameras had proved to be a blank, quite literally. The system was nine months overdue for a service, and all the recording functions were out of order. The security cameras that did work had live feeds and nothing more. None of the guards, of course, had seen the alleged abduction.

'Do you know where the water comes from?' Reshma asked again. The woman stared back at her dully, evidently unaffected by the terrible smell, and shook her head. 'You have to ask Kruger. He knows about these tunnels,' she said at last, as if she was doing Reshma a great favour by talking.

Behind the railway woman was the source of the second part of the olfactory tableau.

There was a series of flashes as one of the warrant officers tried to take photographs of the scene with his phone. Reshma heard him mumble something, either a swear word or a prayer. She looked away for a moment, not quite ready to grapple with what they had found.

Except for the light from Reshma's torch and the blue glow of the officer's phone, the tunnel complex was in darkness.

Behind them, a long-abandoned room led off from the narrow metal staircase down which they had descended into darkness. There was only one entrance to the staircase, a locked wooden door that did not look to be in any sort of regular use, but which had almost no additional security. Reshma had looked for any evidence of recent human traffic as they made their way down, but she had seen nothing.

In the other direction, there were pipes, brick and concrete. Reshma tried to tune out the human noises around her and listen. There was a muted buzz coming from the station concourse, now two storeys above her. She thought she heard water dripping, although that might have been just her imagination. Otherwise there was silence. Not even silence: the absence of noise. It was a dead space. The entire area was cold and damp and unwelcoming. But the cold was also probably keeping the worst of the smell at bay, Reshma realised.

She turned towards the back of the room again. Another flash went off and showed vivid splashes of red against the white of the old plaster. There was more red on the floor. Half-dried puddles of what was maybe blood, maybe human blood at that. The darkness made it hard to see. Another mercy.

The stink and the blood spatters weren't the worst part, Reshma thought, making a sweep again with her torch. The worst was the handprints, smeared across the wall and then across the floor, as if someone had been trying to fight, and then trying to escape. The marks ended in a terrible final smudge at the crumbling yellow edges of the water, although it was impossible for anyone to have escaped that way.

At the centre of the carnage was a small wooden bookshelf that had been pushed up against the wall. There were powdery remains on top, as if something had been burned there. Incense, or Imphepho. The shelf, like everything around it, was covered in spatters. Reshma had already called in the laboratory service – she'd had to make her way back up the staircase to get a signal; there was absolutely no phone reception underground.

She had decided she would wait for the lab to let her know what the red liquid was before deciding how to react to it. People killed chickens, dogs, even sheep and cows in the inner city. It was always better to make sure.

Something under the bottom of the shelf caught Reshma's eye – a pelt, or maybe a dead rat. She moved in closer, trying to avoid getting too much muck on her shoes, and squatted down until she could shine her light right on the floor. For a second she wondered if it might be some kind of animal sacrifice, which might explain the gore, and which would be gross, but surely a better option than the alternative.

Tilting her head, Reshma felt inside her jacket pocket and pulled out an old pen. A cheap Bic, something that could be sacrificed to the cause. She used the pen's tip to dig about under the bottom shelf and pull out whatever it was that was stuck there. The object slid out without much effort, a long tail, soaked in the same red as everything else, leaving a slight trail in the sticky mess. It took Reshma a moment to identify as a piece of hair. Some kind of hairpiece, maybe, or part of a wig.

Reshma was careful not to overbalance in her crouch position. Bloody shoes were one thing, but she didn't want to get the rest of her body involved. She moved the torch closer and lifted the pen so the matted hairpiece was closer to eye level.

Something fell out of the hair, squelching as it hit the floor. Reshma pointed her torch down to see what it was. A second later she wished she hadn't. What was lying on the floor was a human finger. A severed finger, topped with a partly broken fingernail. The LED light of the torch tended to flatten colours in its glare, but Reshma thought it looked like the nail still had the remnants of nail polish on it. Also red. Or that could have been blood.

In spite of her best efforts, Reshma gagged. She tasted vomit in her mouth and swallowed it back down.

She dropped the scalp back to the floor and kept the pen in her hand, held at arm's length like an anti-wand as she stood up slowly, mindful of her balance. When she was certain she was clear, she took

17

a step backwards, away from the mess. She was about to take a deep breath when she remembered that it might make things even worse. She held the scarf over her face again, breathed, counted to ten, and started over. She held the light above her head like a lamp. Then she turned where she stood, breaking up the room into three parts: the upper wall and ceiling; the midline of the room; the floor. Be methodical, she reminded herself. Don't try and take it all in once. Break it into parts.

When she reached the floor, she saw a patchwork of marks emerging from the blood and the dust. Footprints. All sorts of different shapes, sizes, and treads. Reshma did a few calculations in her head and felt a spark of excitement as she looked back to the marks. Her own footprints were easy to spot: boots with a slight heel, flat soles. She could easily make them out on the patch of floor where she'd been standing. The bored railway woman was in a scuffed pair of pumps. Reshma hadn't seen the soles, but she had noticed that the woman's feet were tiny, no bigger than an adult size four, if that. Constable Reynier, and the other one – Warrant Officer Lazar – were both wearing standard-issue service boots. She could see the distinctive cross-hatches on the floor where they had walked.

Which meant that somebody else had to have left the large, flat treadmarks leading away from the bloody area, and off into the darkness. Each of the footprints had a giant star dead centre of the sole, perfectly outlined in blood.

Reshma called her team and told them not to move while she stepped carefully to the closest mark she could see.

She cast her torch around until she spotted the next set of footprints, less clear but still from the same boots or shoes, leading away from the scene where the blood was. More slowly now, Reshma followed the trail, out of the first chamber and into the next. The bloody footprints became less distinct, and harder to see against the grime of the floor. After the second room, the marks completely disappeared. Reshma thought that it was possible that the person had taken off their shoes, but it was hard to tell. She shone her torch ahead of her and looked to see where she was. The beam lit up a small brick arch and, behind that, more darkness. Bad things happened to people who went down tunnels alone. A shiver went up and down Reshma's spine, and she turned back. She would call for assistance.

Reshma made her way back to the first room, careful not to disturb any more evidence as she walked. She was about to ask the rail services person where the tunnel led to, but caught herself, realising it would be a pointless exercise.

'I would like to speak to Kruger,' she said instead, looking the representative straight in the face until it dawned on the woman that she was being asked to do something, and her flat expression animated. Then Reshma turned back to her own colleagues. 'Reynier,' she said, 'go up the stairs – carefully – and call for one of the K9 units. Let's find out if whoever did this is still down here.'

ZEBULON

The missing security guard was 26-year-old Zebulon September.

According to Myburgh, Zebulon's mobile number had stopped working about a week after the guard had gone missing – which was four days after the woman's body had been found in the dam, and three days *before* one of the La Gondola Body Corporate members had found the footage on one of the estate's security videos. Myburgh said all of the estate's CCTV footage was supposed to be kept for at least a year after the recording date and was stored in some kind of server system on-site, which he could email to Ian using a password-protected link.

By Myburgh's account, Zebulon had been scheduled for weekend leave, which he had taken as usual.

'And then he just never came back. Must have been the body that made him nervous,' he said. That had been five weeks earlier. Myburgh said the guard had not formally been charged with anything, but if his absence continued, he would be charged with dereliction of duty for abandoning his post and fired. According to estate rules, Myburgh said, visitors were only allowed in at the express invitation of residents. All employees, including guards, were prohibited from bringing in any visitors, even family members, unless these were cleared in writing, in advance, by a resident or by one of the estate managers.

The implication was that Zebulon had allowed three black women to enter the estate, for reasons unknown and without a resident's approval, and that one of these women had somehow ended up dead in the water. It was not clear, from the way Myburgh explained the potential charges against Zebulon, which part the Body Corporate found more offensive.

'I tried calling him for three, four days after he left,' Myburgh explained, 'and then his voicemail went off, or it was full or something.' The old man patiently dialled Zebulon's number again and let Ian listen to the semi-automated message that played back a voice note with Zebulon September cautiously saying his own name, before it switched back to a robot voice indicating that the mailbox was full.

'I have an address for his aunt in Atteridgeville. I'll send it to you,' Myburgh said. 'He stayed with her there, before he came here. You can maybe start asking by her where he is,' he suggested.

Myburgh said he had tried to speak to Zebulon's aunt over the phone.

'She's old, and a bit deaf. I don't think she knew what I was asking. She's much easier to talk to in person, so you should probably pay her a visit,' he said.

Myburgh also told Ian he didn't want anyone to know that he was investigating the matter.

'The old guys, some of them think I'm a bit of a softy, you know? The young ones, they think I'm too old,' he said, with a shrug that betrayed a mix of annoyance and frustration. 'Some of them think they need to get someone younger to run the set-up,' he added.

Ian could see that this admission came at a cost. Myburgh was either embarrassed, or angry. Or perhaps he was afraid. Ian wondered if the old man was genuinely worried about keeping his job – and, more than that, his fancy house on the estate. The new girlfriend. A whole new life.

'You said he moved. Where did he live after his aunt?' Ian asked as they drove back from the dam in the tiny cart that whizzed along as if everything it did was a great childish game.

'We have staff rooms,' Myburgh answered. 'They're not fancy or anything, but they're clean,' he said. 'The guys only stay here when they're working. When they're on shift. When it's holidays, weekends off, they go back to wherever they live.'

Myburgh described the set-up to Ian.

'We have a 24-hour roster and we have our own guys – they're not contracted out,' he explained. 'They're employed by La Gondola. Or at least, by the property development company. Same guys who hired me. Ex-cops, some of them.'

'See, there's a bus, minibus, comes through from the location at 5 am, all the way to ten at night, and that takes care of all the other staff, the maids, the gardeners, everything. But the security guards can start or finish shift at three, four in the morning. So either the company must pay for special transport, or they have to outsource the guards to another security company that drives its own guys. Or give them rooms. So that was what they did,' he said, turning the cart east and heading towards a large office and admin building.

'My office is in there,' Myburgh said, pointing at a blank wall as they passed.

A hundred metres later, they stopped at a smaller block with small windows, none of which had any view of the greens or the dam.

Myburgh parked the golf cart in front of a very un-cappuccino bare brick exterior.

'This is the staff section. The laundry and utility rooms are in the front,' Myburgh said as they walked round. 'Plus there's a small place for the staff to cook, and to sit and eat if they want. And staff toilets, for the groundsmen and so on. They don't live on the property, though.'

A warm breeze of fabric softener and detergent wafted through the air as Ian and Myburgh passed. There were three women out front, chatting and folding napkins or towels. They didn't stop when they saw Myburgh approach, but paused and nodded in his direction. Ian's presence was also noticed and regarded with mild but relatively well-concealed suspicion. White security men visiting black staff quarters came with a lot of baggage, even a quarter of a century after the end of apartheid.

They turned a corner and reached a concrete courtyard with a neat row of eight almost identical doors. Myburgh fished in one of his pockets and pulled out a key before unlocking one.

'Zeb's room was all cleaned out by the time I got to it,' Myburgh said. He pulled the door open so Ian could see inside.

The room was barely large enough to fit a single bed and a compact bedside table unit. The space looked like it had been cleaned, although there was still a soccer poster stubbornly clinging to the wall. Mamelodi Sundowns, Ian saw.

Ian looked at Myburgh and noticed the man's face was set in a scowl.

'I know it's not much. It's small, I mean,' he said. Ian realised that Myburgh was embarrassed at showing him the size of the room where his employee had lived, presumably for months at a time. His discomfort made Ian wonder about the contrast between the security guard's room and what he imagined Myburgh's own quarters were like.

'It's a job. You know. You try ... you try do what you can for them,' Myburgh rambled. Ian stopped him. He wasn't in the mood for either blaming or excusing his friend.

'He left nothing else?' he asked, even though Myburgh had already said so. The old man gave a nod. 'Ja. Wasn't space for much to begin with. He kept some clothes here. That was about it. Except for a photo of his mom. And that was gone, together with all his other stuff.'

Myburgh closed and locked the door again, and shoved the key back into his pocket, keeping his hand there. He looked back up at Ian, his mouth set into a line.

'I know what you're thinking. That this place, it stops people from being with their families. And you're right,' he said. Myburgh was obviously not unaware of the dynamics at play, but it was evident that they didn't overly trouble him. 'I know this is maybe not the best job, or the best place. I can see it for what it is, you know? But this is what I have to offer these guys. This is what the Board had to offer me. A job, something to be proud of, something they can do well. Something that is supposed to keep them safe. They are good guys, Ian, most of them. They're *my* guys. Zebulon mustn't lose his job like this. If he let that lady in, there must have been a reason for it, I'm sure of it,' Myburgh sounded like he was trying to convince himself.

Ian said he would help, although it was more to ease Myburgh's anxiety than from any sense that he could actually be of use.

Myburgh wouldn't let Ian leave without what he described as a country lunch, which turned out to be a better-than-expected chicken pie in a pub overlooking the Crocodile River.

Except for the view, and the meal, the pub could have been a copy and paste of the drinking hole Myburgh had favoured when he still worked on the East Rand. Except, Ian noticed, Myburgh had switched to light beer, and seemed to have stopped smoking. Ian wondered if this was down to the new location, or the new woman he was plainly seeing. The old man didn't bring it up, so Ian thought it impolite to pry. He let Myburgh rattle off instead about the joys of country life and the funny parts of living on a golf estate, without mentioning dead women and missing men.

But when they parted, Myburgh made Ian promise he would go and see Zebulon's aunt the next weekend. He also told Ian that he would pay him for his time. 'Don't argue with me about this, Cousin,' he said. 'I'm not asking you for a favour. I'm asking you to do this as a job.'

Ian's route home took him through the outer ring of the dam's tourist attractions: more pubs, a few boating sites and caravan parks, and clusters of roadside markets all selling exactly the same tat, from miniature wire windmills and strings of wooden hearts to concrete garden gnomes and ornamental donkeys. On one of the road's curves was another type of curio: a small wooden cross with a photograph stapled on to it, the picture of the deceased long since faded beyond recognition. Ian noticed the marker and was probably not the first driver to observe that it would indeed be easy to go a little too fast around the bend, and wind up in a similar diorama. He slowed down.

As he drove, he spotted other markers of history: there were road signs for the government nuclear facility at Pelindaba; and, west of that, demure signs for Broederstroom where, Ian recalled, an apartheid commando and an arms cache had once found a home. He was almost tempted to drive past the site, although he suspected it was probably another Gary Player golf course now, or something that involved a non-ironic sand trap.

The pie repeated on Ian slightly as he drove past the airport at Lanseria. A few kilometres later, he reached the corner where the old Lion Park used to be, and where only a cartoonish statue of a lion now remained. Ian half-paid attention as the peri-urban edges quickly folded in on themselves, the veld turning into rows and rows of suburbs as he hit Cosmo City.

It took Ian nearly an hour to reach the Westdene Dam. Near the bridge, he could make out two men with fishing poles. Not for the first time, he wondered whether it would truly be considered 'good luck' to catch anything in the dam's waters. Still, the fishermen were out there most days, men standing at the water's edge, passing time.

Today there was also an old white man pushing a wooden trolley across the bridge. Ian had seen him a number of times since he and Reshma had moved to the suburb. The man may or may not have been homeless. He was dressed in an outfit that was more threadbare than eccentric, and he never made eye contact with anything but the ground ahead of him. Ian wasn't sure where the old man went to, or where he came from – there was a small group of men who dossed on the far side of the dam, Ian knew, but they were mostly youngsters, and black. Sometimes they would build a tiny wood and cardboard fort, where they kept mattresses and clothes. Other times the area was swept clean of people by the capricious efforts of the Metro cops. Ian thought it was a pity. The dam itself was cleaner when the young men were there; he had seen them gathering up waste, plastic, and making it into recycling bundles.

From the dam, it was five more blocks to the small semi-detached house with a tiny garden and an even smaller parking area that Ian and Reshma had started renting together six months earlier.

Ian squeezed his car to the side of the driveway, so that Reshma would be able to park inside the gate when she got home later, whenever that was.

She had been seconded to a special new investigative unit two months before, supposedly looking at a growing number of kidnappings, particularly in the Pakistani and Somali communities, but the unit's portfolio had expanded to include everything from child abductions to cross-border smuggling, and anything else the city's central police stations were struggling to cope with. As a result, Reshma's working hours had been more erratic than usual.

Ian dumped his bags inside and set up his laptop on the table while he started preparing dinner – a Moroccan-style vegetarian dish. He let the chickpeas and rice simmer while he went over his emails and prepared for the meetings he would need to attend the following day. He let out a small sigh when he looked at his calendar.

There was a 10 am gathering with staff from the other research units. Then reporting sessions with donors and funders. Then more meetings, to discuss synergy with donor funding applications. All finished up with yet another meeting to discuss HR targets for the next quarter, even though Ian's section only employed two people, part-time.

Just before Ian had finally finished his thesis, he had been approached by an international non-profit organisation and asked if he would be interested in heading up a new project researching violence in communities. Even at the time Ian had known the job would

27

mean more admin and less research, but on paper, the concept still looked good – and the benefits were enticing too, especially for a man who had spent the better part of the previous year in physiotherapy sessions or with his arm in a sling.

Ian's supervisor had encouraged him to take the position. 'The pay's better, and there's more job security,' he'd said, after an hour-long gripe session about the university's latest administrative foibles. Ian was old enough to appreciate the pragmatism in the advice, although if he was totally honest, part of him had wished his supervisor had begged him to stay on, and to pursue his doctorate.

Ian pushed the thought away even as it arose. After he'd been shot, and after Tiny's death on the top of the Northcliff Ridge, Ian had struggled to find the motivation to finish his degree at all. Deep down, he didn't know for sure whether or not he wanted to study any more, but part of him still wanted the accolades and respect he imagined would go with it. For now, he was keeping the door open – but only just. The violence project took up four days of each week and had a work-from-home option when Ian didn't have any meetings, which meant Ian was still able to pick up odd teaching sessions. And, when he chose, he could take on ad hoc investigations – including, it seemed, looking into missing persons.

Ian laughed at himself. The harder he tried to get into a life that made him look and sound respectable, the more he seemed to find projects that would take him back to what he had wanted to do when he had been a cop.

EUREKA

eshma lost track of time underground.

It was ten, maybe eleven in the morning by the time they'd been given access to the tunnels. Now it was well into the evening, and they still had nothing to go on except for the bloody remnants of whatever it was that had happened. Reshma was still waiting for the K9 unit to finish up on an earlier call and help her and her team navigate the darkness underneath Park Station. She had called off any further exploration of the tunnels until they had a better idea where they led – this was to protect the safety of herself and any other officers underground, and also to preserve whatever evidence might or might not have been left behind.

Shortly before 9 pm, JP Kruger arrived in the tunnels. Kruger was a decade-plus past even the most generous retirement age, but he looked neat and trim in an outfit that reminded Reshma of an old railway uniform, but with an incongruous hand-knitted jersey pulled over the blazer. Reshma suspected the jersey was both a quirk, and a practical response to the chill below ground.

Kruger was a mid-level bureaucrat who had been at the railway station 'forever' and had somehow stayed on working on site, most likely because nobody had ever really asked him to leave. As far as Reshma could determine, the man was already on a pension and no longer had an official title, but he arrived for work every day and somehow kept himself both busy and useful. According to some of the older PRASA staff, those who had been at the company during its transition from one state-owned enterprise to another, Kruger *had* to keep working because nobody in the new dispensation would know where anything was without him.

Kruger seemed completely comfortable underground, and was happy to take Reshma on something of a truncated tour. He carried a large hand-held torch, which suggested to Reshma that he was well prepared for such situations. She made a mental note to remember to have her team question him when they started interviews. In the meantime, she let the older man play the part of her guide.

'All the main platforms used to be down here. You would go in through the big entrance on De Villiers, under the animal facades, and then you would go down, four metres, into a giant hall,' he said, his voice becoming animated. He looked over to gauge Reshma's response to the history lesson. She kept her expression guarded but neutral. Kruger took this as a sign to edit the details, and got to the point. 'They sealed everything when they made the new Park Station,' he explained as they walked. 'They blocked off the old halls, all the old passenger tunnels.'

'How long ago was this?' Reshma asked, as they worked their way slowly through evidently long-abandoned spaces.

'Must be fifty years now – a little bit more?'

Reshma's torch caught a wall full of peeling adverts, marketing a long-forgotten brand of whiskey, a type of cigarette she had never heard of, and a poster for the Rand Show from 1954. It was like being in a museum.

Kruger took a left, then a right, then another right, before they reached a smaller room with three more corridors leading off it. The man waved his torch towards a spot on the wall. Reshma made out some kind of diagram and stepped closer.

'This used to be one of the offices. That maps all the old stops, all the tunnels, everything,' Kruger said, proud of his navigation skills and his memory.

Reshma asked him to hold the torch up, and then took a photo of the diagram on her phone, checking to see that the image had come out well enough to study later. 'Where do the tunnels end?' she asked. 'Is there anywhere that someone could get in and out without someone seeing them from the top?'

Kruger thought for a moment, tilting his head as he replied. 'Not that it would be easy, but not impossible,' he said, righting his head again. 'I mean, the train tracks don't go all the way under the city,' he said, 'but then it's not only train tunnels down here.'

Reshma asked him what he meant, and Kruger told her about another system of mail tunnels that linked the train station to the old post office a few blocks away. 'I haven't been in all of them,' he said, 'but I guess people know about them. I don't know where they go.'

'Are those tunnels big enough for a person?'

'Oh yes,' Kruger nodded. 'Definitely.'

Reshma allowed herself a small sigh. The more Kruger explained, the more she began to suspect it was going to be impossible to explore the tunnels fully – it sounded like they extended in a small web all through the immediate vicinity, and possibly into the city centre.

Reshma looked back to the diagram on the wall and thought about the first room they had been in, the one with the blood, and the stinking water.

'Are there also mining tunnels down here?' she asked.

Kruger shook his head. 'They couldn't build the train tunnels too near any of the mining works. That's why most of the tracks are above ground now. There might be other tunnels somewhere else. But not here.'

Kruger walked Reshma back slowly towards the entrance, allowing her time to properly sweep each area, each room, looking for new evidence. She saw nothing except dust and dirt.

It was extremely difficult to search even small spaces in the total blackness of the tunnels, never mind potentially dangerous. Reshma noticed channels of water in several other rooms. Some appeared fairly deep, and several of them smelled particularly foul. When she asked Kruger about the water, he went quiet, and commented only that it sometimes flooded under the station.

'Do you think there's any way we could get the lights switched on down here?' she asked as they reached the room with the blood.

'Luvvie,' he said, trying to be gentle, 'nothing down here has worked for three decades. Everything's dead.'

When they went back above ground, Reshma used the opportunity to check her phone. Ian had messaged her at some point to say that he was home, and that he would make dinner. Reshma checked and saw that he had sent the message a little after five. It was now well after eleven. That meant she had been at the station for over twelve hours. She hadn't texted Ian to say she wouldn't be home for dinner. She thought about texting now, but figured Ian might already be in bed. No sense in neither of them getting any rest.

Thoughts of home and dinner made Reshma realise she hadn't eaten anything since that morning. The food concessions in the station were all closed, except for the 24-hour chicken chain, but there were a few late-night spots in the blocks around Park – not that Reshma would recommend them to anyone, unless they were starving and willing to accept fried potatoes as the closest thing to a vegetarian meal option.

She was finishing a lukewarm Coke and an order of peri-peri fries when she got a message that the police dog and its handler had arrived. She quickly finished her makeshift meal on the walk back to the parking area closest to the entrance to the tunnels – a no-entry zone already conveniently reserved for railway officials and SAPS. There were only three cars parked there, including one Metro vehicle that had been at the station all day monitoring trading on the sidewalk, and which had stuck around out of either professional or prurient interest.

Despite the morning's sighting, nobody had filed a related missing person report at any of the nearby police stations. The blood at the scene suggested that this was more likely a case of a dead person, which didn't warrant more officers than the crimes currently being committed above ground against the living.

In the parking area, Reshma saw an unfamiliar man, silhouetted against the background of spotlights coming off the Queen Elizabeth Bridge, standing next to a small compact painted in police colours. He was in uniform but had no hat, and she could see pale blond hair, thinning on top. He was holding a lead, at the other end of which was what looked like a small ball of wiry fluff. It took Reshma a few seconds to realise the ball was some sort of Jack Russell. Not exactly the impressive German or Belgian Shepherd dog she had imagined.

'What is this?' she asked, careful to keep her voice neutral.

The K9 handler answered in an equally measured tone. He was

obviously used to a certain amount of incredulity. 'This is Stoffel,' he said. The dog looked up at its handler as his name was mentioned. 'Stoffel is trained to detect biological matter – blood, bodily fluids. And a few other things.'

Reshma looked at the officer, and then down at the dog, and back up again.

'I'm Cuan, by the way,' the handler said.

Reshma nodded, and shook his hand.

'Okay, let's show you what we have,' she said, turning around and heading towards the wooden door that led to the narrow stairway that would take them underground.

She could hear the handler and the dog walking behind her. She thought she heard laughter, too. Possibly from one of the Metro cops. She thought about turning her head, trying to see who it was, but she decided to ignore it. If the dog did its job, she didn't care what it looked like.

'Be careful, it's slippery on the way down,' she said, as she stepped back into darkness.

*

Kruger tried to pet the animal but Cuan cautioned him not to.

'Not while he's on duty,' the officer said, not unkind, but firm.

Stoffel paid no attention to anything but the room, and his handler. On Cuan's cue, they started in the gore room, where several battery-powered LED lights had been set up. Stoffel was allowed to nose about; Cuan spent a few moments engaging with the animal when they reached the place where the blood was spattered, and then Stoffel carried on all on his own for another minute or two before lifting his head for further instruction.

Kruger had agreed to take them to and through all of the rooms and tunnels in the immediate vicinity, past the rooms he had showed Reshma earlier, and led the way with his large torch in hand. Cuan and Stoffel followed, with Reshma behind them.

'Does the dog need more light?' she asked.

Cuan said that a little more light would be helpful, but that they would make do. 'They can see better than us in the dark, although it's hard to tell what might be down here. Your crew mentioned some water, rubble, that sort of thing.'

Kruger took them through the rooms and corridors methodically, Reshma checking their route against the diagram on her phone, although she couldn't always make out which direction they were going in, or where they had come from.

They were somewhere south-east of the first room, she thought, when the dog's ears pricked up, and its behaviour became noticeably more animated. Cuan motioned for Kruger to let Stoffel take the lead, which the old man seemed only too delighted to do. They headed into a part of the tunnels that Reshma and Kruger had not explored earlier.

Followed by the light of their torches, Stoffel moved cautiously along a wall, sniffing the edges of an old pipe or tube. When they reached a juncture in the tunnel, Stoffel stopped, then moved in a circle, then sniffed the wall again before darting off ahead, with a loud bark.

Reshma and Cuan raced to catch up, but luckily Stoffel hadn't gone far. The dog was in a semi-crouch, as if about to pounce on something. Reshma saw something move out the corner of her eye, and it took her a moment to realise that it was a rat. Possibly more than one rat. For a second, she thought that was what had caught the dog's attention. Until Cuan shone his torch where Stoffel was staring, illuminating two bodies.

They were both male. Both fully clothed. The one looked shabby, in dirty old work pants, scuffed heavy boots. He was lying on his back, his face mostly smashed in – possibly the cause of his demise. To his right lay the second corpse, this one in smarter clothes. Nice jeans. A brown leather jacket. He was lying face down on the floor, a gunshot wound in the back of the head.

Reshma played her torch over the bodies of the dead men. Not that she was a forensic expert, but the bodies looked like they might have been dead for some time. Certainly longer than that morning. The rats had possibly been having a go for a while, but she saw that both corpses still had their hands and all their fingers intact. Which meant the amputated appendage in the earlier room belonged to someone else.

In the meantime, Stoffel had stopped barking and moved, nose to ground, to the other side of the room, towards an alcove not marked on Reshma's map. It was barely more than a hole in the wall – and, in fact, Reshma noticed that there *was* a hole in the wall, neatly cut, at least sixty or seventy centimetres wide. Stoffel was on his haunches staring at the hole with quiet intensity.

'Is there another body?' she asked, speaking to Cuan.

'No. He would bark if there was a body. Stoffel also sniffs for other things. Ammunition sometimes, money,' he said in a calm voice. 'We don't want the dogs getting too excited, in case they find some-thing explosive,' he said, reaching into a pocket and finding a small bright-coloured ball, which he gave to a suddenly extremely happy terrier.

With Stoffel diverted, Cuan knelt down and shone his torch on the area where the dog had stopped. The floor area around him was, like the other rooms, caked in layers of grime. Reshma flicked her torch around to see if she could spot any marks or footprints, anything that would indicate if the blood-stepper had come this way, but she could see nothing.

Cuan stuck his head into the recess and looked around briefly before turning back to Reshma.

'I think you'll want to see this,' he said, stepping up and back so that she could crouch down in his place.

Reshma shone her torch where Cuan had been looking. Inside the alcove she could make out what looked like a small, neat pile of plastic bags. Some were clear, some were opaque – like the blue and white ones you would get from shops, or even takeaway joints. What she could see in the clear bags, though, made her pulse quicken.

'Hold this for a second,' she said, passing the torch to Cuan while she slipped on a pair of gloves. With a gloved hand, she reached into the hole and grabbed the handle of one of the packets, pulling it out.

'Shine here,' she said, directing the K9 officer to cast his light on the bag's contents.

Inside, each wrapped in an elastic band, were neat bundles of hundred-rand notes. Reshma flipped through them, and thought they might even be genuine.

She remembered a story about a bribe that had been offered to one of the ministers during a corruption case a few years back – about how to fit half a million rand into a Checkers shopping bag. A fact-checking organisation had checked the claim, and proved it was possible. She had thought it was funny at the time. Now, twelve feet underground with a bag of money in front of her, she didn't think it was amusing at all.

Reshma retrieved her torch and examined the bag more closely. She thought she could make out hints of colour on the edges of some of the notes. She took a deep breath and shone the torch back into the cache inside the hole. The thin light disappeared into the darkness behind – what looked like another tunnel, not rough-hewn, but not tiled and concreted like the one they were in. Reshma made a note of where she thought it was on the other map, and decided to worry about where it came from, and where it led, later.

Several of the other bags were poorly knotted, and looked like they contained more bank notes. Other bags were smaller, more closely tied. Reshma had a hunch what might be inside those, but she still needed to check. She reached in and took another bag, this one much heavier. Inside was a 9mm pistol in relatively good condition, and what looked like parts of a shotgun. The guns were bundled together with a Ziploc bag half-filled with loose bullets of different calibres.

'Where are they from?' Cuan asked, staring at the guns more than the money.

Stoffel, excited by his own success, had moved around from behind his handler's ankles to nose at the gun bag, hoping perhaps for another reward. Kruger kept quiet behind them.

Reshma didn't answer, but part of her knew exactly what she was looking at. She was already wondering who she needed to call next – and whether she would still be allowed to remain on the case, if her suspicions proved correct.

'We need to get back above ground,' she said, standing, leaving the guns and the money where they were. 'I need to make a phone call.'

O, FORTUNA

Reshma made one phone call, to a Colonel who was fairly high up in the Priority Crimes section, and whom she had encountered on more than one occasion while working on the court cases against some of the men and women implicated in the poaching scheme she had helped bust a few years before, when Ian had been shot in the arm, and her colleague, Tiny, killed in a confrontation on top of the Northcliff Ridge. The Colonel was not particularly close to Reshma, which was partly why she approached him. He had a reputation for being cleaner than clean, and this was not a personal call.

Reshma knew she was probably going to attract flak for not following the chain, and going via her own commander. But instinct told her that what they had found in the tunnels needed to be cauterised until it could be handled by the right person, or people. She did not say this explicitly to Cuan, but hoped that she had impressed upon him the importance of keeping case details confidential, at least for another few hours.

Oddly, she was not worried that Kruger would tell any tales. He seemed like a man who had held more than his fair share of other people's secrets over the years. Before he left, he gave Reshma a number where she could reach him if necessary. Cuan stuck around, dozing off on the back seat of his car, with Stoffel beside him.

Reshma co-opted one of the police vans and tried to nap in the front. It was now long after midnight, and she had been going since early that morning. Another of Reshma's colleagues stood guard at the door to the tunnels. She hadn't told anyone else about what they had found below, but she had issued instructions to secure the scene until help arrived. Whatever they had found looked like it had been there a while. It could wait another few hours. Plus, it wasn't exactly the easiest place to access – from either the station, or whatever tunnel it was that led off the hidey-hole.

Ninety minutes later, two detectives arrived. Reshma thought she recognised the younger one, a white or Coloured man wearing a suit jacket and blue shirt with a pair of jeans. Her memory bank suggested she might also have seen him around the courts, but she couldn't pinpoint anything specific, not even when he introduced himself as Wayde Claassen.

The older detective was unfamiliar to her – a black man, maybe in his late forties or early fifties. He wore sneakers and a tracksuit, black or navy blue top and bottom, but on him the outfit looked more formal than Claassen's plainclothes. When the man introduced himself, Reshma realised why. His name was Wilson Sobukwe. He was a Major General, but most people just referred to him as 'Super'. Legend was that he avoided being photographed, because he was always involved in some or other undercover operation. 'Super' Sobukwe had worked in the old ICD, handling complaints against police, before being transferred to police intelligence, then back to the 'new' Independent Police Investigative Directorate, moving into Priority Crimes at some point in the last year or two. It was highly unusual for a cop to move between the IPID and any other unit but Super was a notable exception.

Reshma had heard that Sobukwe had clashed with both ousted crime intelligence head Richard Mdluli and former Hawks boss Mthandazo Ntlemeza, but he obviously still had support in high places. In person, she noted, he was appropriately intimidating.

Claassen and Sobukwe invited little small talk. Reshma woke Cuan, so the dog handler could accompany them down the stairs and tunnels again. She had marked and mapped the route, and did not think she would need Kruger this time. On their way down, she filled in Claassen and Sobukwe on the events that had preceded the late-night arms and cash discovery. Both cops remained silent, except for Claassen asking one question about the alleged abduction and the CCTV footage. Neither man commented when they passed the bloody section in the first chambers.

As they got deeper, Reshma tried to provide a summary of what she knew about the tunnels underground, the old railway platforms and the mail tunnels. She told them about Kruger, and said she had a number for the man.

When they reached the gun stash, Stoffel once again showed off his best alert face and was rewarded with another toy from Cuan. Reshma had come better prepared this time, and switched on one of the portable lamps while Claassen and Sobukwe inspected the hole in the wall.

'Are these the only packets you touched?' Claassen asked, gesturing to the single money bag and open bag of weapons and parts, which Reshma had left on the other side of the hole so as not to cross-contaminate.

Reshma said that was correct, and waited to see if any more questions were forthcoming. They were not. The two men spent another ten minutes shining lights into the other packets, and poking bags with their torches or, on occasion, with carefully gloved hands. If they communicated anything between each other, it was in nods or gestures, and the odd muffled noise. The men moved nothing from the hole, but Claassen did take several photographs of the scene with the camera on his mobile phone. For a moment, he appeared to attempt sending the images via a mobile app.

'There's no signal down here. Nothing at all,' Reshma said. Claassen nodded and put his phone carefully back in his pocket.

Eventually the men indicated that they were ready to leave. The group walked silently back to the first chambers, then up the stairs, the only sound coming from Stoffel's claws tap-tapping on the stairs.

As soon as they were above ground, Claassen broke off and made a phone call, out of earshot. When he came back, he flashed a look at Sobukwe. The pair turned to Reshma, with Sobukwe indicating that the dog handler should step away, which, to his credit, Cuan did without any discussion.

Once they were alone, Sobukwe spoke to Reshma.

'You did the right thing, calling us when you did. You know what that is down there?' he asked.

Reshma nodded.

Sobukwe halted before speaking again. 'So, I want you to know that we are very grateful for all your work, Captain Patel,' he said. 'But we will take over from here. Myself or Captain Claassen will let your commanding officer know. We have our men coming to take over the scene. You can tell your men to stand down.'

Reshma knew she had been dismissed, but she still paused, almost involuntarily. She wanted to ask about the forensic scene. About the two bodies, and the blood and the unknown person the gory finger had belonged to, and whether anyone would care to find out if he or she was okay. But Claassen and Sobukwe had already walked away. Sobukwe had his phone to his ear while Claassen spoke to him.

Reshma's murder and missing person problem was small fry compared to the cache underground. Lots of guns and lots of money could mean only one thing: a cash-heist gang was operating somewhere nearby.

SURPRISE

Ian heard Reshma's car pull in to their driveway in the early hours of the morning. He lay half in and half out of sleep, listening for the new-familiar sounds of their house: the key in the security gate at the front door, the soft thud of Reshma's bags being left on the chair in the kitchen, the careful opening and closing of drawers in the spare room that doubled as their wardrobe. Some minutes later, he felt Reshma's body drop into bed and wordlessly curl up next to him without touching.

Ian's internal alarm nudged him fully awake an hour later. The bedside clock said it was just after 5.30 am. He edged out from under the covers slowly, trying not to wake Reshma who was still curled up on her side of the bed, one arm barely peeking out over the blanket. The sun would be up soon, but the bedroom would remain dark and cosy thanks to some heavily lined shades Reshma had made and installed just after moving in, when the sun's summer schedule had clashed with a series of late-night investigations.

Ian tiptoed out the room and closed the door with a soft click.

He checked his emails on his phone while putting on a pot of coffee. There was a message from late the night before, saying that the morning's first scheduled meeting – the planned staff session – had been moved out to the following week due to one of the key people being ill. A new meeting request had already been sent and was lurking in purple on his calendar, waiting to be accepted.

Ian rolled his eyes at the bureaucracy, but was glad to have some free time to work from home. For one, it might mean that he got to see Reshma when she woke up and before she headed back to the station. And for another thing, Ian wanted more time to go over some of the stuff Myburgh had given him the day before, which had started to sound more interesting as the information sifted and settled.

Coffee in hand, Ian sat at the kitchen table and opened up the image and video files from the estate. He checked the time again – nearly a quarter-to-six – and decided he would give himself an hour to go through things again, with fresher eyes.

He pulled out his notebook so he could sketch any thoughts, or things he wanted to follow up on when he went back to Atteridgeville to visit Zebulon's aunt. He knew Myburgh wanted to focus on the missing guard. He'd try to call the aunt later in the morning and see if she would meet with him. But for now, he was drawn back to the photos of the dead woman.

Myburgh's almost complete lack of interest in finding out who she was, who she had been, and why she had just been left, had made Ian feel slightly guilty for being part of a system where any human could wind up as just another dead body. The poor quality of the old man's photos frustrated him even more. He couldn't help but feel it was all part of the same issue, even though he knew it was also because Myburgh was getting old and genuinely didn't know how to take photographs with his new device. But there was something about the victim that hooked him, niggled at his mind.

As soon as Myburgh had introduced the topic of Zebulon's

disappearance yesterday, they had stopped talking about the dead woman – except for Myburgh adding that as far as he knew, nobody had come to claim the body from the mortuary. He had made it clear that in his mind, neither the woman's death, nor solving her murder, were La Gondola's problems. 'It's not my job to do their job for them, is it?' he had asked, without really wanting an answer.

Before Ian had left, he had helped Myburgh to send him photos from his phone via WhatsApp. Myburgh only had two pictures of Zebulon, one plainly from the guard's work identity card, the other with Myburgh and Zebulon standing next to each other, smiling vaguely and giving the camera a thumbs-up for no particular reason Ian could determine.

Once Ian was back home and on a wi-fi network, he had sent all of the images – the ones of Zebulon, plus the dead woman – from his phone to his email address, so that he could look at them on a bigger screen. Ian clicked on the email's ZIP file and downloaded it, and then went through 35 images carefully, of which only about twelve were useful.

He could make out more detail on the computer screen, but not much. The resolution of the phone camera was poor, and Myburgh either hadn't taken the time to make sure everything was in focus, or he'd been taking the pictures without his glasses on.

Ian shifted through the pictures slowly, trying to spot obvious details on the limbs or features that would help him build any kind of narrative about the woman, who she was, what she had been doing on the estate, and why she had died there.

He zoomed in on what appeared to be faint marks on the woman's cheeks, which could be acne or deliberate scarification. He made a note on his otherwise almost blank page to follow up on the scars. He knew that some countries practised ritual scarification, which might correspond – the woman's colouring and what he could make out of her features suggested she could have come from Central or West Africa, although neither Ian's eye nor his knowledge were sharp enough to hazard a guess where.

He added the facial scars to a note about the scars on her wrists, although the latter markings made no sense to him – but that was another thing he was no expert on.

Myburgh had managed to email Ian a link to the CCTV footage. Ian left an image of the dead woman open on the left of the screen while he clicked to open up the video in a new panel on the right.

It took Ian a few moments to open the URL and navigate the password requirements, but once the video was up, it appeared easy enough to look at the clips. Ian scrolled through the footage the same way he had done with the photos, moving forward and backward three or four times. He tried zooming in on the video footage, but it was less effective on his screen than it had been for the stills, and the close-up attempts looked wavy and made some details harder to see. Ian took screenshots of the images that showed the driver of the car – she had short hair and sunglasses, and appeared to be wearing something blue, maybe a denim top. He couldn't make out any more details of the woman on the passenger side past the colour of her T-shirt. It was almost impossible to see her face, and her hairstyle could only really be viewed in profile as the car passed the camera. The quality of the imaging was not particularly good, something Ian found surprising given that Myburgh had mentioned the estate was owned at least in part by a bunch of ex-cops. Maybe they were trying to cut costs – although that didn't match up with the fact that there was an on-site server, and that the camera footage was saved.

Ian dutifully wrote down the registration number and a description of the car the women had arrived in, a silver Toyota hatchback, maybe a few years old. Not the kind of car that would make you stop and notice it on the street.

Ian tried to watch from a different perspective, observing the interaction between the security guard – Zebulon – and the women. He saw the car slow down as it approached the boom. The driver rolled down her window and leaned out almost as if to say hello. He wondered if there was something familiar rather than just routine in the action, as if the security guard knew the women from before. Zebulon, he observed, did not seem to smile very much or show anything except politeness.

The woman in the driver's seat kept smiling and occasionally laughing, as if she was talking to the other people in her car. After a brief discussion, the guard stepped away from the driver's side and walked around to take a scan of the car's licence disc on the windscreen. The disc was on the passenger's side of the car, where the other woman – the woman with the pink T-shirt – was seated. There was one other passenger, in the back of the car. Another woman, judging by her hair.

After scanning the licence, the guard walked back to the driver's side and spoke to the driver again – presumably asking for her own licence. Ian had experienced the same procedure when he had entered the estate, in exactly the same order. The guard's request had caused a short delay. Eventually the driver held out a piece of paper, which Zebulon looked at briefly, but did not appear to scan before handing it back. After a few more seconds of discussion – the video didn't record sound, just images – Zebulon waved the car through. As soon as the car was gone, he walked back to the small security station between the booms. Nothing that Zebulon did was remarkable; he was neither negligent nor overbearing.

After the third viewing, Ian rewound the security tape back thirty minutes and watched as Zebulon sat mostly in his security station, waving three cars out. For cars wanting to exit, there were fewer procedures, no scanning of licences.

There seemed to be very few people driving in or out of the estate at that time of day. Ian did not know whether that was usual or unusual. He did notice that Zebulon seemed attentive and engaged in every interaction on the tape. Ian made a note to ask Myburgh for the security logs, to see who else had entered and exited that day.

There was nothing on the screens to show what had happened in the eight or nine hours after the women had passed through the boom, or how a passenger went from being alive to dead in the water, without anyone saying anything.

Next, Ian watched the car's exit video repeatedly – although it was devoid of colour in the night camera mode – and wondered how or why the women in the car had left the complex so easily, and without any apparent signs of concern for their missing friend. Zebulon had gone off shift a few hours before their departure, and the guard who had let them out didn't see any need to do a head-count on who was leaving. Security was about keeping people out, not keeping people in.

Ian returned to the daytime video and tried once again to zoom in on the passenger side of the car as much as the file would allow. After several tries at stopping and starting the film footage at different moments to get the best possible clip, Ian gave up.

He looked at the time and thought he would pause and take a shower before making more coffee. He wrote one more note to follow up, to see if the cops had traced the registration number of the car – otherwise it was something he could try and do himself. If he could track down the driver, perhaps he could find out who the dead woman was, what she had been doing at La Gondola, and why her friends had been so happy to leave her behind.

Under a spray of hot water, Ian started compartmentalising his day. He pushed thoughts of the Hartbeespoort Dam and Myburgh and Zebulon September and the unnamed dead woman to the back of his mind, and tried to switch focus to meetings and reports and funders. To himself, Ian acknowledged that part of the appeal with the missing person–dead woman story was that it allowed him to justify avoiding thinking about work. Or, at least, the admin of his work. There were several big issues he needed to raise, and maybe deal with, over the course of his afternoon's meetings. None of them were particularly serious, but all of them required attention and needed to be managed now, before they became bigger problems further down the line.

Not for the first time, Ian wished he had taken a few management courses at university. He also wanted to find solutions to the increasingly onerous admin requirements that came with dealing with some of the programme's funders – he was spending more and more time doing paperwork rather than the research he was supposed to be producing.

By the time Ian stepped out of the steamy bathroom, his mind was already halfway along a stream of thoughts involving optimistic and imaginary solutions, and grateful or at least empathetic principals.

His thoughts were disturbed by the sounds of clinking noises coming from the kitchen. For a moment Ian wondered if the shower had woken Reshma, before he realised that the noises were of dishes in the sink, and Reshma never washed the dishes unless compelled to do so. A half-second later, he registered that it was Thursday, and the noises meant that Surprise had come to clean the house – she had her own keys so she could let herself in and out, and would often pop in early if she had classes later that morning.

Ian stepped back into the bathroom to retrieve one of Reshma's dressing gowns, which would offer more coverage than the small orange towel wrapped around his waist. Once he was modestly covered, he stepped past the kitchen door and waved hello to Surprise. She was in a set of yellow patterned overalls that looked like they had belonged to someone's grandmother, and was preparing a foamy sink of hot water for the dishes. He could see a pair of white and red headphones snake from her pocket to her ears. Surprise nodded her head to acknowledge him, but waved a pair of soap-covered wet hands, indicating she couldn't take out her earphones.

Ian pointed at the door to his and Reshma's bedroom and pantomimed that Reshma was still asleep, gesturing that Surprise should be quiet. The young woman nodded and continued bopping along as she washed and rinsed glasses in the sink.

*

Surprise was the youngest sister – a surprise last child – of the late and formidable policewoman Tiny Madibela, who had given her life defending Ian and Reshma, along with a group of others, from a wildlife poaching syndicate. Surprise was studying criminology and law at the University of Johannesburg, and took on occasional odd jobs during the week to help cover the ends that didn't quite meet between her nominal bursary, her student fees, and her accommodation. She didn't like waitressing, because the shifts were either during lecture times or too late at night, so she'd asked friends if they would consider using her for housework and babysitting services.

Reshma and Ian had figured that with the new house, Ian's new job, and Reshma's unpredictable schedule, having the student come in to help out was a good investment. It also, in some small part, helped Reshma in particular manage the lingering guilt she felt over her colleague and friend's death.

Both Ian and Reshma soon discovered that Surprise was just as sharp and proactive as her 'little big sister'. She borrowed Ian's old textbooks and Reshma's crime novels, and constantly tried to fish for information about their work, claiming that it would be good for her studies.

Ian dressed quickly. By the time he came out of the spare room and back into the kitchen, Surprise had put the glasses to soak in hot water, and had a new pot of coffee on the go.

'You want another cup?' she asked Ian. He nodded.

Surprise was pouring coffee for both of them when she casually asked Ian about the women in the photos.

'Why are you looking at women with braids?' she asked. For a moment Ian rebuked himself for not closing his laptop when he had gone to shower – he had left all the images, including of the dead body, right out in the open.

He didn't reprimand Surprise for poking about on his computer. She was naturally curious about the images, and he couldn't really scold her for sticking her nose into the business when he'd basically left it for anyone to see.

'Not women. Woman. A woman who drowned in the Hartbeespoort Dam a few weeks ago. I'm helping an old cop friend look into it,' Ian said. He already felt a twinge at giving the impression he was investigating a woman's death, rather than the disappearance of a security guard who, as far as anyone knew, was still very much alive.

Surprise paused, and gave Ian a disapproving look. She handed his mug back to him, picked up her own and walked around to where he was seated in front of the screen.

'You say this woman,' she said, pointing at the close-up of the pink T-shirted passenger in the vehicle, 'and *this* woman,' pointing at the dead woman on the shores of the dam, 'are the same person?' she asked, quick on the uptake.

Ian confirmed this, but more cautiously. 'The timelines match. They're wearing the same clothes. And look, here,' he said, pointing to one of the screenshots he'd taken earlier, 'you can see the hair.' He felt off-kilter, somewhere between being annoyed with Surprise for suggesting that he might be missing, or mistaken about, something, and worried that she had seen something he had not.

Surprise's face remained impassive. 'You have more of the video footage?' she asked. Ian nodded.

'Can I watch it? Look at what else you have with this woman?' she said, deadly serious.

Ian decided to let her watch the clip.

Surprise sat down in front of the laptop. Like Ian had done before, she scrolled forward and backward through the images, letting the video play for stretches in between. She sipped her coffee while she watched, but was otherwise silent.

After she had watched the clip for the third time, she turned and looked up at Ian as he stood at her shoulder.

'These are not the same women,' she said, with complete and utter confidence. She didn't wait for Ian to interject before she continued. 'You see here,' she said, pointing to the passenger woman's head in part of the video. Ian nodded, although he was not sure what he was looking at. Surprise clicked back to the images of the dead woman's face.

'You see her hair? I mean, I know the shots aren't great, but can you see here and here?'

Surprise pointed to the top of each woman's head. Ian nodded, but still had no idea what he was looking at.

Surprise carried on. 'If you look at the woman in the car, the moment she drives past? You can see where the end of her hair is. You see that, like that feathered-out bit?' she asked, drawing a circle with her fingertip around a close-up of the passenger's head, silhouetted against the daylight as it passed.

Ian wasn't entirely sure about where Surprise was going, but he could see what looked like a loose piece of hair. He made a vague noise of assent.

Surprise turned to look at Ian's face, her own expression changing from serious to slightly smug as she realised he hadn't been able to see what she had.

'I'll tell you what it means, Detective Jack. It means that the woman in the car had box braids – hair extensions. They get attached to her real hair at the base, but they can be brushed out. That's how she got the smooth feathery ends like you see there. They are called feather tips. Now the other woman, the dead one,' she said, clicking over to the other image, the octopus tentacle-like one, 'she has dreadlocks. Not box braids. Her locks come from her own hair, plaited, matted, knotted, twisted. You can't get the same feathered effect, not unless you want to ruin your style. And look at her hair – there's no straight bunch of ends there.'

Ian looked at both photos, and realised that what Surprise was saying seemed to match what was shown in the pictures.

'Let me guess,' she asked. 'Everyone else who looked at this video was white? And probably male?'

Ian flushed even though he knew Surprise was partly teasing. It was a necessary reminder, though, that he needed to open up his point of view even when he thought he knew what he was seeing. Particularly when he thought he knew what he was seeing.

'Black women's hair is not really your strong point, is it?' Surprise asked, bluntly.

Ian agreed. He wasn't troubled by conceding the point. He was more interested in what it might mean for what he was looking into. If the passenger in the car was not the same as the dead woman who had wound up on the embankment of the dam, then who was the dead woman and how had she gotten into the water? And – another realisation now troubled Ian – if the little silver Toyota had left La Gondola without one of its passengers, what had happened to the other woman in the pink shirt who had entered the estate that day?

ROOTS

R eshma woke with a start, literally catching her dream-self as she fell down the spirals of the staircase that led below Park Station. Her hands were still clenched, as if she was trying to grab a railing. She turned her fists face-up, forcing her fingers and arms to relax. She flexed her fingers a few times to make sure the blood was circulating, then rubbed her hands together, checking she was still at home, in her own bed.

Reshma could hear voices through the bedroom door – a conversation, although she couldn't make out any words. Ian and Surprise, both talking softly so as not to wake her up.

Reshma rolled over to look at the alarm clock on Ian's side of the bed – she was too lazy to reach out to her own bedside table and tap on the screen to wake up her phone.

It was a little after seven. Reshma hadn't had enough sleep, but she wasn't likely to get any more. With a small grunt, she sat up and levered her legs over the side of the bed. She dragged one of the fleece blankets off the covers, draped it around her like a cape, and made her way towards the kitchen to make herself a cup of tea.

Ian and Surprise both stopped talking the moment she shuffled into the room, and he immediately began apologising for speaking too loudly.

Reshma shook her head, not quite awake enough yet to deal with Ian's constant need to be the good guy. 'It's not always about you,' she said, only half-joking. 'My mind is just busy. With work, I mean.'

She retrieved her mug and a fresh teabag from the cupboard. As the kettle boiled, she put out her hands on the kitchen counter to steady herself. Her mouth was dry, and her stomach was in a knot nearly as tight as her fists had been. She stared at the wall as her mind replayed the night before in sped-up time. She caught flashes of blood. The yellow water bubbling up from the ground. The smell of rot and death. The bodies. The carelessly discarded finger. The guns and the money. Giving the case away.

A sour taste-feeling rose up from her stomach and pushed into her throat. She still had not checked her phone. There was bound to be fallout as a result of what she had done or, more importantly, how she had done it. Reshma knew that calling in Sobukwe had been the right thing, even if she hadn't necessarily gone about it the right way. She thought she could live with her decision without losing much more sleep over it, but she wasn't looking forward to the inevitable short-term consequences, which would, more than likely, include her immediate commander either shitting on her, or giving her the silent treatment. In the police force, being excommunicated could be a dangerous sentence.

As Reshma sipped on her too-hot tea, she realised that she wasn't in the mood to talk. Not to Ian, not to Surprise, not to anyone. She took an extra two seconds to make up an excuse before she faced the kitchen audience, who had resumed their conversation in even more hushed tones. 'I'm sorry, I have to get going. There's a court thing today,' she said, making what she hoped was an appropriately apologetic face before heading off to the spare room to choose a fresh set of clothes.

Reshma was in and out of the courts all the time, usually to testify about something minor, often for cases that were several years old, which meant it was unlikely Ian would ask about it. She grabbed her clothes and took them into the bathroom with her, turning on the shower and climbing in before Ian could follow her and try start a conversation.

By the time she was out of the water and dressed in jeans and a clean shirt, Reshma felt slightly more human, but still not in any mood to make small talk. The events of the night before scratched at her, unsettling her. There were too many unknowns, and the stakes might be higher than she had realised.

She thought it was probably best to get the discomfort out the way, and mentally steeled herself to go straight into Joburg Central, where her unit was based.

She kissed Ian on the cheek as she left, and waved goodbye to Surprise. She could see disappointment on her lover's face, and hoped her hasty departure hadn't been too rude. She just didn't have the energy to put on more than the barest facade of a polite face.

On the short drive to the station, Reshma tried to dull the edge of her anxiety by reciting a Coleridge poem she had learned at school.

In Xanadu did Kubla Khan.
A stately pleasure dome decree:
Where Alph, the sacred river, ran
Through caverns measureless to man
Down to a sunless sea.

She recited the first stanza out loud and then went blank. She enjoyed grasping for the phrases, a good distraction. By the time she reached the parking at Joburg Central Police Station, she'd skipped most of the middle, but remembered the last few lines:

Weave a circle round him thrice,
And close your eyes with holy dread.

Reshma took the lift up to the seventh floor, where their unit had been given temporary offices for the last few months. The 'facilities' extended to an open-plan room with a few tables, telephones, six working computers, and eight desks, none of which were occupied when she walked in.

She checked the time. It was just after eight – the only advantage of going to bed late and waking up early, she told herself. The others would only get in around nine. Reshma was grateful for the quiet time. The unit's head, Colonel Noma, had her own office next door, but the door was closed and Reshma didn't knock to see if she was in. Noma was a good commander, and Reshma enjoyed working with her for the most part. She hoped she hadn't done anything that would sour the relationship permanently.

Although the unit occasionally shared workstations, Reshma had part-claimed one desk as her own. She kept a stash of muesli and nut bars locked in the middle drawer, the key clipped onto her already jingling lanyard. On the top of the desk, not quite obscured by the computer screen, was a small succulent plant – a gift from Ian – that was bravely clinging to life, and a small Ganesh icon that had been a gift from her mother. At least two other team members had stapled multi-coloured quotations from the Bible on the room dividers, so Reshma felt the elephant god was an appropriate contribution to the monologues.

Reshma switched on the computer and waited for it to whirr into life. That the computers *and* the internet both worked on a regular basis still surprised Reshma, who logged in with no clear idea of what she was looking for, or who might be looking for her, just so that she had something to do.

First, she clicked through to her email. To her relief, there was nothing except the routine stuff, and nothing from Colonel Noma, not yet at least. There was also an email about an actual hearing that was taking place that day, and which gave Reshma a brief moment of panic when she thought that perhaps her white lie to Ian had tripped her up. She took a short breath and forced herself to re-read the mail, realising that her guilty conscience was connecting the wrong dots. She had almost no connection with the case that was being heard, and was off the hook.

From Outlook, she clicked through to the online internal message board, and spent another fifteen minutes checking to see if there were any important announcements or upcoming events she needed to make a note of. There was an announcement from IT, warning everyone about digital hygiene and not sharing passwords. There was also an alert reminding everyone that there were repairs scheduled on the water mains in a week's time, and that the station would be without water services between 6 am and 6 pm, if the job went according to schedule. The notice said that temporary toilet facilities would be provided in the lot outside the building, and that everyone should be aware there would be no water in any of the taps – for hand-washing or coffee-making, for instance. Reshma made a note in her calendar to stay as far away from the building as she could. She had spent two days working in the Sandton police station when there had been an emergency shutdown due to a burst pipe that affected the whole area and most of Alex. After eight hours, the unflushable inside toilets had become cesspits. Reshma thought of herself as pragmatic rather than cynical, but she didn't see half of Joburg's finest taking seven, or more, flights of stairs to take a pee.

Reshma tapped her fingers on the desk and allowed her mind to wander along a thread that led from the thought of dank toilets to the underground chamber from the night before. She couldn't go digging around the crime scene now, not without possibly attracting more censure. But she was curious about the one unrelated detail, the foul-smelling water underneath Park Station.

She looked online to see if there was anything in the news about a sewage leak, or something similar at Park Station. She saw that a few years before, the entire station precinct had undergone a massive upgrade to its storm-water drain and sewerage systems, including replacing manhole covers in between the rail tracks.

When she looked up 'yellow water' and 'Johannesburg', something else came back. Pictures of kids smiling and swimming in the toxic run-off from mine dumps. There was an entry from Greenpeace about polluted water welling up below the city. It was yellow or orange in colour.

Reshma recalled that when she had asked the bored railway official about the malodorous water, the woman had fobbed her off and referred her to Kruger. Was it possible they were covering up something? Environmental stuff wasn't really Reshma's area, but she felt an urgent need to get away from her desk. And surely this fell outside of whatever Sobukwe and his team would be investigating.

She wondered if it was too late – or too early – to try the old man. She found the mobile number Kruger had given her the night before and sent a message, asking him to call or text her when he had a moment, as she had a question.

Kruger's reply came less than a minute later. Obviously also not much of a sleeper either. He had left the crime scene at around the same time she had, and perhaps he hadn't left the station at all. Kruger said he was free to meet Reshma any time, and that he would be around that morning.

Five minutes later Reshma had logged off from her user profile, grabbed a muesli bar from her desk, and was headed back to Park Station.

The railway terminus was less than a ten-minute drive from the police station, although with the morning traffic it would take her double that. Still, in Joburg you never walked when you could drive.

In the morning light, the streets and city grid looked brighter than they had the night before, the optimistic energy of a fresh start in the City of Gold. By the late evening, the energy would transform again, the goodwill carried away by the sunset.

Eighteen minutes later she pulled her car into the same lot she had used the night before. The Metro car from the previous evening was still there, but there were no other vehicles. There was one warrant officer in her uniform standing at the door to the underground section, but that was it. Reshma hoped she would be able to talk to Kruger without bumping into Claassen and Sobukwe, who plainly were not interested in having other people or other units on what was now their scene. Reshma allowed herself a temporary exemption from their rules, seeing as she had been the one who had handed it over to them.

Kruger was waiting in the parking lot, wearing a new set of clothes that were only different from the night before because they were different colours, but were otherwise almost identical in composition: blue trousers, a grey V-neck jersey, a blue shirt, and a grey tie.

'Do you mind if we go and speak in your office?' she asked, realising as she spoke that she was not even sure if Kruger had an office, or where such an office might be. 'I just need to talk to you, ask you some questions about the property – we don't need to do it in the parking lot,' she said, trying to make her request sound more reasonable.

Kruger shrugged and indicated that Reshma should follow him back into Park Station. They went up the escalators to the mezzanine level above the main arrival hall, and then took another set of escalators to a floor Reshma had never been to before. The noise fell away as they went higher. At the top of the escalators was a small landing and a sign for the company that managed the rail services properties. Kruger stood at a set of glass doors and placed his thumb on a biometric reader. A green light went on, and the door clicked. He pushed it open and gestured for Reshma to follow.

Kruger navigated through a short maze of blue and brown walls. When they reached a dead-end, he reached into his pocket and drew out a key attached to what looked like a small model of a train, and opened the door.

'I sit here,' he said, gesturing for Reshma to go in ahead of him.

Kruger's office was tiny, the space restricted further by floor-to-ceiling shelves on two of the walls, where all of the available shelf space had been neatly packed with books, papers and files. In one section,

Reshma could make out what looked like year books, the dates clearly stamped in gold on the sides of the spines.

'Is this like a library?' she asked.

'It's part of an archive. What used to be *the* archive. A century of trains and train tracks coming to and from Johannesburg. I look after the bits that I can,' Kruger said.

Reshma thought that Ian would have loved to learn more about the history of the station. She was more interested in the present, though. 'The woman from last night. She said you knew about the water. The yellow water in that room. You know what I mean.'

Kruger waited nearly a minute before speaking. 'You think you know what it is?' he asked.

Reshma gave a small nod.

'Then why ask me?' Kruger said, impassive or cautious – she didn't know him well enough to read his mood. The guardedness of his response made her wonder if she had accidentally asked something that made him uncomfortable. She changed tactic.

'I guess I was just curious,' she said, trying to make her voice sound lighter. 'There was a lot going on down there. I think with the ... with the forensic stuff, it was just overwhelming, and it was something I hadn't seen before. I didn't know there were mines under the city, you know,' she said, trying to sound more absent-minded than she felt.

As soon as she mentioned the word 'mine', she knew she'd lost the chance to ask any further questions. Kruger's face shut down.

'I thought you had a question related to your investigation,' he said, standing up, making it clear the discussion was over. 'I make every effort to help where I can, but I look after history and archives. I can't help you with water or pipes or whatnot,' he said, making it sound as if her query itself had been vague and confused. Which, she realised, it had. 'I'm afraid I have other work to do now, Captain,' he continued with a polite but forced smile. 'If you or your ... other colleagues have any further queries, I am sure they can send them through to Ora. She will assist you.'

Kruger walked Reshma back to the glass door and repeated his goodbyes before placing his thumb on the reader, opening it for her. He did not offer to accompany her back down the escalators.

Reshma was surprised at how quickly the conversation had been terminated. She responded with the barest polite thank-you and headed back down to the growing noise of the main atrium.

When she got back to her car, the woman from the day before was waiting for her in the small parking lot. Although she hadn't caught the woman's name at the time, Reshma assumed that this was Ora.

Reshma greeted her and waited for a response. When none seemed forthcoming, she started digging in her handbag for her car keys. Trying to draw people into a game of who-blinks-first was obviously some kind of internal railway strategy, and Reshma was too tired from the night before to enjoy any sort of game.

Ora spoke at last. 'I just spoke to Mr Kruger,' she said, acknowledging the obvious. 'We've had some issues with sewage before. It happens in the CBD. Old infrastructure. Our tunnels are the lowest point, so the water and everything else drains there. You can speak to Joburg Water if you need to.'

The woman paused before speaking again. 'We don't need a problem. We have over two hundred thousand people coming through here every day. It's important we don't make some kind of panic about nothing. You understand?'

Reshma was about to ask about the sewerage repairs she'd read about in the newspapers, but decided rather to stay quiet. Ora took this as a sign of dissent.

'This is a National Key Point, you know. You should be careful about what you think you want to look into. Whether you have any ... authority,' Ora said, glancing over at the officer still guarding the door to the stairwell. 'Stick to your crimes, Captain. Or you might find this a difficult place to work.'

Ora turned and headed towards the interior of the station, presumably back up to the company offices.

Reshma wondered why the property officials were so concerned about a pool of dirty water tens of metres underground. The woman had clearly been warning her off. Ora's comment about the National Key Point had been pointed too, and gave Reshma pause. If it wasn't directly relevant to the crime scene, did she have any right even to be asking? And, given that she had basically given up the entire criminal case, did she have any right to be asking about the crime scene either?

Reshma got into her car and turned on the ignition. The trip had been frustrating and a waste of time. On cue, her phone buzzed. It was a message from Colonel Noma, asking Reshma to call her or come see her once she was at the station. Reshma's stomach clenched right back to where it had been that morning at her kitchen counter. The tone didn't indicate anything either way, but Reshma couldn't think of any other reason her boss would want to speak to her.

She looked at her phone again and checked the time. It wasn't even 10 am. Too early to call it a day. She would go and face whatever was waiting for her on the seventh floor.

Reshma was still holding her phone when she reversed out of her parking space, making a wide arc as she pulled out. She felt the back of her car bump into something, stopped and pulled up the handbrake. She turned her head but couldn't see anything behind her. It wasn't until she climbed out the car that she could see she had reversed right into a yellow and black chevron that marked the edge of the tar. She hadn't even noticed it when she'd driven in. Now there was a small black smudge on her back bumper. Reshma touched it to see if it would rub off. It wouldn't.

She looked around and saw that the warrant officer who was guarding the door had noticed her, and presumably her little accident. Reshma pretended not to have spotted the officer watching her, but her entire face burned with the shame of being a bad driver and being foolish all at the same time. The damage to the car wasn't serious, but it was enough to be more than an annoyance.

Reshma swore, got back in her car, and started reciting Coleridge again as she drove back through Xanadu.

FLIGHTS

By the time Reshma got back to Joburg Central, there was no parking close by, and she had to leave her car in one of the half-managed lots a few blocks away – a site where there had been a building until fairly recently. Now the landowner was renting it out for parking income while trying to sell the space to a developer who would build something new to cover up the gravel and rubble left behind.

She half-marched back to the police headquarters, her tension building. Waiting for the lift to get to the ground floor made her anxiety start to twist into irritation, and so she decided to take the stairs.

By the time she reached the seventh floor, some of the tension had been blown away by her huffing and puffing. Reshma wasn't unfit, and had even started running with Ian on occasion, but stairs had never been her thing – nor anyone else's in the building, she gathered, judging by the fact that she didn't pass a single person on the entire journey.

She took a moment to catch her breath on the landing so she wouldn't head into Colonel Noma's office sounding like an asthmatic. She took one extra breath just for luck and walked down the corridor.

Noma's office door was slightly ajar, but Reshma knocked anyway, the tap pushing the door a little wider – just enough for her to see that Noma was talking to someone sitting on the opposite side of the desk.

Reshma didn't have enough line of sight to see who was in the Colonel's office, but Noma gave Reshma a short look of just enough annoyance to let her know that she was not required or desired at that moment. Reshma wondered briefly if it was because she didn't want any interruptions, or because of what Reshma had done the night before.

Slightly chastened, she headed back to her own section. From the other corner of the office, one of the team's lieutenants waved at her – Elliot, a smart youngster who had grown up in Eldorado Park. Other than him, the room was empty.

Reshma went to go and get a cup of water from the cooler, and then sat back at her desk. Out of boredom more than anything else, she ate half her nut bar. She checked her email again. There was nothing new. Not even Ian had messaged her, which was unusual for him. She remembered him saying that he had a bunch of meetings, and she felt bad that she had been so caught up in her own anxieties that she hadn't shown any interest in his work. She hadn't even asked how his visit to Myburgh had gone, and she cringed at her own rudeness. She would remember to apologise later, and ask the right questions, sound like a good girlfriend instead of one who only cared about her own stuff.

Reshma was about to deconstruct the remaining half of her nut bar when she saw movement at the office door. She was expecting Colonel Noma to walk through, coming to call her in for a kakking-out. But she was surprised to see Claassen from the night before.

He nodded at Reshma, as if he had been looking for her. Reshma could see him scan the office. He clocked Elliot in the corner but did not acknowledge the younger policeman. Then he walked over to Reshma's desk, positioning himself so that his back was towards Elliot, and his side shielded by one of the blue room dividers.

'Howzit. Do you mind if we have a quick chat?' he asked, pulling up a chair even though Reshma hadn't said yes.

Reshma felt the knot twist in her gut again.

'I have a meeting with Colonel Noma – I'm just waiting for her to finish with whoever she's seeing now, and I can't be busy when she's done. But I can talk if it's not going to take too long,' Reshma said, trying not to sound too abrupt, but also not needing to be overly friendly. She'd done her duty and didn't consider it necessary to be more than polite about the fact that she'd given up what was probably a very big and important case.

Claassen made a movement with his mouth that was an attempt at a smile, but too guarded to come across as friendly.

'She's already done. She was meeting with me. That's what I want to talk to you about. Can I sit?' he asked, pointing to the chair.

Reshma nodded, and her anxiety-knot split – one strand was panic, fear that somehow Claassen and Sobukwe had found out about her unsanctioned visit to the station. The other was all excitement and curiosity. Something else might be happening here.

Luckily for Reshma, Claassen didn't play railway games and got straight to the point.

'You know what we do?' he asked.

'Kind of,' Reshma said, after a second's pause.

She had an idea, but it wasn't informed by much more than what she'd read in the newspapers and picked up around the table at work. She knew that there was a group, not always the same group, but some group within SAPS that was tasked with trying to stop the spate of cash heists that had been taking place over the last decade. It wasn't a new crime, but over the past five years it had been happening more often, and the attacks were becoming increasingly violent as it became harder to get into the heavily armoured vehicles – the gangs' response to improved security measures put in place by cash transport companies that were losing tens of millions a week. Often the only way was for them to force their way in – by ramming a car, using industrial cutting tools if they had time, or using explosives if they didn't. It was all much easier if they could just get the guards inside the vans to open up for them. Which they usually achieved by threatening horrible violence, something it turned out none of the heist gangs had a problem with. The month before, two guards had burned to death when the gang attacking their convoy set the main cash van alight after not being able to get into the vault inside. They'd also shot the driver at point-blank range, and shot and injured a witness who had been on the opposite section of the highway when the attack took place and had foolishly stopped to try and film it on his phone.

Reshma followed the stories but knew there was a lot of information that never made it beyond the case officers. There were rumours that some of the heists involved inside informants. Including security people. And ex-cops. Cops, even.

That was why she figured guys like Sobukwe were now involved. Nobody liked Sobukwe, but most people respected him. Or feared him. He wasn't the kind of guy who seemed corruptible, which made him scariest of all to certain factions.

And now here was his junior, wanting to talk to her.

It took Reshma another second to realise that Claassen was probably coming to warn her off talking about what she and the dog handler had seen the night before. Their unit surely didn't need any loose lips spreading the word that there was a cache of guns and money hidden under the bowels of Park Station, a hundred metres away from a cess-pool of yellow water.

'You don't have to worry. I won't tell anyone about what we found,' she said, unable to stop herself from claiming subtle ownership of the discovery and the crime scene, even if she had handed it over.

Claassen gave Reshma a proper smile this time.

'I know you wouldn't. That's why we ... I actually came to ask if you would be interested in joining our task team.'

This was not where any of Reshma's various thought-streams had led, and she found herself stalled, her fingers about to pick at an exposed piece of nut.

'Your commander knows, if that's what you're wondering about,' Claassen continued. 'Look, I can't say she was, uh, *excited* about what you did last night. But it impressed Super. And me, of course. You think straight, you do the right thing for the case even if it's not the right thing for you personally. You're smart, you know how to handle a lot of work. You've used your firearm before. These are attributes we need.'

He finished his sales pitch. 'So, you interested?' he asked, still with the same smile.

Reshma was already processing what he'd mentioned about his chat with Noma, and realised that even if she wasn't tempted by the chance to work with one of the best cops on the entire force – General Sobukwe – and on one of the most elite task force teams, the realisa-tion that her relationship with Noma would probably be a little sour for a while, whichever option she took, helped to sell the deal.

'I'd be a fool to say no,' she said, looking back at Claassen. 'When do I start?' she asked, suddenly aware that the set-up, the impromptu offer, was extremely unusual in the context of the way the department liked to do things. Although it might just be how things were under the General's command.

'You'd start now. As in, you leave your desk and follow me to our offices. You still think you'd be a fool to say no?' Claassen asked. 'Because you won't get a chance to pull out once you leave.'

Reshma gave a nod, more for herself than for him. 'Now. That's fine,' she said, surprising herself as the words came out. Not that she was agreeing to the opportunity, but that she was doing it without second-guessing herself. She would have plenty of time for that later.

Claassen stood up and smoothed the palm of his hand against his leg. 'Excellent,' he said.

He looked over the desk, and around Reshma.

'You don't bring anything from here unless there's something personal you want to keep. We'll provide everything – computer, all of that. Is there anything you need?' he asked.

Reshma removed the desk key from her lanyard. 'Hey Ell,' she called over to the younger cop, who was trying very hard to pretend he wasn't dying to know what they were talking about. Elliot immediately perked up and looked in her direction.

'There's muesli bars and stuff in the drawer. You can have them, or share them out or whatever, okay?' Almost as an afterthought, she asked if he would take care of her plant. She picked up the small succulent and walked it over to his desk, with only a small twinge as she handed it over. Ian wouldn't mind. She could always get another one.

On her way out, Reshma doubled back and grabbed the small icon of the elephant-headed Ganesh. Ian might forgive her for leaving his plant behind, but her mother would never let her hear the end of it if she didn't take the deity to her new desk. Wherever that was. She shoved the icon in her jacket pocket and thought she might even take it home.

'That's it. I'm ready,' she said, hoisting her bag over her shoulder as she prepared to follow the detective out the building.

DYNAMITE

It was early afternoon by the time Reshma drove into the parking lot of a small industrial office complex somewhere near Modderfontein. Claassen had driven almost painfully slowly on the route between the CBD and the East Rand, constantly checking in his rear mirror to see if Reshma was behind him.

Claassen's white hatchback pulled up outside a face-brick building that had a sign for an IT services company next to the front door. He indicated for Reshma to park in one of two spaces that were marked 'VISITOR', and then made a three-point-turn before reversing into one of three shadecloth-covered bays marked 'RESERVED'.

While Claassen parked, Reshma took off the jacket that had become too hot in the highveld autumn midday sun, and draped it over her arm so it wouldn't crease. She took her handbag from the boot and was ready by the time Claassen approached the front door.

'You ding your car?' he asked as he walked past, noting the yellow and black smear on her bumper. She cringed inwardly but nodded.

'Close encounter with a stationary object,' she said, hoping Claassen would leave it at that.

He looked sympathetic. 'This is us,' he said, pushing the door open a narrow second after Reshma heard the lock buzz.

The inside was veneer flooring and drywall, with the same

company sign behind a too-large reception desk. A diminutive woman, swamped by the supersized table, pointed at a registration book that lay open next to her computer.

'She doesn't need to sign in, Celia,' Claassen said. 'This is Reshma Patel. She's going to work here.'

The woman smiled and offered a quiet hello as they passed. Two metres behind the desk was another door, which buzzed again – Celia, Reshma assumed. Claassen let Reshma go first although she had no idea where it was exactly that she was supposed to go.

'Just head straight,' he offered, not unkindly. It wasn't supposed to be some sort of test, Reshma realised, just politeness.

At the end of the corridor, Claassen told her to turn right. The carpeted hallway gave way to a large and well-lit open-plan office, where Reshma saw six desks, all pushed together into some kind of geometric formation. Only two of the desks were occupied, but the rest all had various combinations of laptops and piles of files, with a knot of cables joining the computers in the centre of the desk.

The men seated at two of the computers looked like cops who had tried to dress as IT professionals, but hadn't quite managed to pull it off. One was in jeans and a check shirt; the other was wearing beige slacks and a green jersey that looked like it was related to Kruger's. Both men had headphones on, and were evidently engaged in something that was either important or riveting on their computer screens. Only one of them lifted his head to acknowledge Reshma and Claassen's arrival.

'Boardroom in five,' Claassen announced, unbothered as to whether they were paying attention – or, assuming that they were paying attention. He indicated that Reshma should follow him. As they walked past, Reshma caught a glimpse of what Jersey Guy was watching: CCTV footage of what looked like the forecourt of a petrol station. There were several cars, one van or truck. As Reshma watched, she caught a flicker of movement, and thought she could see a body move on the tarmac. She turned her eyes back to Claassen, who was heading towards an office door in the corner, next to what appeared to be a glass-walled boardroom.

'We'll meet in there now,' Claassen said, indicating the larger space. 'I'll introduce you to the others when we sit down.'

He tapped on the office door before walking straight in.

The office belonged to General Sobukwe, who was seated behind a desk that looked almost identical to the ones outside, except it had two computers on it – one Mac, one PC – and a similar mound of paper and tangle of cables trailing off to the floor.

On the wall behind Sobukwe was a giant map of greater Johannesburg, tacked up with what looked like a combination of masking tape and duct tape. There were red and black pins dotted all over the paper, like an army of malevolent ants. Reshma assumed the pins marked crime scenes, cash heists.

On the opposite wall were several smaller maps that had been tacked together to make a larger one. Reshma thought it looked like parts of Mpumalanga, stretching into southern Limpopo – she could just make out Witbank-Emalahleni, Groblersdal and Marblehall, but they were almost obscured by their own red and black pins. There were other colours, too, which Reshma couldn't guess the meaning of.

'So. You said yes?' Sobukwe asked, pausing his work to address her. It was a friendly question, and Reshma answered with another yes, and a smile that she hoped didn't come across as obsequious.

'I told them to meet in the boardroom,' Claassen repeated to his boss.

Sobukwe nodded and bent his head back to whatever it was he had been busy with before Reshma's arrival. There was no formal dismissal, but Reshma took the hint and followed Claassen quietly out the door. Nobody in the group seemed much for small talk so far, which suited her fine.

Claassen walked her through to the boardroom. 'You can sit here and wait for the others,' he said, gesturing to the empty space. It felt like a room for bland ideas, and Reshma wondered how come it was housing a supposedly elite crime unit – one that only had four members, as far as she could see.

'You want coffee? Tea? Something? There's a fridge in there, behind you,' he said, pointing to a veneered wall unit that matched the desks, 'and there's water inside if you want. Grab a seat and make yourself comfortable. I'll be back in a second.'

Reshma put down her bag and got a plastic bottle of water. She hadn't eaten except for the half-bar of nuts and was regretting handing over her snack drawer contents to Elliot. But at least the water was cold, and it took some of the edge off the lingering heat of the cross-town drive, and the residual anxiety and strangeness. She sat and stared at the incongruous space around her, wondering if she'd acted too quickly in agreeing to join.

It was natural to want to be part of the unit – anyone would want to work in this team, with this boss. But she wondered if she should have waited, even an extra hour, made a proper farewell, and gotten some closure with Colonel Noma. She didn't think the woman was the kind to take things personally, or hold grudges, but it dawned on Reshma that it might have been a little foolish to walk out of Joburg Central without so much as a goodbye to anyone.

Her train of thought was interrupted by the arrival of the two other men. Both greeted her, their tone somewhere between friendly and cautious. Reshma wondered if this was the entire team. She wasn't sure what she had been expecting, but it definitely wasn't four men and a fake computer company.

After their initial greeting, both men remained silent. Another two minutes passed and Claassen returned, then Sobukwe joined them from his office next door.

'This isn't the whole team,' Claassen started, answering Reshma's unvoiced question. 'Scott and Dube here are the IT experts,' he said. Scott was the one in jeans; Dube was the one in the jersey.

'They're running footage, a whole bunch of documents we got scanned. They're looking through everything on their computers. We have a few other people who are out in the field, looking at crime scenes, doing interviews. There was another robbery yesterday near Midvaal, so two of the guys are there. Another two are at Hammanskraal, from last week. You'll get to know the team as you go along, but there's not a lot of us really. We work as sort of the core investigation outfit, and with whoever the local detectives are when something happens.'

'What Wayde is saying is that we are the team trying to stop these things before they happen, Captain Patel,' Sobukwe spoke. 'That means that this team, this unit, has to be on top of all the intelligence we get, from everywhere. And we have to produce enough paperwork for our friends at the NPA to prosecute, and get a conviction,' he said.

The way Sobukwe spoke, Reshma wondered if the relationship between the unit and the National Prosecuting Authority was cordial or frosty. She didn't know how to read the man.

Claassen jumped back into the conversation, and introduced

Reshma to Scott and Dube. 'Captain Patel has been with the kidnapping task team at Central,' he explained. 'She was the one who found
the stuff at Park Station last night. You want to tell them about what
happened?' he said, turning to Reshma.

Reshma paused for a moment, then explained, as quickly and simply as possible, what had taken place – from following up a suspected
kidnapping and the gore-fest underground, to the sniffer dog and the
discovery of the weapons and money cache. She tried to tell the story
in a way that didn't centre the case around her involvement. And she
said nothing about her botched follow-up visit, and the polluted water
underground.

Both men nodded, but appeared only marginally interested.
Perhaps they were eager to get back to their work, Reshma thought.
She could google both men later and see if she could figure out their
backgrounds; but if they were from IT, there was a good chance there
would be no information about them.

'You find the missing woman?' Dube asked. Perhaps he had being
paying attention. Reshma shook her head. 'Cameras at the station
were down, and we found nothing in our sweeps. Might just have been
a nuisance call,' she said, although she didn't really believe that.

Reshma stopped talking and waited for Claassen to take over, but
the gap stretched into a soon uncomfortable silence. 'Do you have any
questions about us?' he said, at last, looking from her to his boss.

Sobukwe smiled at Reshma blankly, not unkindly, but with a tiny
hint of impatience, as if he had work he needed to get back to.

Reshma didn't like being put on the spot. It made her feel defensive, which she couldn't admit out loud. She hadn't asked to join the
team, but here she was. She paused before saying some of what was on

her mind. 'How come you work in this place, here?' she said, gesturing to the space around her.

It was Dube who answered.

'It's from a case we—' he looked over at Scott – 'worked on a few months ago. Fraud. No one ever worked here. Just office space. We got phone lines, fibre put in.'

'I chose for us to work here, because it keeps our investigations out of the way of people who ... should not really be interested in what we are doing,' Sobukwe said, his voice slow and measured. 'This way, people know about us, but they don't notice us. They don't know what we are actually doing. And we don't tell them.'

Something about Sobukwe's last sentence gave Reshma pause.

'Captain Patel, we know that there are informers. On the inside – people inside the security companies, for sure. Even people inside our own force. Not everyone got caught in Operation Spikiri last year.'

Operation Spikiri had been a major sting, one that had seen three high-ranking cops and four more non-commissioned officers arrested and charged for various crimes related to cash-in-transit heists. Some of the information about the busts was still coming out, but Reshma knew that at least three of the suspects were accused of murder and attempted murder – and that two of their victims had been cops.

'There is something maybe Claassen should have told you before you said yes. So I will say it now, because you should know this before you make up your mind. Once you start working with us on this, it will be too late to back out,' Sobukwe said, his face suddenly grim.

'What we do, what this team does, is not a game. There are people who will happily kill us. People who will try to kill us. Because we might be that last thing between them, and the greed and avarice that drives them morning and night. And whatever you have seen before now,' he said, 'you have never seen greed like these people have. They will kill without provocation. They will kill to steal money, and they will kill to stop you from stopping them. So whatever we do in here, whatever we say, whatever we see, it stays in here. Right up until the time, when not if, right up until the time it gets to court. You do not discuss anything that happens in these rooms, you do not share information, you do not mention locations, you do not even mention that you are working on these cases. Do you understand? You don't share it with your mother, your lover, your friends ...'

Reshma nodded that she understood. She got the importance, and the risks. Or at least, she thought she did.

'Do you have any more questions?' Claassen asked.

'Why me?' she said, as serious as Sobukwe had been a moment before. She had what she thought was a reasonable amount of confidence in her own work, and her abilities as an investigator and a police officer. But she wasn't sure why this unit wanted her to work with them – unless, again, it was to keep tabs on her. Maybe the underground cache was much more important than she had realised.

Claassen chirped back. 'We needed more women on the team. HR said we weren't representative,' he said.

Reshma didn't laugh. She had been the only woman on the team more often than she would have liked. She had also meant: why had they chosen *her*?

Sobukwe must have seen something in her expression, because he answered. 'Seriously?' he asked. 'Because after last night I asked around, asked about you. You have a good record. And you made a decision that was the right one, but would not have been a popular one. I like that. And we need people like that here. This is a chance to do good, maybe great, police work. But it's not a popularity contest.'

After a second, he added, 'Also, you have experience under fire. You know what it's like to be shot at, and to have people shot down next to you. You had that, and it didn't stop you from being able to take the shot you needed to. I need people who are calm under fire. And who can take down an armed suspect without flinching.'

Reshma knew Sobukwe wasn't just talking about arrests. He was telling her, in veiled terms, that if her life or the lives of her colleagues were going to be at risk, he was expecting her to fire back, and shoot to kill.

DONOR FUNDS

Ian's afternoon meetings had gone well right up to the point where the South African compliance officer working with one of the smaller American-based NGOs had started complaining about the recycling guys who pushed and pulled their trolleys around the city.

'It's on our neighbourhood WhatsApp group. They said it came from SAPS. These guys leave codes, like clues outside houses – but they do it in rubbish. Like, messages for robbers and hijackers. If they leave a red thing, a can of Coke, it means they should avoid your house. But if they put out something green – Sprite – then it means that your house is a good one to target,' the woman said, her expression ludicrously earnest.

Ian was about to explain that most modern criminals worked with cellphones – which were much easier to use than imaginary coded trash and had the added advantage of not broadcasting your criminal intentions to the rest of the world – when the woman continued, saying that her own neighbour had recently been a victim of crime, and that she was convinced the local recycling guys had acted as lookouts, but the police had refused to arrest any of them.

'We just want them to clean up the streets,' she said, indignant, looking at Ian for approval and agreement.

The irony of her statement wasn't lost on Ian. The Reclaimers – as the trolley-powered recyclers called themselves – were responsible for keeping a considerable portion of Johannesburg's trash contained, and also saved the City hundreds of millions of rand a year through their collection and recycling efforts. Although, individually, there was no rule that any of the Reclaimers were saints, as a group, Ian also knew that men on trolleys were not the ones who were responsible for the increased spate of muggings, attacks and home invasions taking place in the suburbs. Most serious suburban crimes were vehicle-based – at least one, sometimes more of the perpetrators were in a car, or a motorbike. A foot-propelled trolley carrying a couple of cubic metres of recyclable plastic wasn't high on the list of things Ian was scared of. But he realised, looking at the lipstick on the teeth of the compliance officer, no matter how carefully he phrased the facts of the situation, she would be unlikely to listen to what he said unless it agreed with what she already believed. And, plainly, she believed that the men who cleaned up her trash were a threat to her wellbeing.

For a moment Ian felt trapped, reluctant to alienate someone who represented an important work partnership – although he didn't have to work with her directly, he reminded himself. In the end, he gave an awkward shrug and spread his hands as if to indicate that it was not something that was in his area of interest, or control.

After the woman had left, Ian admonished himself for staying quiet, and for being a coward. It made him anxious to think that he had potentially changed his behaviour towards someone because she had a hand on the purse strings, for a purse his work group needed, and because a bigot had some degree of impact on how much or how little money the organisation she represented would choose to disburse to support his team's work.

Ian compromised by writing up a short email to the woman – in polite but unambiguous terms – explaining his position, and his discomfort, and providing links to several recent reports from both Wits University and the Council for Scientific and Industrial Research, about the Reclaimers and their recycling efforts. He wondered if the woman would even read the articles, but he pushed 'send' anyway. Ten seconds later his mailbox pinged with an out-of-office reply from the compliance officer's address, saying the she would be on holiday in Plettenberg Bay for the next ten days.

Ian sighed, but even as he experienced a jab of frustration, he realised he felt a larger sense of relief at avoiding confrontation. For some reason, the contrast appealed to him, as if it was a marker of pushing Ian the Cop further and further to the back of his CV. He would have to work out how to make Ian the Bureaucrat a little less boring as he went along.

Almost as a reward, Ian allowed himself to open up the folder where he had moved all of the pictures and video clips from La Gondola. As he did, he realised that he had forgotten to call up Sylvie September, the aunt of the missing Zebulon. He checked the time and saw it was just before 5 pm. He looked up the number Myburgh had sent him, and pressed dial. The phone rang twice before someone answered. Not an old woman, but a young girl.

Ian asked if it was Sylvie's phone, and the girl said it was, but that Sylvie couldn't hear very much, so could she help? It took Ian two more questions to ascertain that the phone answerer was named Thandeka, that she was Sylvie's next-door neighbour, that she was in high school, and sometimes came over to help Sylvie.

87

When he explained what he needed, Thandeka passed on the information and came back a few moments later to say that Sylvie would be very happy to see Ian any time on the weekend except on Sunday morning when she went to church. Ian said he would come on Saturday, and took down Thandeka's number in case he needed it. He thanked her for her help before ending the call.

Something about the exchange gnawed at him – not worry, more the opposite. There was nothing in Thandeka's tone that suggested Aunt Sylvie was terribly concerned about her nephew's disappearance. Which made Ian start to think the missing person investigation was going to turn out to be a bit of a damp squib. Still, if that was the case, then he could report back to Myburgh and possibly use it as an excuse to follow up on the unidentified body from the dam. He sat and imagined himself somehow solving the case of the dead woman's identity, unable to work out whether this small goal meant he had lowered or raised his own bar.

Ian drove home with the setting sun nearly directly ahead of him. The late-afternoon trolley guys were on their way back to Pageview and Vrededorp, cautiously confident as the motor traffic curved its way around them. The section over Empire was blocked off by roadworks that had started without warning and stretched into months. Ian turned left and detoured through the bottom of Auckland Park, taking a back route between two of the monolithic buildings of the public broadcaster.

The streets turned orange as the sun touched the horizon. For a moment Ian tried to picture a city without the traffic, without the trolley-preneurs. It would feel sterile, isolated, and deeply boring. He wondered if that was the kind of Johannesburg the compliance woman and her neighbours longed for, the neat green lawns and orange-blue-and-white postcards of the past.

He headed over the dam again – today there was only one fisherman – and arrived back to a beautifully clean, neat and empty home. There had been no word from Reshma, which he tried not to take personally. He wondered if he would be eating alone again, or if she would be joining him. He reasoned that he didn't have to wait for her to make contact. He sent her a message asking if she wanted to have dinner at home, or maybe eat out. A minute later she pinged him back, to say that she would be home just after six. A second message, a second later, said 'LUCCI?'

Lucci's was a mostly Italian restaurant run by a proper Italian, Luciano, who swore that the only way to cook a proper pizza was in an electric oven. Cooking directly over flames or with coals, he insisted, was a shortcut to poisoning, and he refused to poison his customers. The restaurant had recently moved from Westdene to a new location in Brixton, near a renovated office-share slash coffee shop, after his former premises had been sold to a property developer.

Ian and Reshma had become regulars at the Westdene location – mostly because it was one of the best vegetarian-friendly places in the area – but had only been once to the new spot. Reshma's suggestion to go there cheered Ian a bit. They were overdue for a dinner date by a few weeks at least, he reckoned. Between her schedule with the kidnapping unit, and him being expected to attend after-work functions, there had been little opportunity to spend time together except for over the breakfast counter.

Ian thought back to the quick escape Reshma had made earlier that morning, and wondered if she had been anxious because of the court case she mentioned, or because of something at work. He realised that he barely knew what Reshma was involved in, that he hadn't discussed the matters she was working on, and didn't even know what it was that had kept her away from home until after 3 am the night before.

He also hadn't filled her in his trip to Hartbeespoort, or any of Myburgh's problems. Not that it was quite as exciting as the work Reshma would be doing. Perhaps 'exciting' was not the right word to describe a dead woman and a missing security guard, Ian told himself.

Reshma squeezed in through the gate just before seven. Her face was a mix of excitement and apology.

'I am so sorry. There was so much traffic coming back from Modderfontein. Why do so many people have to work late?' she said, giving Ian a peck on the lips as she walked through the front door and dropped her bags on a chair.

Ian didn't ask what Reshma had been doing in Modderfontein rather than the Magistrate's Court, or Joburg Central police station.

'I'm surprised you're still standing,' he said, attempting some form of good humour, but unable to veil his frustration. 'You only got about three hours of sleep. Busy day?'

Whatever barb Ian was hoping to land, Reshma either deliberately ignored, or she was genuinely too tired to notice. 'I am *finished*,' she said, 'and I am starving. I haven't eaten anything since half a nut bar this morning. Do you mind if we just go straight there?' she asked. 'I really am sorry I'm late. But I can fill you in much better over food, I promise. Just let me use the bathroom, and we can go.'

Reshma drove them in her car, up past the University of Johannesburg, and along the Brixton High Street. Even at this time of night, the road was still busy with people, buying airtime, having their hair cut. The furniture shops were open, and so were the taverns. Ian stared out the window like he used to as a child, and wondered about the lives other people lived.

Reshma turned up the hill, moving away from the clamour and towards the ridge. The new restaurant was a few blocks down on Caroline Street. A car guard in a yellow reflective vest gestured frantically for them to park in a tiny spot that was too close to a corner for Reshma's liking. She drove past while the guard continued to make hand gestures and shout, before circling back and parking half a block away.

The restaurant was busy, but not full. Outside, under a candy-striped tarpaulin that barely covered the stoep, a table of students were sharing pizza and sangria and smoking cigarettes. Ian briefly wished he could do the same, but Reshma had expressed strong feelings about his occasional smoking habit, and the evening was already only just on the right side of thin ice. Ian caught a draft of smoke as he walked past. It would have to be enough.

Luciano came to greet them personally and ushered them to a table that was in the good corner rather than by the bathroom doors. His enthusiasm lifted whatever residual tension was lingering between Ian and Reshma, and by the time her wine arrived, together with a bowl of breadsticks and a little tub of butter, it was starting to feel more like a date than a peace-making mission.

They ordered a vegetarian calzone, and a baked spinach and tomato pasta to share. Luciano insisted on adding a salad, which they agreed to.

While Luciano cooked, Reshma began to tell Ian about the cash heist unit and their strange offices in Modderfontein Office Park.

'I don't even know if I'm supposed to be telling you any of this,' she said, chomping on a breadstick.

She made the remark half-jokingly, but the comment put Ian on edge again. 'How come you got to meet Sobukwe?' he asked.

Reshma paused, obviously considering how much to tell – which gave Ian another pang. After a moment, she told him about the grisly underground discovery from the previous evening, and the arms cache hidden in one of the tunnels. Reshma kept her voice low, which made Ian wonder if she thought that he perhaps was not to be trusted with the information.

'Your guys must have flipped when they realised you handed the whole case over to Sobukwe,' Ian said, half-laughing. He saw Reshma blush.

'Yeah. I think Colonel Noma was about to give me a very solid talking to, but then the CIT guys came in and said I had to leave ... so, she's probably still pissed, but I don't have to deal with it,' she said, shrugging.

'And the other guys? Charles, Elliot?' Ian asked, trying hard to remember any of the other names Reshma had mentioned. He could have sworn Reshma blushed at the question, which didn't make any sense.

'Ja, no. Most of them weren't there. They were all at court. That thing I told you about,' she said, not quite looking Ian in the eye. 'Turns out I didn't have to go after all. Not my case. Stupid, I should have slept in more.'

When their main courses arrived, Reshma started telling Ian about the video footage she had watched that afternoon courtesy of

Scott and Dube, who she said were some kind of IT and multimedia specialists.

'Ian, you must see the stuff they have – it's bloody scary. Dashcam videos from the armoured money cars. You see these guys run out at them, firing. Non-stop. Trying to force the guards to come out the van. They ram the money van, to make it stop. Or they block it off, and then they have to try get the guards out so they can get the keys to the vault in the back. They can go through a hundred bullets, easy, on a job. Explosives too', she said, cutting herself another wedge from the calzone.

'If they can't get the guards out, then they blow up the sides of the trucks. You've seen pictures, right? There was that video online. But these guys, the heist guys, they are so organised. So connected. They have the right guns, all the ammunition, cars. And they know every-thing about the vans, where and when they are going to be, how many guards. It's an operation', she said, her cheeks flushed with a combina-tion of excitement and exhaustion and wine.

'And Super Sobukwe? What's he like in person?' Ian asked, trying hard not to feel jealous.

'He stayed in his office most of the time, didn't talk much. He's bloody intimidating', Reshma answered. 'He has these giant maps on the wall, and he's always staring at them, moving pins about. Like he's some old-fashioned battle general.'

Ian couldn't help but wonder if that could have been him in another life. If he had stayed on in the force, then maybe he would have also been working with – or been one of – the elite outsiders. Or, he acknowledged, maybe he would have been pushed out, like many others before him. Ian knew that he had never been particularly good at playing the political game that most of the big cops needed to know how to play these days. His father's generation hadn't been like that. Not the detectives, anyway. His dad, guys like Myburgh, they had just been cops. Sometimes they were brutes, sometimes they were clever. Sometimes a little too much of both.

Listening to Reshma talk, Ian couldn't help but think about his own work day. The passive-aggressive funder with lipstick on her teeth and a fear of anything outside her suburban cocoon. He thought about the CCTV footage from the housing estate he had been watching earlier that morning. Definitely on the boring side, compared to Reshma watching bullets hitting armoured glass.

He gave her a potted summary while she ordered tea. She seemed interested in the Jane Doe from the dam, less so in the fate of Zebulon September.

'I saw somewhere that ten per cent of bodies that go to the medico-legal labs, they don't have identities for them,' Reshma said. 'Imagine, dying and nobody knows. Nobody even cares, maybe. You say you think she's a foreigner?' Reshma asked.

Ian nodded. 'I'm going to Atteridgeville on the weekend. To speak to the aunt, where the security guard used to live. If you want to come? You're always good at asking questions,' he said, feeling momentarily inspired at the prospect of a joint investigation.

'Shit. Sorry, Ian. I'm going to be working the whole weekend,' Reshma said, as one of Luciano's waiters put a pot of tea and a cup in front of her. 'That's why they made me go in today. There's a big briefing tomorrow, with more of the guys. Saturday we're going out to go and look at one of the safe houses they found. I mean, after it had been used. They've been working with this task team for weeks, all the others. I have to sit and go over all the security footage, get familiar with everything. And I can't take anything out of the office. I'm the only woman there, Ian,' she said. 'I need to catch up, so I don't look like the stupid apprentice.'

It wasn't a rejection, just a disappointment. Ian had always known that Reshma's job was not just equal to his, but probably more important. Definitely more important. He'd felt smarter, above it when he was a student and a lecturer. Now he was an NGO worker in an office in the suburb, trying to tell people that the colour of their trash was not a security issue.

Since the shootings on top of the Northcliff Ridge, Ian had stepped back from more hands-on security-type work, while Reshma had gotten a lot of attention for her role in the same operation – one that had taken down the small but deadly poaching syndicate. Ian knew it shouldn't bug him that she was going to be spending her weekend doing work with the potential to stop a really big crime, while he went to find an employee who had gone AWOL.

'You okay?' Reshma asked once they finished their meal and paid. She borrowed Ian's jersey because the night air had gotten cold, and she had left her coat at the task team office. She looked disarmingly vulnerable, draped in the too-large knitted sweater.

He confessed that he was also tired. 'Long day fighting bureaucracy,' he said, and meant it.

Reshma rested her head against Ian's shoulder as they walked to the car and he wrapped his arm around her, feeling somewhere between protective and affectionate – both of which made him feel good. He checked his phone and saw it was only a little after 8.30 pm. There was a moon somewhere in the evening sky, but it was hidden by clouds or smog, or something in between.

'I'll drive,' he said, and held out his hand for Reshma's keys. Just as she reached into her handbag, a figure fell out of the bushes and lurched towards them.

'Thank you, sir. Thank you, madam,' the zombie figure called, his arms waving about him.

It took Ian a second to realise that it was the car guard from earlier, coming to ask for a tip for watching their car. Ian dug into his change pocket and found a single five-rand coin, which he handed over.

'Ag, sir, don't you have some more,' the guard asked. 'Please man, I just need ten rand. Ten rand more to buy bread and milk. I don't buy booze.'

Reshma had by now moved out of Ian's embrace, and was standing at the passenger side of the car.

'It's open,' she said, looking at Ian, the keys in her hand.

Without making further eye contact with the car guard, Ian made a half- apology, saying it was all the change he had.

The guard started to mumble. Ian thought he caught the tail end of the word 'poes', but figured it wasn't worth responding to. There was already enough aggro in Joburg without him adding any more.

Ian climbed into the car before the guard got more confrontational. Reshma was already inside, and locked her door as soon as Ian was seated. They shared a look of mutual annoyance and embarrassment: the same conversation, the same avoidance, acted out five, ten times a day. She handed over the keys, and they drove home in silence, Reshma half-dozing against the window as they moved.

'I have to sleep,' she said as they walked through the door, her voice faltering under the weight of staying upright and conscious. She managed to brush her teeth and change into pyjamas before collapsing into bed. Ian came in to ask if she wanted another cup of tea, but she said no.

'I'll have in the morning. Love you, Ian,' she mumbled, drifting off.

For no good reason, Ian went over Myburgh's CCTV footage one more time before he went to bed. He saw nothing new, but for some reason, the action calmed him.

SEEING DOUBLE

Reshma thought if she stared at her screen any longer, she would start seeing double.

She had spent almost her entire Friday looking at video footage of three cash heists and an ATM robbery, switching back and forth between the film clips, together with copies of the police dockets, plus another case Sobukwe suspected was related. And most of them were not good dockets. They were sloppy dockets, dockets with messy writing, dockets with missing information.

Sobukwe's unnamed special task force had also compiled its own files on each incident, which Reshma was trying to review and integrate with the videos and the original case notes. It was now approaching ten on Saturday morning, and she had already been staring at her computer for the past three hours, trying to get her head around the MO of the robbers, and the different crime scenes.

The scheduled trip to the suspected safe house was delayed because Sobukwe had been called to some important meeting – a mayor or a Minister, Reshma couldn't quite tell – so she was using the extra time to get up to speed. In addition to Wayde, Scott and Dube, there were two other detectives they would meet in Vereeniging. She hadn't even had a chance to ask about the arms and money under Park Station.

The video footage she was reviewing was a compilation of files that

Scott had handed over the day before: a mix of CCTV feeds, dashboard camera recordings, and cellphone clips shot by witnesses who obviously had more interest in going viral than staying alive.

Scott had told her that the reason she needed to look at these five incidents in particular was that Sobukwe suspected they were all somehow linked to the same gang, which was also connected to the property they were going to visit, a safe house they suspected had been used before and after a highway heist that had taken place near Ogies.

Not all of the footage Scott had given her was useful, which made Reshma feel like she was being tested – as if there was something she was supposed to spot.

In two of the incidents, the dashboard cams captured little more than the impact and motion as the money truck was rammed. In the first case – the one near Ogies – the truck had driven over a spiked chain before being rammed, almost at the same time, by an older-model Volvo station wagon. The impact had caused the van to flip, hitting a culvert on the side of the road as it landed. All the front-facing footage after that was pretty much of a seam of concrete meeting a line of tar somewhere on the N12, and the sound wasn't much to go on either.

Both guards in the front of the van had been hit by airbags, released at the moment of impact and entirely blocking the interior-facing camera's line of sight. Paramedic reports from the scene said the guards might already have been unconscious when they were dragged out of the cab, through a buckled window, but this was hard to establish because both men had also been smacked in the back of the head with something heavy, possibly one of the weapons the robbers were carrying.

Neither man been shot, although the reports said that the robbers had threatened to shoot the unconscious guards to convince their colleagues at the rear to open up. There were two guards in the back with the vault. One had not been wearing a restraint and had been injured quite badly during the impact, but the other, by some miracle, was able to open up and get his colleague out the van before he, too, was hit over the head. All four of the guards had been hospitalised. The only guard who had been able to give any information was the one who had been at the back, who had said he thought there were six to eight assailants, that they were all wearing balaclavas, and that at least one of them had an AK47 rifle.

In the second incident, the ramming vehicle had struck the target van nearly head-on. The cash van had gone into a spin, but somehow remained upright. The front-camera gave a tantalising glimpse of the attackers' cars as it panned in two full circles. The task team's file included blurry stills from those frames, showing two cars closing in plus the ramming vehicle (a Mercedes, its entire front crumpled in, which was abandoned at the scene). The truck's interior camera had malfunctioned and recorded only sound. Before the van had even come to a stop, a series of shots could be heard – several of these had been fired at the driver's side, using heavier ammunition. At least one of the attackers had also emptied a magazine from a pistol into the van's engine block and bonnet. Two of the bullets had ricocheted into the windscreen, leaving giant spiderwebs of fractured glass. The police docket noted that together with twelve 9mm casings, four rifle shells had been found at the scene, probably from an AK47.

Through the damaged glass, the front-facing camera had continued to film its angled view of the other side of the highway, which was separated by a three-metre grass verge. The whole incident had lasted less than a minute-and-a-half, and during that time, not one car passed. Eyewitnesses said that they had spotted the scene, seen the cash van and men with guns, and either reversed or turned around to beat a hasty retreat. The guards had been pistol-whipped, but no serious injuries were recorded. There was a large splash of blood on the airbag of the abandoned Mercedes, which could have been a broken nose or a more serious injury for one of the robbers.

One attack had happened on the N12 heading east nearing Ogies, the other two hundred kilometres away on the same road west, just after Potchefstroom. But the MOs were similar, or similar enough, that Sobukwe was convinced it was the same gang.

Based on the various accounts of how each attack had unfolded, Dube explained to Reshma that the gang would have had to set up the ambush fifteen minutes to half an hour before each attack.

The attack spots had been chosen carefully, on sections of the road where there was an exit relatively close by, and where it was also easy to cross over to the other side of the highway. The preparation time was mostly guesswork, but was also informed by the schedules of the local highway patrol. Not all of the stretches of road were covered, but there was sporadic traffic monitoring, particularly near Potchefstroom, which meant the robber crew wouldn't have been able to hang about for a lengthy period. This meant that in the hour before the attack, the robbers would most likely have had to have been driving on the road somewhere to avoid attracting any suspicion.

The use of the spiked chain also meant that the robbers would have had to have known exactly when the van was approaching. To do that, either a guard inside the van would have to tip them off – which was not impossible, but seemed unlikely – or there was a spotter car on the same highway. Scott mentioned that they thought the spotter could possibly be the ramming vehicle, or a back-up vehicle.

The cars that had been used for the rammings were both mid-range older models. Each car had been hijacked in the week before the heist, and their number plates had been changed. Apparently the older models – like the Mercedes and the Volvo – were favoured because they were heavy and powerful, and packed a punch, but they had to be new enough to have airbags that would work, protecting whoever was unlucky or stupid or foolhardy enough to drive a car into an armoured van at full speed.

Once the money van had been forced to stop, the robbers swarmed the outside and made the guards at the front get out of the cab. After that it was easier to compel the guards in the back to open up and give up – both times robbers had threatened to kill the drivers if the other guards didn't comply. The incident near Potch had happened less than two weeks after the Ogies robbery, and so the guards probably had it in the back of their minds that they would be lucky if they escaped without serious injury. All of the security personnel seemed to know that if the heist crew killed one of them, there was a much higher chance that others would get shot. Some cash-in-transit gangs would kill everyone, just to avoid leaving any witnesses.

The third incident had taken place near the centre of the town of Klerksdorp, also linked via the N12. A smaller security van had been travelling along a side road when a sedan had pulled out in front of it. Dashcam footage showed the robbers – all in balaclavas – climbing out the front car and firing immediately into the windscreen, which was bullet-resistant, although the rest of the van was only lightly armoured.

The interior camera showed the driver freezing for the briefest moment as he registered what was happening. There was another half-second's hesitation as he realised that he wouldn't be able to reverse out of the ambush quickly enough – at which point he simply exited the vehicle and ran. The assailants luckily ignored him, and grabbed several cash bags from the cab before making a getaway.

Security footage from CCTV cameras a block away showed that the dark green Camry that had been used to block the van had parked and waited on the side road for more than half an hour before the van had finally driven along. From the vantage of the office block, two other cars could be seen racing away. As in the other incidents, the Camry had been hijacked that morning in Johannesburg. The registrations of the other cars were still unknown.

Claassen had explained that the security companies themselves were still playing it tight on the amount of money that had been in each van, but that each big job was estimated to have netted between five and eight million, with the Ogies robbery even higher, possibly over ten million. The Klerksdorp robbery was much smaller – maybe only a hundred thousand, or less. Almost as if the gang needed petty cash, or just wanted an excuse to let off a load of bullets.

The last one, the ATM van robbery, had gone down slightly differently, but Scott and Dube – and, as a result, Claassen and Sobukwe – were convinced that the footage showed that at least two of the crew who had done the ATM job were the same as in the van heists. That, plus the location, at a petrol station just outside Parys, made them think that it could be the same team.

The robbery had taken place when a cash van had come past the petrol station to refill the bank machine inside the convenience store next to the forecourt. Access to the ATM was through a safe door on the inside of the building, near the doors to the men's and ladies' bathrooms. CCTV footage of the petrol pumps and the front of the store showed nothing unusual before the attack – people moving in and out to get coffee, snacks, use the bathroom. When the ambush happened, it was like a perfectly co-ordinated criminal flash mob.

The money van had parked near the safe door, taking up two parking spaces that were supposed to be for store customers only. Two guards had exited the van – one with an R4 rifle, the other with the moneybag to make the service drop. The guards had gone inside and completed their drop-off without any problems. It was only once they came outside and re-opened the truck's back doors that a group of armed men suddenly materialised out of the human traffic. Three of them swarmed the guard with the rifle, who had been standing lookout. Two others went to disarm the guard who had been wheeling the moneybag. He was taken down in a matter of seconds, his faced mashed into the concrete with a gun held to his head. Three more men had simultaneously moved to the sides of the van, securing the cab doors and making sure the driver and a fourth guard were unable to get out to assist their colleagues. At almost exactly the same moment the men had taken their positions on foot, a car had pulled up in front of the van, blocking it from driving off.

Within fifteen seconds, four bags of cash had been removed from the back of the van and taken away to another waiting car, together with the one guard's rifle.

Reshma paused the video a number of times as she watched and re-watched, working out that the crew involved at least ten men that she could see. As soon as the cash bags were gone, the other men

peeled off in a staggered withdrawal, groups of them running to waiting cars before zooming off. Reshma upped the tally in her head to
include at least another three drivers.

As with the other attacks, the entire scene started and finished in
less than sixty seconds. The guards were up as soon as the robbers had
left, the CCTV footage giving their movements a slightly jerky quality
as they ran around the side and then the front of the car, taking cover
while they checked the assailants had left. The cash van itself briefly
stop-started, as if the driver had thought about giving chase before
deciding not to risk any pursuit.

What was important about the petrol station robbery was that
because it had been in a public space, none of the gang had worn
balaclavas or masks. This wasn't to say that their faces could be seen
properly. At least half of them had been wearing hoodies or beanies,
and two had peak caps, which obscured their features. But at least two
of the gang – the ones who had been acting as lookouts and giving
cues to the rest of the group, and to the drivers – appeared on camera
for long enough to make it possible to identify them.

'You see him there,' Scott said, 'if you watch, you can see him turn
around and look inside the store so he can watch what the guard is
doing.'

Scott apologised before reaching over Reshma and pausing the
footage. He skipped back a few seconds and hit pause again just at the
exact moment a man in blue trousers and a short-sleeved shirt turned
around, clearly showing his face.

'Would be even more helpful if the camera wasn't cheap shit,' he
said, standing back. Reshma looked at the screen. The man's face
should have been easy to make out, but the paused frame was almost

misty around the edges and in the centre.

'The shops, they install cameras that display on these tiny screens in their back rooms. The second the screens get bigger than a paperback, you see the kak camera quality. Still, it's more than we got from the other recording,' Scott said.

A separate incident had occurred two weeks earlier in North West, near Brits, but there was no footage, because the dashboard-mounted device had been destroyed in a fire that that raced through the front cab and the vault, burning two of the security company's guards beyond recognition, while a third had died from smoke inhalation. Reshma had kept the photographs of the scene until last, and was working through them slowly and methodically. The case had made all the news headlines, but it was the first time she had seen the extent of the carnage.

Either Dube or Scott had been reviewing the docket from the North West job a few weeks later, as a matter of course, and had identified a ballistic link to the ATM incident.

'They set fire to the van to try and force the guards out. Only, something went wrong. Another guard got shot – he survived, oddly enough. He says he got off a few rounds, hit some of the robbers. They found blood at the scene, but nothing else. Still, pretty shit to have to look at. Worse to have to live through,' Scott said, his voice thoughtful and not at all flippant.

'You want some tea?' he asked. Surprised but grateful, Reshma said yes. The footage and the pictures had left her feeling jittery – not scared, but restless – and the weather had turned overnight. The fake fancy IT office had not come with equally fancy heating options, and she was wearing her coat indoors.

She was halfway through a sweet and milky mug of Five Roses, and a rusk, homemade by Scott's wife, when Sobukwe and Claassen returned and announced that it was time to head out to Vereeniging.

They went in three cars: Sobukwe on his own, Scott and Dube in one vehicle, and Wayde and Reshma in the third car. Reshma had offered to drive, but Wayde declined.

'Your car has a dent on the back. Not sure if I should trust you,' he teased. When Reshma scowled, he reassured her that he was just joking.

'Seriously, I'll drive this time; you can do it next time. It's not a woman-driver thing,' he said, immediately making Reshma wonder if it actually was about that. The thought annoyed her, but it wasn't a battle she was in the mood for fighting. There were lots of people, lots of men she had worked with, who were the same. Barbed comments about women in general, and women as cops. If you wanted to get anywhere in the force, it was usually wise not to complain about it.

But she never forgot it, either.

DERBY

It took Ian and Surprise more than forty minutes to get through the knots of traffic around Fourways and onto the Western Bypass. The scenery changed from dense clusters to office parks, and back to clusters again as they headed onto the N1.

'My mom used to take me to the Snake Park here when I was a kid,' Ian said, pointing at a row of warehouses now owned by a German multinational.

Surprise shrugged. 'I remember Tiny taking me to the zoo, but she never really liked snakes,' was all she said.

Surprise had volunteered to be Ian's assistant for the day, convincing Ian that it was always a bad idea to go alone to a strange location, and that her Sepedi was no doubt superior to his extremely patchy isiZulu. Ian had agreed on that basis more than anything else.

They followed the N1 and split off towards the west, the N14 stretching out, surrounded by the endlessly repeating brown and green of veld and gum trees. They turned off at Groenkloof, passing the Voortrekker Monument. Surprise pointed it out and said that she had never been.

'Is it somewhere that you want to go?' Ian asked. Surprise said that she wasn't sure.

'Maybe it's worth seeing, maybe it's not,' she said.

As they cut around the west of Pretoria, the landscape started changing. It had been cold and overcast when they left Johannesburg, but now it was noticeably warmer, and the clouds had given way to open skies. There were more acacias in the islands between lanes. On Ian's left, small koppies rose and fell, brown and yellow and dotted with scrub. It wasn't even a hundred kilometres out of Joburg and the entire microclimate was different. Ian rolled down his window, letting in fresh air that still smelled faintly of morning fires.

The entrance to Atteridgeville was unofficially marked by a row of giant electricity pylons. Two white SAPS vans were parked on a patch of red sand a few metres away. Ian wasn't sure if the police presence was normal for the area, or if it was because of the xenophobic riots a few weeks back. A number of Somali-owned shops had been trashed and looted, and one young man had been shot in the commotion.

The winter sunshine made the scene look cheerful rather than threatening, the space all neat and contained by grey brick sidewalks.

At the cemetery, Ian and Surprise turned right, heading up Khoza Street and following the signs for Kalafong Hospital until they reached the traffic circle next to the Shell garage where Thandeka had suggested meeting them. The intersection was busier than the shops had been, and there was a constant flow of cars and minibus taxis and pedestrians moving through the space. There were two more SAPS vans under the trees. Surprise looked at Ian to gauge his reaction, but it was his turn to shrug. As far as he knew, the area was quiet. Also, a white man usually got less trouble than a black man from north of the Limpopo river.

Thandeka was waiting on the wooden fence opposite the petrol station, wearing denim jeans and a thin denim jacket. She was a few years older than Ian expected – her voice had sounded quite childlike over the phone, but she told Ian and Surprise that she was eighteen, was finishing matric, and that she hoped to study nursing the following year. She and her mother lived next door to Sylvie and helped out whenever they could because of the older woman's disabilities, which restricted Sylvie's mobility. Thandeka added that Sylvie had also worked as a nurse before her accident. Thandeka did not explain anything more about Sylvie's accident, and Ian decided to wait and see Sylvie in person before asking further.

From the back seat, Thandeka guided Ian and Surprise away from the garage and towards Saulsville. As they drove, Ian noticed pockets of youngsters with soccer shirts and flags. When he asked, Thandeka said that a big derby was scheduled for later that afternoon at the Lucas Moripe Stadium. Mamelodi Sundowns were playing their rivals SuperSport United. According to Thandeka, this was the reason for the extra cop vans, in case the rivalry between fans spilled into something more serious.

When Ian asked her about the previous weeks' looting, she said it had been a problem at the time, but that it had been quiet since then. She pointed at one shopfront window, now boarded up, where she said the owners had been chased and beaten.

Sylvie September's house was on a corner, a modest white-painted home that looked conspicuously older than its larger face-brick neighbours. Flowers grew over part of the palisade fence around the property, and there were three fruit trees at the back, partially hiding the boundary wall. There was a small driveway leading to a concrete courtyard, but Thandeka said that Ian should park on the pavement.

Ian's presence attracted a few looks from passers-by. One of them called out to Thandeka, saying words that Ian didn't understand. She simply laughed as she opened a small metal pedestrian gate and gestured for Ian and Surprise to go through.

Surprise looked over at Ian, a small grin on her face. 'He said you look like a cop,' she explained, as they went through the gate.

Sylvie was waiting for them at the front door. She was wearing a navy skirt and shirt, and a small hat, perhaps some kind of church uniform. Ian put her somewhere in her mid- to late-sixties, which didn't make her quite the ancient granny Myburgh had implied. But as he approached, he could see that the woman was supporting herself on a cane, and that she had what appeared to be burn marks on several parts of her skin.

Surprise stepped forward and politely introduced herself and Ian to the woman. She greeted them and asked them to come in, heading into a small sitting room where a three-piece lounge suite, coffee table and television just managed to fit. On the coffee table was a tray with a glass jug of what looked like Oros, the top covered with a lace doily with beads hanging off the edge, and a plate of biscuits.

Sylvie made her way to one of the single chairs and carefully took a seat. The light was not particularly good in the room, but Ian could see that she had burn marks on the right side of her face, and on her hand and wrist on the same side, which suggested an extensive past injury. Below the hat, Ian could also make out a hearing aid hooked over Sylvie's right ear, which was also damaged.

'Please, you are welcome,' Sylvie said, looking at Thandeka to offer Ian and Surprise a glass of cooldrink, and a biscuit. Ian accepted both, although he was not particularly hungry or thirsty. The simple ritual of hospitality gave him something that he realised the rest of his week had been missing.

He took a sip of his Oros and was about to start talking when a car drove past, blasting music from a loudspeaker. The bass was so heavy, the juice glasses rattled on the tray. Ian waited for the thrum to fade.

'Thank you for seeing us, Mrs September,' he said, speaking slowly, unsure of how much she could hear. He looked to Thandeka for reassurance, and she nodded at him to go on. Ian explained, briefly, that he was helping the head of security at La Gondola, and that he was looking for her nephew, Zebulon.

'Mr Myburgh tells me that he didn't come back to work after his long weekend in April,' Ian explained. 'And if he doesn't come back soon, they are going to fire him from his job.'

Ian was trying deliberately to emphasise the risk to Zebulon's employment, rather than the matter of the disciplinary hearing, or the dead woman at the dam.

Again, he checked whether the older woman could hear him. He pointed to his own ear and asked if she had heard what he had said. Sylvie nodded in return.

'Mrs September, Mr Myburgh, he doesn't want Zebulon to lose his job. He just wants to know if Zebulon is alright, or if something happened, or if he has another job. His cellphone isn't working, and we don't have any other way of finding him. Do you know where he is?' Ian asked.

At his question, Sylvie turned in her seat towards where Thandeka was sitting and made a face – and then she started laughing. She turned back to face Ian and Surprise, and put her glass down on the table. She wiped her hands on her skirts before she spoke. Her tone was warm, but rather bemused.

'You know, Zebbie, he hated that job. And it was me who made him take it. I said, go, go to Myburgh,' she said, 'and he went there because of me, and he stayed there because of me, but that was never in his heart. Hey, Thandeka – you can tell them the same thing. That boy, he was never a guard.'

The schoolgirl nodded, obviously familiar with Sylvie's point of view.

'He was in the choir,' she said, encouraged by the invitation to talk. 'He used to look after me after school, make me food. And he was always playing music, making up his own dances. Or drawing pictures of his favourite soccer stars. He wanted to be an artist, a performer,' she said.

'So, you're saying that he left because he was bored? Because he didn't like it? But then why didn't he tell anybody?' Ian asked, almost angrily. He was already discouraged by where the conversation was leading. If Zebulon had left – without saying a word to Myburgh or any-one else – because he didn't feel like being a guard any more, then Ian could only think that dismissal was the most suitable option. Which made his involvement and Myburgh's anxiety both futile and wasted.

Thandeka looked concerned at Ian's obvious annoyance, and she was about to speak again when Sylvie interrupted her.

'No. No, Mr Jack. That is not what Zebulon did, and that is not what I was explaining,' she said, cutting into his temper so sharply that Ian actually sat up straighter. He paused and took a breath.

'I apologise if I jumped to a conclusion. Could I ask if you would mind explaining what you meant?' he said, after another beat. He was strongly aware of Surprise beside him, and suddenly had an extremely strong urge not to be thought of as a bully, or an arsehole – not by anyone, but particularly not by her, even if she was only informally his assistant.

Sylvie broke the tension by smiling again.

'You don't have to apologise. Just don't be so impatient, like every-one under the age of fifty. Of course you are frustrated, and Myburgh also, because Zebulon did not communicate with you. So, I am tell-ing you that he never really wanted to be a guard, but that is not why he left that job – because whatever his faults are, he is loyal, and he understands duty. He left because he had no other choice; he had to go. He had dreams,' she said.

Ian frowned, still unclear of what Sylvie was trying to explain to him. Did she mean Zebulon had dreams of something better, a differ-ent line of work?

Surprise broke into his confusion. 'He is undergoing ukuthwasa,' she said. It was a statement, not a question.

Zebulon's aunt nodded, but her smile became serious.

'He did not think that Myburgh – that they would understand,' she said.

It took Ian another few seconds to piece the words together and realise that what the women meant was that Zebulon had left to train to become iSangoma – a process that could take months. And which also meant that it might be an equally long time before Myburgh or Ian, or anyone not involved in his training, would be able to speak to him.

Surprise, who seemed to understand Ian's problem, asked if it was still possible to speak to Zebulon directly. Sylvie did not answer imme-diately, and Ian decided to jump in with more information.

'I know I said it was just his job. But we also need to ask him some questions. There is a woman. Women,' he corrected, looking at Surprise, 'who went missing, a few weeks before he left. He might have been one of the last people to see them,' Ian said, sharing enough to give Sylvie an impression of urgency, even if she did not appear to be particularly worried about her nephew's employment prospects.

She appeared to think about Ian's question, but then shook her head again.

'I don't think so,' she said. 'He hasn't even told me where he is, what he is doing,' she said. 'But he promised he will come back to church with me when he is finished. My church meets every Wednesday evening, and on Sundays. Maybe you can come and join us when he's back,' she smiled.

The visit ended with Sylvie walking Ian and Surprise back to the car and Thandeka asking for a lift to the Chicken Licken on their way out. He shook Aunt Sylvie's hand, but couldn't entirely let go of the deflated feeling their conversation had left. He made a vague promise to come and meet Zebulon once he had returned, and to attend a Sunday service – with Surprise, who was also included in the invitation.

They dropped Thandeka at the fast-food place and thanked her again for all her help, and then they headed back to Johannesburg.

Ian was quiet, trying to think what he could do next, if anything.

Surprise tried to fill the space with a proactive approach.

'Maybe you can ask another sangoma to talk to this guy?' she suggested as Ian stared at the road ahead, distracted by a sense of what felt increasingly like a failure.

Eventually Surprise gave up trying to talk to him and switched on the radio. They spent most of the journey listening to Classic FM, which made the silence seem more heroic than it actually was. Halfway home, Ian paused his brooding long enough to suggest stopping off for a toasted sandwich.

By the time they got into Johannesburg, it was already late afternoon. Ian switched on the news as they took the Smit Street off-ramp and went under the highway back towards Westdene.

The lead on the bulletin was a breaking story about a cash-in-transit heist that had taken place somewhere near Meyerton. The newsreader said that a police officer had been shot and wounded.

DISCOUNTED LIVES

Even in spring, the drive south of Johannesburg was a monotone affair. In June, it was more khaki than anything, a mix of yellow, brown, and grey, with a slightly insipid green from the persistent blue gums, and the reeds that had been used to stabilise the sides of the mine dumps. Even the grass on the verges seemed to be struggling to make an effort.

Although it wasn't yet midday, there was a distinct smudge of brown on the horizon, smoke from fires made for cooking, and to keep out the capricious bite of winter.

Reshma's map said that the section of road they were on was called the Sybrand van Niekerk Highway. She wondered exactly who Sybrand was and why he had earned such an invisible honorific, to have lent his name to a flat stretch of the R59 near Alberton. She googled the name on her phone and saw that there was also a Sybrand van Niekerk High School in Mpumalanga, but she was still none the wiser.

'Wayde, have you ever heard of Sybrand van Niekerk?' she asked Claassen. He shook his head, and so Sybrand remained a mystery.

The interior of Claassen's car was impossibly neat, like it was a thing for him. It smelled of cleaning materials rather than the traditional fabric-softener hack, which Reshma's nose and head appreciated. There was a box of tissues, open and neatly placed between the two front seats, and even a special Velcro holder for a portable radio unit that was tucked beneath the dashboard on the passenger side. Reshma held hers in her lap. Both radios were currently off. Sobukwe had issued clear instructions for radio silence, except in case of real emergency. Everything else was communicated via WhatsApp or text.

'There's spare cuffs and thick cable ties in the cubby,' Claassen had told her when he noticed her looking around. Reshma nodded, and was secretly grateful that they had not, in fact, taken her rather messier car.

Claassen and Reshma had taken the lead while the others followed. Just after Meyerton, Claassen took the Redan turn-off and followed a narrow flat stretch that ran parallel to a train line. Reshma's view of the tracks was interrupted by a large wall and a sign for a bird sanctuary and housing estate. The road curved past a nursery, a wheel-bearing business, and an animal hospital, before they hit a T-junction, behind which Reshma could see tilted roofs of corrugated aluminium sheeting, and some impressive steel towers that looked like part of some fancy industrial complex. She checked her GPS and told Claassen he should take a left.

Vereeniging lay north-east of Vanderbijlpark and north of Sasolburg, the three areas making up the Vaal Triangle, the centre of the province's heavy industry. The house they were heading to was in a well-to-do part of Vereeniging called Three Rivers, named for its location between the smaller Suikerbos and Klip rivers, and the larger Vaal River.

The town planners for Three Rivers had obviously decided that traffic circles were essential to preserve the suburban qualities of the area, which seemed to feature mostly large and slightly dated houses with long stretches of lawn.

Reshma and Claassen curved around the wide road lines until they reached a pink gingerbread house with green palisade fencing. A silver Golf was waiting across the road and Claassen waved at the occupants. Reshma assumed these were some of the other team members – the ones Scott and Dube had mentioned – but she also noticed a yellow construction hat wedged on the car's dashboard, so she wasn't entirely sure.

A pair of estate agents' signs were neatly hammered into the verge outside the house. One said: 'FOR SALE' and gave the name and phone number of the responsible agent, together with a photograph of her face, a woman smiling from the metal board as if it was both a painful and joyous experience. The second board informed potential buyers that the property was a double stand, zoned for sub-division and development.

Wayde took out a set of keys with a keyring bearing the same estate agent's logo, and aimed a black remote at the gate. On his second try, the palisade started moving with a wobble and the driveway gate slid open. Wayde drove through first, going around the pink house towards the back of the property, which had been partly blocked off by a prefab wall. He parked on a large bricked section of courtyard and waited for the others to join them.

Scott and Dube were first behind them, and made predictable jokes about Claassen's 'nice place'. From the back of the house it was clear that while everything was intact, nothing in the property had been updated since the 1970s. The Golf pulled up next, and two men climbed out. Reshma thought that one might have been considered Coloured, but it was rude to speculate publicly. Both men stood around six feet tall, medium to heavy build, with dark hair, and moustaches. They were clearly not related, but the similarity between them was amusing. Claassen introduced them as Lt Colonel Smit, and Captain Kaye.

'Ryk,' Smit said to Reshma, 'and Mark,' he added, nodding towards Kaye. 'Good to meet you, Captain,' he said. Reshma smiled back in greeting.

Sobukwe was the last to arrive, pulling up behind the others in a Subaru station wagon.

Wayde had explained on the drive out that the house was, as yet, untouched – by the cops at least. It had been on the market for over a year and was being renovated by the current owner – someone who'd bought the place at an auction of a deceased estate. The owner was apparently hoping to improve what had apparently been slow sales prospects.

Sobukwe had received a tip-off from a very reliable source that the property had been used as a safe house on at least one of the recent heist jobs. It had taken several days to get access to the site without having the estate agent accompany them. Reshma got the impression that some of the preparation work had been done by the twins, which might also explain the yellow hard hats. But if they had been posing as property developers, they didn't say anything about it.

Sobukwe wanted to go through the location with his team, to see if there was anything inside that would give them more information about the identities of the gang – and to see if they could find anything that could link the crew to more of the jobs.

Because the scene hadn't been secured, there was no way of knowing if or to what extent it had been contaminated. In the car, Claassen had explained that Sobukwe was making a point of hiding their unit's interest in the property, in case it was a good tip-off and the arrival of a team of cops alerted the robbers, or exposed Sobukwe's informant.

That meant they couldn't tape off the house unless they found something important. Still, Dube dug a box of gloves out his car, cueing more jokes from all the men, and handed them to everyone. Sobukwe added a note for the team to document as much as possible on their phones, in case it was needed later.

Claassen, hands all gloved up, took a fumbled extra moment to find the right key on the estate agent's bunch, but eventually he got the back door open and let the rest of the team inside.

Reshma moved for a light switch, which was on the wall near the back door. Thankfully the power still worked, and the illumination showed off a perfect melamine kitchen in becoming shades of guava and beige. Reshma almost burst out laughing at the thought that hardened criminals might have made their tea or cooked a meal in such a kitsch environment.

'Split up and go room by room. Reshma, start at the bedroom side. Wayde, you take the lounge and dining room. Jake, I want you to do the kitchen and bathrooms,' Sobukwe said, calling Dube by his first name, which jarred Reshma for a moment.

'Scott, you go with Ryk and Mark, and cover the outside areas. Start with the construction. And take it slowly, work in three levels,' Sobukwe said. 'I want you to scan the floor, the midline, and the ceilings and curtains if you are inside. Look for anything. I'm going to move between where you are. If you need something, call for me. Any questions?' he asked.

Ryk raised his hand. 'Elmanie, the estate agent lady, she says that aside from the construction guys, nobody has been here for ... maybe three, four months,' he said.

'Do the construction workers have access to the house?' Reshma asked. 'I mean, do they come in to use the bathroom, and so on?'

Ryk shook his head. 'Not as far as I know. There was a port-a-loo on the side of where they were digging foundations. But I don't know when that was,' he said. 'We can go look,' he suggested, keen to get moving, or perhaps just to get out of the slightly oppressive colour scheme of the kitchen.

Leaving Wayde and the others, Reshma made her way down a brown carpeted corridor to what she assumed were the bedrooms. Although the house was empty apart from the officers, she was cautious. She moved slowly and quietly, and kept her right hand cradled over the grip of her holstered gun.

The house had two bedrooms, and the doors to both were open. Although it was daylight outside, the rooms were both dark, gauze curtains muting whatever illumination tried to make its way in. Reshma turned on the lights to see better.

All the furniture had long since been removed, but there were pale gouges in the carpet – the same economical brown as the corridor – where a bed and two bedside tables had obviously sat, probably for many years. Reshma noted other faint marks on the carpet, possibly more recent, that suggested a single mattress or something similar had been in place long enough to flatten the pile.

She took her time with her sweep, going level by level to make sure she didn't miss anything. She checked behind the curtains and looked at vents and plug sockets. When she'd finished with the first bedroom, she shouted that it was clear. A few seconds later, Claassen shouted that he had finished with the dining room.

The second bedroom was smaller, and equally empty, except for a waste bin hidden away in the corner, concealed by a gather of fabric at the end of the curtains.

The bin was a cheap plastic job, and probably not original to the house going by its blue colour. Reshma peeped inside, hoping to discover something interesting, but saw only a few tags from a discount building store. Still, they might turn out to be useful if she could match them up to items. She took a quick photo of where the bin had been placed, and then picked it up and carried it back to the living room, where Claassen was finishing up.

The living room bore the same deep marks of old and long-gone furniture – darker patches under what must have been an old three-piece suite, the slight fade the only evidence that, at some point at least, the previous owners had allowed natural light to enter the premises.

There was a small plastic table and a few kiddies' chairs, all in a similar shade of blue to the bin Reshma was carrying. The children's furniture looked incongruous and wrongly proportioned in the old-fashioned brown house. The cheerful plastic items made the drab room seem creepy. As if to emphasise the contrast, there was a copper ashtray shaped like a fish on the table – it looked like something from a bad antique shop, or perhaps it came with the original house fittings. There was no cigarette butt, just a small worm of half-crushed ash that suggested it had been used in the last few weeks.

'Strange, hey?' Claassen asked. He paused and looked at the scene in front of him. 'But I suppose it's also cheap, and you can buy this shit anywhere, and no one's going to ask if you actually have kids or not, are they? Plus, you can still sit on it,' he said, pulling out one of the chairs and sitting down.

'It's even quite comfortable,' he said, grinning. 'What you find?' he asked, pointing at the plastic bin in Reshma's hand.

She looked down, almost surprised to see herself still holding the bin. The sight of Claassen perched on a blue kiddies' chair was somehow unsettling. 'I don't know. Price tags. From Bargain Build,' she said. 'I haven't looked yet.'

Dube joined them to say that the bathrooms were empty.

'Did you check for hair in the plug hole?' Claassen half-teased.

Dube nodded. 'You're always welcome to go back and do a deeper search, Claas,' he retorted.

While they waited for the outside crew to complete their sweep, the three of them swapped and went over the others' areas again. Never trust one pair of eyes when you have more. Dube agreed with Reshma about the marks on the carpet pile in the bedroom. Wayde managed to produce a clump of something disgusting, and possibly containing hair, from under one of the bathroom drains.

They sat on the children's chairs and waited. After a few minutes, first the twins, then Scott and Sobukwe joined them.

The house held very few clues – but hinted that people had been around. Places in the grass held new marks like the carpet pile, signs that something, some things, had been there, until very recently, or the grass would have grown over. Sobukwe's best guess was that there had been three or four cars parked on the section at the back, and that they had been there for at least a few days.

Ryk and Mark had made a much more important discovery – a bullet, lying in the grass next to the port-a-loo (which, they both commented, appeared to have been recently cleaned, which meant that a service company had been out here). Ryk thought that whoever had used the toilet might have been carrying loose ammunition in his trousers, and that perhaps a single had fallen onto the grass when he had been pulling up his pants. It wasn't an implausible suggestion, but it wasn't conclusive of anything.

In an outside drain cover, Scott had found traces of what looked like animal skin, and some clumps of hair. 'Could be a goat?' he suggested, holding a rangy strip of tan and white hide in his gloved hand. He had no theories about why there would have been a goat. 'Well, it can't have been a cow, because the neighbours definitely would have noticed that,' he added.

Sobukwe said they would have to take the organic matter back to Johannesburg for forensic technicians to examine. He was more interested in Reshma's discovery. He made her tip the Bargain Build tags onto the plastic table, and slowly sorted through them with gloved fingers. There were twenty-three different tags in total. None of them had a description on it, but each of the tags carried a product code that Reshma thought she could follow up with the store.

Nine of the tags were for the same item. Two hundred and seventy-nine rand each, and the same item code. Next to the number was an asterisk and the word EMERALD.

'Any idea what these are?' Sobukwe asked. The others shook their heads.

'You'll call the store and ask?' he said, looking at Reshma. 'And see if there's a way to figure out which store it came from. If they got everything from the same store, maybe someone would remember them. Where's the nearest Bargain Build?' he asked.

Claassen whipped out his phone and searched online. 'Says there's one in Powerville.'

He clicked on his phone again, and then pinched on the screen to zoom. 'It's between here and Sharpeville,' he said. 'Should we go there?' he asked, looking back up at the rest of the team.

Sobukwe thought for a moment. 'No. Not now. Saturday, it's going to be busy. If we go in asking questions, someone will notice. We'll go Monday or Tuesday. Reshma, you can come down and go with Ryk or Mark, or both of them.'

Reshma nodded, pleased to be delegated a task already.

The team walked around the property again, marking the entire perimeter, and working a grid through the grass and concrete of the back, working their way towards the street. They found nothing else.

They gathered in the brown living room for one last discussion before moving out. Reshma checked the time – it was closing in on 3 pm. She had the tags in an envelope in her bag.

Sobukwe looked resigned, not quite glum, but not happy. He had obviously been hoping for more.

'Either we got the wrong house, or these guys are smart. And organised. Which is a bigger problem,' he said. 'We need to try figure out what these ... small details are. Then, if it is our guys, work out how they got access – I mean, what the link to this property was. And we can also interview the neighbours. But not in a gang – we don't want anyone knowing what we're doing. We need to go super slow on this, in case we move too fast and it jeopardises something we're not even aware of yet.'

The departure happened with a lot less energy than their arrival. Mark and Ryk stayed behind, but the rest of them were headed back to Joburg.

Sobukwe's deflated mood was contagious. Even Claassen was frowning. Reshma wondered if she should offer to drive. But it seemed like it would have been a hollow gain if he had said yes.

Sybrand van Niekerk and his brown grass verges were ready to welcome them as they joined the road heading north. Reshma tried to switch her mind back into some kind of constructive thinking mode, rather than just staring out the window.

She thought back over the videos and the reports, about the comments the investigators had made, the fact that the attackers were on the road before the money trucks. She wondered if they just drove about, or if they ever stopped. She looked suspiciously at every car stopped on the roadside, but they were mostly just drivers taking a pee. Men didn't care about unzipping their trousers in public.

Weekend traffic was constant, but fairly light. There was a regular stream of taxis taking people up and down between Sedibeng and the East Rand. There were every shape, size and colour of sedan, and the odd fancy car with vanity plates. There was also a large number of cars towing boats of all shapes and sizes in both directions. Reshma didn't see the appeal in fishing or water sports, and had never spent much time with people who felt otherwise. A smaller number of commercial vehicles chugged their way through the commuter and leisure traffic. Builders, painters, people who made poles and pipes and bearings. Workers perched on the backs of open bakkies, carefully holding onto the sides, either laughing and talking among each other, or staring blankly outward, showing no sign of anything, especially not the cold.

Reshma pulled her jacket closer just looking at them. She thought about the building store tags that were now in her bag and wondered what the crew – if it was a heist crew – might have been buying. Angle grinders? Would they need so many? What about welding equipment to get into the vans, and the vaults? As if to punctuate her train of thought, she saw a TBR money van on the other side of the highway heading south, a boxy Lego tank on wheels.

Claassen saw it too and shrugged.

'Once you start working this team, you see them everywhere. They don't have standard routes, and they don't tell us what they are or where they're going,' he said.

Reshma made a mental note that during the coming week, she would need to learn more about how the trucks were constructed, the positioning of the vaults, the seats, everything. The only way to defeat the crooks would be to know more than them.

Wayde drove on, and Reshma's eye caught a small white cross in the grass island between the lanes. There were bright plastic flowers on the marker, both sad and gay.

A few metres ahead of the cross, a cloud of dust and dirt was being raised by an over-sized V6 bakkie with four or five labourers in the back. The vehicle was slowing to make an illegal U-turn between the north and south lanes. Wayde reduced his speed as the traffic shifted around the obstacle.

The grass island, dirt at this and most other times of the year, did not prove much of a challenge to the bakkie's large tyres. Reshma heard tiny stones flick against Wayde's windscreen as they drove past. He swore, softly and concisely, probably because the dust would mean he would have to wash his car again.

She turned back to look at the offenders, unable to contain her irritation at people who broke laws so easily. She wondered if the driver was as callous about the safety of the men on the open back of his bakkie. The passengers seemed unperturbed. All of them were sitting upright, staring intently ahead down the stretch of highway where they were turning.

As the traffic started to flow again, the penny dropped. Reshma kept her sights firmly on the bakkie behind them as she spoke. 'Wayde,' she said. 'I think I know what they brought from the building supplies.'

BULLETPROOF

Reshma wasn't big on psychic powers, or magic, in spite of what she had seen on the Northcliff Ridge, where witches and a sangoma had battled the poachers who had killed Tiny. But she did believe in her gut feel. And the second she realised that whoever had been staying at the creepy house in Three Rivers had bought nine identical workman's overalls in Emerald Green, it all clicked into place. To his credit, Claassen did not doubt her for a second. She hoped it meant that his gut was telling him the same thing. Although, if they were correct, it meant that they were about to drive into a live firefight – one in which they would be badly outnumbered.

Claassen drove five or six kilometres before pulling over under a pedestrian bridge, making sure that nobody had clocked them. Reshma had sent out an unspecified emergency call on the radios and switched to mobile.

Reshma put Sobukwe on her phone's loudspeaker and explained what she had seen, and that she suspected an attempted heist was imminent. Sobukwe, who was somehow already halfway back to Joburg, said that he would contact the Meyerton SAPS commander directly, and that Reshma and Wayde had the go-ahead to turn back, and to engage with the robbers if anything happened. He reminded them, again, not to discuss anything on the radios – which could possibly be heard by other parties.

'There's too many security employees involved,' Sobukwe said. 'And cops,' he added, almost as an afterthought.

Reshma asked if they shouldn't notify TBR, to let the guards on board know that an ambush might be imminent. Sobukwe barked out an immediate negative.

'They have guys on the inside, Captain. We give this away to the wrong person, everything goes wrong. We need to keep this contained. It can't go through triple-one, or any regular unit. Understood?'

Reshma and Claassen both said they understood.

Sobukwe said he would call station command at Meyerton and get back-up without going through the switchboard. But he had no idea how long it might take the local crime squad to respond – especially as no crime had taken place – yet.

Ryk and Mark were still in Vereeniging, and Scott and Dube were thirty kilometres away, grabbing snacks at a One Stop. That meant Reshma and Wayde would have to go in on their own, and hold their ground until back-up arrived.

Claassen went to retrieve two bulletproof vests he'd stashed in the boot of his car, together with (he told Reshma) a mini first-aid kit, a torch, and an extra peaked cap.

One of the vests was Kevlar; the other had armour plates. Both were slightly too large for Reshma, but the armoured one had more reticulation, which made it easier to put on. The pair of them suited up between open car doors, obscuring any view of them from the road. Claassen helped Reshma tighten the fit of the straps over her shoulders. When she stood, she checked her belt to see that her holster and magazine pouches still sat right before pulling her coat over the vest, leaving it open at the front. Claassen did the same with his jacket before walking back briskly to the driver's side. The moment his door was closed, he engaged gears and moved almost seamlessly back onto the highway. A few hundred metres later, he executed a U-turn not unlike the one made by the truck Reshma believed was carrying a crew on their way to a robbery.

It would take ten or fifteen minutes to catch up to the bakkie and the cash van heading south, oblivious to what was on its tail. The plan was that Scott and Dube, coming from the other direction, would hopefully intersect with either the money van or with Wayde and Reshma before anything bad started happening. But they would all have to play it by ear.

Reshma had no idea where the crew would be planning their ambush. It was clear to her that the bakkie with the men on the back had performed its manoeuvre in order to chase the target vehicle. That meant there would probably be a ramming vehicle already on the road, and another ambush vehicle up ahead, maybe at one of the bridges, or near one of the off-ramps they had passed. She was annoyed with herself for not paying more attention to the places they had passed.

After a few seconds, the irritation gave way to excitement as adrenaline started to wash through her system. Reshma wasn't stupid enough to actively seek out fights with crews of heavily armed men. But some part of her was looking forward to the battle. She ran her thumb lightly over the back of her pistol, and double-checked her magazine pouches.

Claassen hadn't spoken since he'd crossed the island, which was fine with Reshma. Her throat was tight with anticipation, in between panic and pleasure. Somewhere in the back of her mind, she wondered if she had gotten it all badly wrong. If the bakkie with the workers on the back was just another driver who thought the rules didn't apply to him, taking a shortcut home on a Saturday afternoon. If that was the case, Reshma couldn't decide if she would be disappointed or relieved. She figured she could live with the jibes from her colleagues. But she would never live it down if they missed their shot at the gang.

'Do we have a plan?' she asked, as Claassen focused on the road ahead.

He looked at her and said, seriously, 'Don't get shot.'

Whatever Claassen was going to say next was interrupted by a Toyota Tazz with its hazards on, driving the wrong way down the highway, heading straight for them. The Toyota flashed its lights at their car as Claassen swerved out of the way.

Something was happening up ahead.

Claassen slowed slightly and rolled down his window. Reshma followed a few seconds later. Wind buffeted the inside of the car, whipping her hair around her face.

'You hear that?' Claassen asked.

Reshma paused. It was there even against the noise of the outside air and the tyres on the road surface. Popping. Like Tom Thumbs.

Gunfire.

Up ahead, another four cars were trying to get away from what was happening. Three cars had pulled onto the island and had their hazards on, not moving – the owners panicked, either paralysed or too slow to work out how to get out of the way. Another car was reversing, backing into traffic that was no longer even hooting at the unexpected disregard for the rules. As the reversing car passed, Reshma could see the passenger filming whatever was ahead with a mobile phone. Two more cars were trying to pull the same trick as the Tazz, except they had managed to cross over the island and join traffic heading in the other direction.

From five hundred metres away, Reshma and Claassen could see the money van, facing sideways and stopped dead in its tracks. Twenty, thirty metres in front was a white sedan, maybe a Nissan, stopped across both lanes, blocking anyone still stupid enough to try and drive north. To the right of the Nissan was an old Camry with a missing front bumper – possibly the ramming vehicle. There were two other cars, forming a loose laager around the security van: a dark-blue Golf, and the bakkie they had seen before.

Four men were near the van, one at the Nissan and another at the Camry. Reshma figured there were probably also drivers inside each car. She had no line of sight beyond the back of the security truck, and she shouted to Wayde that there could be additional men on the other side.

Wayde had slowed down, hanging at the periphery as if they were part of the mess of confused and terrified bystanders. 'Call it in,' he instructed.

Reshma shook her head at herself for forgetting basic protocol. She grabbed Claassen's radio and shouted that there was a heist in progress.

'You got your seatbelt on?' Claassen asked. He didn't wait for an answer, but changed gears and gunned straight for the scene.

None of the attackers noticed Claassen's car zoom up on them until the last hundred metres. Reshma pulled her firearm and cocked it.

'You waiting for an invitation?' Wayde asked, as he pressed his foot flat.

Reshma took aim as best she could and fired out of her open window.

The watchman at the Nissan dived out the way as Claassen used his own vehicle's speed and momentum to take out the stationary vehicle's front end. Claassen played it smart with the angle of impact. Reshma's body pushed only lightly against her belt, like they had been playing dodgem cars. Wayde let the car carry on moving forward as they passed the truck, and he turned gently into the swing as they curved back towards the attackers. They were maybe a hundred metres away on the other side when he brought the car to a halt.

Reshma, hyper-alert, kept her eyes fixed ahead of her. She'd fired off three shots on the approach. She didn't want to waste more bullets, but there was a lone gunman on the blind side of the van, about ten metres away from the vehicle. He was facing outward, looking straight at Reshma and Claassen. A second later, he brought up a rifle and pointed it at their car. The R4 had a range of over five hundred metres, if you knew what you were doing. Something pinged off Claassen's side mirror, which was a sign the robber might indeed know his way around a rifle.

Reshma swore, partly out of shock, but also out of anger. She shot back, and the rifle man ducked.

The rest of the crew remained focused on the money truck. None of the guards were out, yet, and three of the robbers appeared to be doing something to the front cab. The sight of the men, swarming the cab in their overalls, triggered memories of the photos Reshma had been looking at just that morning. Dead men. She couldn't let more men die while she watched.

'We have to stop this!' she shouted.

Wayde nodded. Then he dipped his chin slightly, like a child setting off to do something with great determination. And he drove almost straight towards the man who was repointing the rifle at their car. Another shot nearly found its target, leaving a bullseye of fractured glass on the top of the windscreen.

'Move a bit to the right,' Reshma shouted as they closed in. She leaned out of her window, just enough to get a good arm position. It was difficult to get a clear shot, with the angle and the movement of the car, but she fired off three more shots, hoping they would inter-rupt the gunman's fire. The rifle man flinched again, buying them a few more seconds' grace.

Claassen took the movement as a cue to speed up. He braked just at the last minute, in time to hit the surprised attacker – not with full force, but enough to send him flying backwards. He landed on the tar with an audible thunk, dropping his rifle as he fell, and didn't get up.

From where they were, Reshma could hear the noise of van through her open window, the du-du-du-du of the diesel engine. The vehicle was still running, it just couldn't move. Up close, she could see the tyres were not just shredded, but that the front axle appeared to be caught on a chain.

Her and Wayde's antics had finally caught the attention of some of the other crew. Three men peeled away from the cab and started towards them just as Wayde changed gear.

'You shoot, I'll drive,' he shouted. 'We can't take them all on. Let's just keep them from killing anyone until some back-up gets here,' he called, stepping on the accelerator and reversing faster than the men could run.

There was a bridge about three hundred metres away where they might have better cover. Wayde was trying to reverse using the wing mirrors, so that he could keep his eyes on the attackers up front. Reshma fired, four rounds, evenly spaced.

Before they'd covered half the distance to the bridge, the car hit something. There was a loud thunk, then a crunching sound, then the sound of Wayde swearing even louder than Reshma had a minute before.

'We're stuck,' he said, revving the car, trying to change gears again to see if he could go backwards, or forwards, or anywhere out of the line of fire.

The armed attackers had slowed down when they saw the car speeding away, but now they started to approach again, cautiously, not running at first. Wayde, still swearing, got out of the car. He told Reshma to do the same, and she did, her weapon in ready position.

Once they were out of the car, the problem was easy to spot – there was a rock, the size of a medicine ball, joined by four other rocks of almost equal sizes in a zig-zag on the side of the slow lane. They hadn't fallen there by accident, but were presumably part of the ambush plan – a back-up in case the spiked chain failed, Reshma guessed. Distracted by the gunmen, Wayde hadn't seen the hazard behind him.

To get away, Reshma and Wayde would either have to lift the car off the boulders, or steal one of the attackers' cars. Neither scenario seemed likely. Which meant they would have to engage – or run for it. Reshma looked behind them to the bridge, and possible safety. It was a two-hundred-metre sprint, in the open. She turned back to the scene, to the two men advancing slowly but surely towards them. The third had turned around and was running back towards the truck. Eyes on the prize. With their car out of action, Reshma and Wayde were sitting ducks.

'We staying or we going?' Wayde asked, looking over at Reshma. He was crouched behind the open driver's door, his pistol out and ready.

The decision was taken out of their hands when the lead man opened fire. Luckily for Reshma, he was a terrible shot. The bullet went completely wide. At forty metres, the shooter wasn't able to get even close to his target. Reshma noticed he was also firing with one hand. Either he was injured, or stupid. She would use either option to her advantage.

'I got the front,' she called to Wayde, as she took up position behind the passenger door, using the frame of the open window as a prop to keep her hands steady. She kept her sights firm and squeezed carefully on the trigger. She exhaled and popped three more shots in quick succession. The first man went down just as Wayde let off a burst at the second target. The second man, who was slightly further away, spun as the one bullet clipped either his arm or his shoulder. Wayde corrected his aim and followed up with two more shots, this time hitting the man in the back. The attacker crumpled as they watched.

That was three, maybe four down or at least incapacitated – Reshma hadn't seen what had happened to the Nissan driver after his car was taken out. But there were more men at the van, presumably still trying to get to the loot inside. Whether it was to avoid Reshma and Wayde or because of something else, the robbers had moved to what was now the far side of the van. The armoured panels were sheltering them from Reshma and Wayde's fire, and also blocking Reshma's line of sight.

She guessed it had been less than three minutes since they had arrived at the scene. She tried to count off in her head how long it would still take for Scott and Dube to arrive, or how long it might take for the Meyerton SAPS to respond. She couldn't work out if they should wait.

The photos of the burned corpses lingered in her mind. If the heist gang was using some kind of explosive or incendiary device, they would never be able to get the guards to safety once things were on fire. The only way to prevent that was to stop it from happening in the first place. But the odds of her and Wayde taking out the rest of the armed men on their own were small. There was no more element of surprise, and the gang was cleverly working where it was impossible to reach them.

Reshma wondered if they should try and get the security guards, still trapped inside the van, to join the fight – that way, they wouldn't be so outnumbered. But getting the guards out of the truck might be a death sentence on its own.

'What do we do now?' she asked, looking at Wayde.

'Don't get shot,' he said again.

He pointed at the messed-up Camry, still stuck on the side near where the van was. And, twenty metres before that, the R4 rifle that was lying unclaimed in the middle of the road.

'If we run there,' he said, pointing to the Camry, 'and use that for cover, maybe we can lay down enough nuisance fire to keep them from blowing shit up.'

Wayde obviously had the same concerns she did. And it was a smart idea to get the rifle, which would give them much better fire-power. If there were extra bullets, of course. It was a risk, but it would certainly be better than trying to hold the scene with just a pistol and a bullet-resistant vest.

Reshma's ears were pounding with a wash-wash of blood and

adrenaline. Her gun felt good in her hands. Her target work had made her feel confident. She gave Wayde a nod, and he took off first, zig-zagging slightly, picking up the R4 and then neatly cutting across to the Camry. Reshma followed a slightly different route; her gun was out, and she felt ready for anything, like she was untouchable. Right up until the moment her boots hit a smooth patch of tar and stone and she went skidding, her foot slipping out from under her. She landed hard on her left side, the impact driving her magazines straight into the side of her stomach. It hurt so much, and so fast, she didn't even cry out. She just opened her mouth in silence, trying to let air into her pain.

'Come *on*. They're coming,' Wayde called from behind the back of the Camry.

Adrenaline was a better prompt than pain. Reshma's eyes were blurred with tears, but she pushed herself up into a crouch and managed to sprint-scamper the last few metres to relative safety just as Wayde took aim with his pistol and fired at a figure that appeared around the corner of the van.

Crouched behind the wrecked car, Reshma could see the driver, still in the front seat, his head lolling to the side and a blossom of blood on his forehead. It wasn't a bullet mark. The injury matched a bloody spiderweb on the car's windscreen. The driver looked like he could be dead, but might have just been knocked out. Reshma couldn't find it in herself to worry about checking his vital signs. It would have to happen later. For now, he was out for the count one way or another.

Wayde was busy checking the rifle. While he did, he asked Reshma to creep forward and see if the driver had any weapons they could use. She moved in slowly, opening the door cautiously in case the maybe-dead man was roused by the movement.

She tried not to look directly at the body in the seat, reducing the person to a collection of details. She forced herself to slow down, be methodical. Her eyes moved from his bloodied head, down his torso and legs, to his feet. He was not wearing a seatbelt, a foolish action on any day, but particularly on the day you choose to drive a car into what is basically a small tank.

The man's hands were hanging limply at his side, and on the floor near the door was a pistol that looked like it had seen better days. She held her own weapon in her right hand and reached for the dirty gun with her left. She pushed the mag release, and a full magazine popped out. Dirty or not, these people had bullets to burn. She shoved the magazine into her coat pocket, and carefully racked the slide twice, to clear any bullets that were in the chamber. Only one popped out, and she put that into her pocket too, before slipping the unloaded firearm underneath the car, near the wheel well. She hadn't seen the driver breathe once since she'd been up close, so she was betting on his being dead, and hiding the gun on the road was easier than having to tuck it into the back of her jeans.

She crouch-walked back to Wayde and told him about the pistol, and the dead guy. After a moment, she added that the pistol had been a Z-88. A cop's gun.

'But it was dirty, like earth-dirty. Maybe it had been buried,' she said.

Wayde nodded at the information.

'How's the rifle looking?' she asked, her voice soft. The scene around the van was suddenly quieter. There was no pop-pop, just the sounds of male voices, and the noise of metal on metal, which was almost worse than gunshots. From where Reshma and Wayde were positioned, they still had no direct line of sight. Reshma's imagination was working overtime.

'The guards are all still inside, right?' Wayde asked.

'Far as I can tell,' she said.

'How long you think we got before the others arrive?' he asked.

'Could be five minutes, could be longer. Your guess is good as mine.'

Unspoken between the two of them was the possibility that nobody else might arrive in time, and that it might just be them.

'You think we need to draw them away, draw them out a little?' Wayde asked. 'Get them out from behind that tank?'

Reshma nodded. They needed to stall for time.

Wayde holstered his pistol and then took a kneeling position, rifle up at his shoulder. Slowly, with his focus on the van, he edged to his left, keeping his position until he had a clear shot. He fired three times, and immediately drew back to the cover behind the Camry. A few seconds later, he repeated the exercise. The R4 rounds would deliver a lot more punch than a pistol, Reshma thought. The second time, his tactic seemed to get the gang's attention.

A man stepped around from behind the truck. He was tall and well-built, wearing the same green overalls as the others. Even if he hadn't been holding a shotgun, Reshma would have been wary of him.

Behind him was another figure, smaller, lighter, carrying a pistol. At that same moment, the sun broke through a cloud and the afternoon light briefly scattered over the gunmen, breaking up their bodies into patches of light and dark, as if they were made of pixels. For the briefest of seconds, it looked like there was only one man. Reshma shook her head, and there were two again. Both of the men began to raise their weapons, perfectly in sync.

Reshma didn't need to think, she just took aim. The tall man with the shotgun was right in her sights. She squeezed gently on the trigger, and then pulled. Her shot went wide, as if she'd been shooting at thin air. Reshma's stomach turned, and she cursed herself for being over-confident. The gunman kept moving, coming closer and closer to her and Wayde.

Reshma checked her sights again. The light was in her face and she wanted to wipe her eyes, but she kept both hands on the grip, her right finger caressing the trigger as she pulled again.

There was a click. From her own gun. She glanced down and saw the slide was all the way back. She hadn't been counting how many rounds she'd shot off.

One of the gunmen laughed. She couldn't tell which one. She called out to Wayde and reached for the spare magazine on her hip with-out looking. The pain from earlier was already gone, blocked out by adrenaline. She pushed the release button and caught the empty mag-azine as it dropped, inserting a new one in its place with a neat click. She jammed the empty magazine into her pocket. As she did, Reshma could feel the loose single bullet from the maybe-dead driver, her fin-gers brushing over it like a talisman.

At that moment, she realised that Wayde hadn't fired a single shot while she'd been changing her magazine. In fact, he hadn't fired since the men had stepped out from behind the van.

'Are you okay?' she called to him. But Wayde either didn't hear her, or he wasn't listening. She glanced over at where he was crouched. She could see his mouth opening and closing, rolling over shapes that might have been words. His hands were completely still, rifle aimed, but his finger was off the trigger. He'd frozen.

When she looked back at the attackers, the tall man was nearly on them, a balaclava covering his face leaving only his eyes visible. Behind him, the small man was still crouched at the edge of the money van, his pistol aimed straight ahead. The space around them went dark, as if the sun had been blocked out by another cloud. She shouted to Wayde as she got her own weapon up again, the shotgun man in her sights.

Third time lucky she thought, as she was about to pull the trigger. But something made her pause. It was as if there was something wrong with the tall man. Because she could almost see through him. Reshma blinked, and for a second the tall man faded from her vision completely – and there was just the shorter gunman, behind the truck. He was still there, and he was about to shoot a bullet straight towards where Wayde was squatting.

Reshma had a second to choose. She switched her sights and issued a prayer to any deity that was listening. And then she took her own shot just as the small man fired. She saw his movement, the slight recoil of his pistol. There was the briefest of pauses before he gave a cry of surprise, falling back and down as her bullet struck him. Reshma turned her head towards the second target, certain that either she or Wayde were about to get hit point-blank by shotgun fire. She was about to shoot when she realised that there was nothing ahead of her, only air – and a hundred metres behind that, Scott and Dube's car screeching up and over the traffic island, a plume of dust in their wake.

'About fucking time,' she called, jubilant, looking over to where Wayde was huddled. Which was when she noticed that he had been shot and was bleeding onto the grey tar.

HEADLIGHTS

Ian fetched Reshma from the hospital. She had said that he didn't need to, and that one of her colleagues would drive her back to Johannesburg. But he had wanted to. He had needed to.

Reshma's phone had rung and gone to voicemail when he had tried to call after hearing the news on the car radio. It had been excruciating, sitting and listening to the updates that didn't really tell anything.

Ian had dropped Surprise in Westdene, and headed south as soon as Reshma had called him back. She was at a private hospital in Vereeniging. She said she wasn't hurt. Ian mostly believed her.

At the hospital, he'd had to make his way past two news reporters and a bunch of men in blue, who were doing double duty keeping people out and keeping the injured robbers in.

Reshma was sitting in the waiting area, her coat and armoured vest over her arm. Ian offered to carry both.

'You got a weapon in here?' he asked, feeling the weight in the coat pocket. Reshma whispered, 'Shit,' and took the coat back.

'Hang on a second,' she said. 'I just need to give something to someone. Come with.'

They walked around until Reshma managed to find Super Sobukwe, who was talking to another cop, an older white guy with lots of brass. Sobukwe stepped away for a moment while Reshma introduced Ian, and explained that she had one of the robbers' magazines in her jacket pocket.

'It already has my prints on the outside,' she said, adding that the firearm was still under the Camry's wheel, as far as she knew.

Super nodded, but barely acknowledged Ian's presence. He wasn't overtly rude so much as busy.

He took the magazine with a handkerchief. Nobody said anything about the chain of custody. The crime scene itself had been utter chaos. Reshma still wasn't sure how many robbers there had been, how many were in hospital, and how many had gotten away.

'Hang on, there's more,' Reshma said, reaching into her pocket to pull out the single bullet she'd racked from the dead driver's weapon. But when she opened her hand, there were two objects in it. Cradled next to the bullet was a small bronze statue of a human figure, looking back at her with an elephant face.

Reshma looked at the figure of Ganesh with surprise.

'What's that?' Sobukwe asked.

She looked up. 'He was on my desk. I put him in my pocket and forgot I had him with me.'

On the way out, Reshma told Ian that one of the men they had arrested had been found with body parts in his pockets. 'They said he had an eyeball. Like with blood and tissue and everything. Apparently they think it means that no one could see them. Imagine that,' she said with an awkward laugh. 'These guys, they are so stupid.'

Something in her voice sounded off to Ian. He wanted to press her, but guessed it was a bad time for questions.

On the drive home, Reshma stared out of the window, watching car lights pass on the highway. The crime scene was still cordoned off and the north-bound road had been turned into a two-way section for about a kilometre, which caused a traffic jam even on a quiet Saturday night.

For some reason, Reshma asked Ian if he knew who Sybrand van Niekerk was. He didn't.

She kept checking her phone for updates on the cop who had been shot – Wayde Claassen. She said he was still in surgery. Ian had met two others, Scott and Dube, at the hospital. They were the ones Reshma said had arrived literally as Claassen was hit. The security company guards had used the subsequent distraction to make their own way out of the driver's side of the cab, and the remaining attackers had been surrounded, except for one car that had gotten away. Nobody was sure how many men had been in it.

Reshma said the Meyerton and Vereeniging cops only arrived fifteen minutes later, the same time as Claassen's ambulance. 'Bloody useless,' she said, 'and now we've had to hand most of the scene over to them.'

The scene itself was a mess. It seemed like at least three men dead, four others arrested, three of them injured – including the eyeball guy. They were in the same hospital as Wayde, but would be moved soon; and apparently the injured cop would be transferred to Joburg in the next day or so, as soon as he was stable.

'He just fucking froze, Ian,' Reshma said, trying to tell him what had happened.

Ian could see she was struggling to get the words out. 'It wasn't your fault, you know. It wasn't your fault he was shot. You did what you could,' he said, hoping to say the right thing.

Reshma nodded, but her expression showed that she had doubts.

Her face was drawn, and she had been frowning since Ian had collected her from the hospital.

'You want to go over it again?' he asked, 'Or do you want me to shut up?'

Reshma was quiet for a while. 'I don't want you to shut up,' she said, at last, 'but I don't want to talk about ... *this* right now. I need some space, because otherwise I won't be able to think straight. How about you tell me about your day instead? You find your missing guy? Or girl? Shit, sorry man, I've had so much on my mind,' she apologised.

Ian brushed it off. After the day Reshma had had, he was just happy she was still around. He told her so, and she gave him a smile for the first time since he'd fetched her.

He spent the rest of the trip going over what had happened in Pretoria, the cop cars all over Atteridgeville, the auntie and her sweet Oros. Then he told her about the sangoma part.

'So you can't speak to this guy because he's gone to do his initiation?' Reshma asked, slightly incredulous.

Ian nodded.

'Maybe you should speak to MaRejoice, you know? Get some help?' she suggested, although it sounded like a question.

'Surprise said the same thing,' Ian said. 'I'm going to visit MaRejoice tomorrow – you can come with if you'd like? If you aren't ... if you're feeling okay, I mean,' he said, stumbling over his own stupid enthusiasm, as if he'd forgotten that three hours earlier, she'd nearly been killed.

Reshma stared ahead. 'Maybe,' she said, not really meaning it. 'I might just ... you know, stay in. Get some sleep. It's been a rough week,' she said, turning to face him.

Ian nodded.

'Actually, I think I would like a bit of quiet, if you don't mind,' she said.

When they got home, Reshma disappeared into the bathroom and took a long shower before crawling into bed. She put her tiny statue of Ganesh on her bedside table, but didn't say anything more.

Ian made tea without her asking. His mind replayed his own afternoon like a car crash, the agony of hearing the news on the radio, the long drive to Meyerton. The relief of seeing Reshma sitting on a chair, unhurt, in the hospital.

He hugged her and she winced. He pulled back, afraid he'd done something wrong.

'I fell, on my side. When I was running. It was stupid. It's just bruises, nothing bad,' she said, taking the tea. 'I love you, Ian,' she added, leaning forward and kissing his lips before sitting back and sipping.

She held the cup in one hand, and Ian's hand with her other. They stayed silent until she finished her drink. She held onto his hand even when she lay down and turned off her bedside light.

'Stay here with me,' she said. Ian lay beside her and held her until her breathing slowed. Eventually he closed his eyes and went to sleep too.

*

Ian woke with morning light creeping down the corridor past their bedroom. The knot in his stomach resurfaced as soon as he remembered what had happened the day before. He gently touched Reshma beside him, needing reassurance that she was really there.

'Do I get more tea?' Reshma asked, evidently already more awake than he was. 'I'm too lazy to get up. How long do I get special treatment for not getting myself killed?'

Ian could picture her smiling. He leaned over and kissed the side of her face before agreeing to tea, and anything else she wanted. The kiss turned into something longer and deeper, their hands reaching over the blanket, under the sheets, finding each other, touch as much about an urgent need to be alive, to do something alive, as desire for each other.

Afterwards they lay on the bed together, half-naked, until Reshma complained about being cold, and her now extended lack of tea. Ian laughed and got up to put on the kettle. For a few moments, everything felt normal between them. Normal in a good way, like two people who were in love, not two people who had to carry guns and kill other people so they didn't get killed first.

Ian knew that Reshma wasn't a violent person. At least, not in the way he believed violence lived inside him, at times. But he knew she wasn't afraid of it. Maybe part of her even liked it. The task team she had been asked to join represented an important step in her career, a recognition of how good she was as a cop. But it also meant putting her in the direct path of more violence.

Violence he wouldn't be able to step in and prevent. Hadn't been able to step in and prevent.

Once Reshma had finished her tea, she told Ian she was going in to work. The look on her face made it abundantly clear she wasn't interested in hearing any argument from his side. 'I have to write down statements about yesterday, I need to look over who has been arrested, who was killed. I need to ... I need to try and figure out what the hell happened with Wayde,' she said.

Ian nodded. He hadn't really expected her to stay home the day after a big bust. Although part of him had hoped there would be a little more time for things like tea and lying in bed.

'That's fine,' he said, quick to hide any disappointment. 'I should go and visit MaRejoice anyway. You sure you don't want to come?' he asked, only partly teasing.

Reshma gave a grimace in return. 'Tell her I send my love. But I'm not in the mood for her ... for her looking at me. Sometimes it's like she's staring right through me, you know? But you can drop me on the way – my car's still in Modderfontein. You're going to Alex, right?' she asked, sliding off the bed and groaning as the movement caught her bruised side.

Ian nodded, and left Reshma to get dressed.

He did know how Reshma felt about MaRejoice, but it was also precisely the reason why he always felt so comfortable with the sangoma. Because she could see exactly who he was, and it never frightened her.

*

MaRejoice was the only person Ian had really stayed in contact with after the pursuit of the poaching gang that ended in the Northcliff Ridge shootout. She had come to Reshma and Ian's new home once for tea, after they had moved. He'd developed a friendship with the sangoma that felt, at times, like an apprenticeship. Or, at least, that he was a student and she was the master, even though he had no ambitions to go through ukuthwasa himself.

Now, at the sangoma's house on the East Bank, MaRejoice's

grandmother, too old to answer the door to random callers, sat in the living room engrossed in a soap opera on the television. She waved at Ian as he stuck his head in to say hello.

'She's watching *Muvhango* now,' MaRejoice said. 'Before that, it was *Isidingo*. Like she didn't already watch the same shows during the week.' She made a sort of tutting sound, but it was obvious that she enjoyed her grandmother's pleasure.

'Uyalifuna itiye?' she asked the old woman, before asking Ian if he would also like some tea. Both Ian and the granny accepted, and Ian followed MaRejoice into the small kitchen.

While she boiled the kettle, Ian gave her a basic outline of the missing Zebulon September.

'I told Myburgh I would help find him, because the guy is about to be fired if he doesn't come back to work,' he said. MaRejoice knew a little about the history between Myburgh and his dad, and she understood something of what he felt towards the older man.

She poured a small amount of boiling water into the pot and then swirled it a few times before pouring it out again. She carefully added two teabags and more hot water before looking back at Ian.

'So let me understand: you have a security guard who says to his aunt that he is going off to thwasa and he just leaves his job, and you think I can find him and speak to him for you?' she said.

She paused for a beat before she lifted her left hand and, sticking out her baby finger and index finger, mimed making a phone call.

'Yes, Mr Jack. Let me just use my secret sangoma phone,' she said, before cracking up with laughter, smacking her own thigh. Ian flushed, and knew immediately that his whole face had gone visibly red, which made MaRejoice laugh even harder. She carried on laughing as she took the tea to her gogo, and while she ushered Ian into the quiet space of her ndumba.

Not much had changed since the last time Ian had visited. He noticed a pair of fleece-lined slippers beside MaRejoice's mat and sitting cushions, a concession to winter. There were also new bunches of herbs hanging from the ceiling, and a few fresh plants gathering sun on the windowsill.

She gestured for him to sit on a cushion opposite her, and he sat down cross-legged while she poured their tea and finished chuckling.

'I'm sorry, it was a stupid question,' he said, at last.

MaRejoice gave him a look. 'There are no stupid questions, Ian. But, no, not all izangoma know each other. And I don't know how someone will feel if I am going to be asking questions about their sons. But because it is for you, I will at least find out who I must ask. And if they are reasonable, I will do what I can,' she said.

Ian thanked her and took a sip of his tea, feeling slightly less embarrassed.

MaRejoice was still staring at him. 'Tell me why,' she said, suddenly. 'Tell me why they think this young man went missing. There's something else going on here. I can't help if you make me guess, Ian. I'm isangoma, not a psychic,' she said, subtly rebuking him for only telling her half the story.

Ian apologised again; he was spending too much time on the back foot this morning. He told her about Myburgh's request for help, about the trip to the dam, and how strange the place was. And then he told her about the dead woman in the water.

'Nobody knows who she is,' he said, adding that he thought the woman had come from somewhere else in Africa.

'You saw her?' MaRejoice asked, her eyes wide with curiosity.

Ian shook his head. 'No, only pictures. Cellphone photos Myburgh took. But you could see her face. Her hair. And she had these marks,' he said, pointing at his cheeks, and then his wrists, 'marks like tattoos, or scars. Deliberate ones, not accidents.'

MaRejoice was frowning now, and sitting very upright. 'When did she die, this woman?'

Ian thought back through the calendar for a moment, the DD/MM/YY stamped on the corner of security footage. 'March? April? I'm not so sure any more. They had footage on their security camera of a group of women driving in, but we don't think it's the same woman now who was with them. Actually, that was why Myburgh thought that Zebulon had left – because he let these other women in, and apparently he wasn't supposed to,' he said.

MaRejoice raised her eyebrows.

'So, this missing man, he was working at a place where he wasn't supposed to let in *black* women?' she asked.

'Basically, yes,' said Ian, embarrassed to be helping Myburgh and, by extension, the racist old farts who no doubt ran and owned the estate. 'Why were you asking about the dead woman?' he said, steering back to safer ground.

MaRejoice showed her teeth, not a grin or a grimace, but like she was going to say something strange. 'There was a woman in the Jukskei River, last week. Some children saw her. They were picking up scrap from the river, doing normal things young children do when they are playing where they are not supposed to be playing. They saw an arm – a hand really, that was what they noticed, in the rubbish. Fingers, a hand. Then they saw her arm. The one boy, he lives just here with his mum,' she said, gesturing vaguely. 'He said that the body in the river had marks on it. But I don't know if it's the same thing. Maybe bodies in rivers just have marks. But he said that he didn't know the woman – I mean, that she was not from here, from us. He said she was mak-werekwere. A foreigner.'

MaRejoice almost spat out the last word, as if to express her dis-taste – not for foreigners, but for the boy, and his family's obvious dislike of them.

'And the others? You said children found her? Did they also see marks?' Ian asked. He could feel tension radiating out from his stom-ach, across his chest. Not quite excitement, but a feeling of something important about to come into view. 'What did the other children say they saw?'

At this question, MaRejoice's expression changed. 'The girls who saw her said she was a mermaid.'

She was looking Ian straight in the eye, and with such a serious expression that he couldn't be sure if she was taking the mickey out of him again.

'A mermaid?' he asked, incredulous. The image that popped into his head was of a pale-skinned blonde woman, long hair curling dis-creetly over her nipples, and a fish tail instead of legs. Something out of a Hans Christian Andersen story.

MaRejoice went on. 'They said her feet were tied up in a plastic. So maybe that was why they thought it was a mermaid, like from a cartoon or something,' she said, making a fish-like movement with her arm.

The mention of a plastic bag on the woman's feet made Ian pay even closer attention. There had been a plastic bag near the dead woman at the dam – he had thought it was just trash, human detritus.

'I've never seen one, here. A mermaid, I mean. Actually, I have never seen one at all,' MaRejoice continued, almost as if she was talking to herself. 'But I can't think why a mermaid would come to the Jukskei when they have all those nice pools in your suburbs,' she said, flashing Ian a grin to let him know she was joking. 'The river here, it's full of shit. Even those children shouldn't have been playing nearby. There was a boy, eleven years old, who got caught and drowned in a flash flood when it rained in the summer. It's not safe.'

She paused again. 'It was probably just another dead woman. There are a lot of those. Some of them are bound to wind up in the water,' she said, looking at Ian. 'But this one, the one in our river here – maybe there is something about her that is like the dead woman you found in your fancy dam place?'

Ian nodded, increasingly certain that the identity of the dead woman was the key to something – something important, even if it wasn't the answer to the mystery of the missing security guard.

'You think any of these kids – the ones who found that woman in the river – do you think any of them could tell me what they saw?' Ian asked, feeling a slight twinge of guilt at asking MaRejoice's help to compel children to talk about dead bodies.

He was weighing up the ethics of the approach in his head, then reminded himself that he wasn't an academic, nor was he a cop. In this situation, he could ask whoever he wanted for help. Plus, if MaRejoice knew the children's parents, he figured that she would be responsible enough not to abuse whatever trust came with being the neighbour-hood gogo.

She looked at him as if she was reading something important on his face before she nodded. 'We can go ask them now. But you will have to come with me, Mr Jack,' she said. 'You're not making me into one of your investigators. Just like I'm not turning you into isangoma,' she said, the chuckle from earlier rolling up out of her chest and into her throat as she rose.

MaRejoice's granny was dozing in front of the television when they left. The shows had switched over to cartoons. Outside it was sunny, but there was still a bite in the air. If anybody on the East Bank wanted to stare at Ian Jack walking down the street, they did so covertly, avoiding the eyes of MaRejoice.

The pair walked past a small crèche, its white walls painted with bright primary-coloured murals of toys. A few houses after that was a hole-in-the-wall kiosk manned by a gangly boy of about eleven or twelve – Ian was not good at guessing children's ages. The table in front of the boy held four types of sweets, plus a couple of bags of popcorn. Business seemed slow, but Ian couldn't imagine Sundays would be particularly busy.

MaRejoice spoke to the boy in isiZulu. The boy listened and nodded while MaRejoice explained what she wanted. Then she pointed at a plastic jar holding blocks of what looked like homemade fudge. She reached into her pocket and handed over two five-rand coins. The boy opened the jar and gave her two squares, each wrapped in plastic. MaRejoice waited, the fudge held between her fingers, and stared at the boy. Almost with a start, he put the jar back on the table and edged off his stool before running into the house behind him.

'You scare him off?' Ian asked, as MaRejoice handed one of the plastic packets over to Ian.

'He will call the others,' she said, unwrapping her own square and nibbling on the caramel sweet inside. 'His aunt makes this. It's good,' she said, encouraging Ian to try his.

Ian had finished the entire piece and his mouth was longing for cold water to take the edge off the sugar, by the time three children arrived – the skinny boy, and two girls – all chattering with each other. The girls looked about the same age as the boy, maybe one was younger, one was older.

Behind them trailed an older woman – a parent, judging by the slightly circumspect look on her face. The woman and MaRejoice exchanged a few words, in the middle of which MaRejoice pointed at Ian. The only word Ian could pick up was when she mentioned the Jukskei River. At this the children became more animated, and started to jostle each other slightly, almost impatient to tell their stories. At last the mother, or whoever she was, relented, and apparently indicated to MaRejoice and the children that it was okay to talk – although she did give Ian a very intense once-over before withdrawing.

With the other adult gone, MaRejoice asked the children to talk in English.

'This is Mr Jack. He helps me sometimes,' she said.

'Is he a policeman?' one of the girls asked, her eyes wide, her face excited, but not scared.

Ian dipped his head in acknowledgement. 'Once. A long time ago,' he said. 'Now I'm just ... a helper,' he said, looking over at MaRejoice.

Rejoice told the children to tell him about what they had seen in the river. 'Do you remember the woman?' she asked.

The children all nodded enthusiastically, as if a corpse was something interesting rather than just scary. After another short negotiation with MaRejoice, they agreed to walk her and Ian down to the river and show them where they said they had found the body.

The children walked ahead, occasionally stopping to look over their shoulders and see if the sangoma and the white man were still following them. They made a dog-leg over a bridge, then onto a footpath that ran perpendicular to the main road. There was a small playground next to the path. The children ignored the roundabout and seesaw, and carefully worked their way down a wall of mesh and rock gabions, gesturing for MaRejoice and Ian to follow.

Under the bridge, the river was easily accessible, the pathway hidden from view. Anyone could have gotten there with little effort – which meant the body could have washed up, or it could have been dumped. The children pointed to a clump of evidently new rubbish, clinging to a broken branch dangling on the river's bank. The body had been near there, they said. Ian thought he could detect the flutter of chevron tape against the piece of wood. Nothing else marked it as having been a crime scene.

'Could you tell me about it? Tell me what the bo— what the woman looked like?' Ian asked, trying to keep his language neutral.

The kids nodded again, and the smaller girl started talking. 'Lebo saw the hand,' she said, pointing at the other girl. Ian still couldn't tell if they were sisters, or friends.

The one the younger girl had called Lebo spoke next. 'I saw it because it had nail polish. Like with red glitter.' She held out her own nails for comparison. They were painted a shiny blue colour, slightly chipped at the edges. 'She is Portia,' she said, looking at her friend and then withdrawing her hands abruptly.

The girls giggled again.

'Did you see more than her hand?' Ian asked. 'Did you see her arms? Or her face, maybe?' he asked, touching each body part as he named it.

The children gave small nods, and he saw the three of them exchange glances with each other.

'You could tell me – or you could draw me a picture?' he suggested, reaching into his pockets to see if he had a pen or pencil somewhere.

He was still looking when the boy reached into his own pocket and pulled out a cracked smartphone. The girls looked at him, and the three of them all nodded again, giving approval to sharing whatever was on the gadget.

'You have photos?' Ian asked, suddenly understanding.

The younger girl – Portia – spoke again.

'We found this phone. Before. There's no SIM card – we only use it for games,' she said. Her voice dropped down to a whisper. 'We took photos of her. Of the mermaid,' she said. Now her voice really did sound almost afraid.

Ian asked if he could see them. 'It might help me – help with something else I'm working on,' he said.

The boy tapped on the screen, and expertly scrolled through the phone menu until he found what he was looking for. He handed the phone over to Ian. 'We didn't mean anything bad,' he said. 'We just never saw a body from the water. We didn't touch her.'

It was hard for Ian to make out anything on the left side of the screen, which was covered by a web of fine lines radiating out from the top corner.

Even with the crack, the photos were still marginally better than Myburgh's. And, also more jarring. Ian wondered if it was because of the frames the children had inadvertently chosen, or because he knew the pictures had been taken by children. He thought perhaps it was both.

There was, as the girls had said, a woman's hand, bright ruby red nails in stark contrast to the lifeless brown skin. Her other arm and most of the rest of her body was caught in and under a raft of plastic and cardboard and unidentified objects. There were straws and pieces of polystyrene. Empty bread bags. Cardboard take-out containers and cooldrink bottles. The woman had been wearing light blue trousers, maybe some kind of denim, which had partly blended in with the mottled colours around her, hiding the corpse. At the woman's feet, as MaRejoice had mentioned, was a giant blue plastic bag – not a shopping bag, more the size of a trash bag – which had obviously managed to trap some water, and then gotten twisted, until it did indeed resemble some kind of grotesque fish tail.

The dead woman was almost face-down – her face was half-buried in the small island of rubbish that had washed up against her, or which had been tangled around her in the water. It was hard to see much from her profile – one eye was almost visible, but it was mercifully closed. Dead eyes could haunt your dreams for a very long time, Ian knew.

There were no visible injury marks on her head, or anywhere else that he could see, but they might have been obscured by her hair. The dead woman had a medium-length bob, and he couldn't tell up close whether it was a wig or natural hair. He had been trying to be more aware of the difference ever since Surprise had given him a short lesson, but he realised that what he knew about black women's hair was less than nothing.

Ian went back to the picture of the hand, imagining its owner almost reaching out, reaching for help. He thought, with a small blip of adrenaline, that he could make out a line on the woman's wrist. The same, or similar to the ones he had seen on the photographs of the woman dragged out of the dam. He would need to compare the photographs more closely. Even better, he would need to see the actual bodies. Not that he was sure how he would manage that on his own. Unless Reshma was prepared to help? Maybe if he could show her two women's bodies, both with similar marks and deaths, she could take an official interest.

'Can I take this with me?' he asked, looking up at the children. He needed to get the photos off the broken phone, and onto another screen – perhaps his own computer. Even if the kids' phone had no SIM card, he could still download the images if he plugged the device into his laptop.

There was a brief moment of hesitation – reluctance on the part of the children to part with their secret toy.

'I just need it for a day, maybe less. I can have it back to you this afternoon,' Ian said, looking at MaRejoice, hoping that she would back him up, or put in a good word.

'You'll bring it back today?' the smaller girl asked. Ian nodded. He was pretty sure he could get what he needed off the phone in a matter of minutes. He just needed a computer and a USB cable.

After a moment Portia nodded.

'If it will help you catch whoever killed the mermaid, you should take the phone,' she said. Then she looked up at Ian. 'Are you going to catch who did this?' she asked.

Ian didn't have an answer, and he didn't want to lie. So he told the kids that he didn't know. Portia looked like she knew that at least he was telling the truth.

SANCTUARY

Scott and Dube were already at work when Reshma arrived. She wasn't sure if it was passive aggressive one-upmanship, or if they genuinely loved being at their desks. Sobukwe arrived five minutes later and stomped into his own office before pointedly closing the door.

Dube was wearing a new jersey, but the same aesthetic as before – West Rand government official. Reshma wondered if he was being ironic, but had no one to ask.

'We found your woman,' Scott said, turning on his chair to face her as she stared at Sobukwe's closed door. She had thought that at very least, the big boss would want to talk to her about yesterday. Being ignored stung more than a little. She only realised a few seconds later that Scott had said something to her, and that she hadn't responded.

'Sorry, what was that?' she asked.

Scott gave a smile – not a mean one – and repeated what he'd said. 'When we first met, you said your team got a tip-off about someone trying to abduct a woman at Park Station. We found her for you,' he said. 'At least, I think we did.'

He called Reshma over to one of the four screens spread across the complex of desks he and Dube had commandeered.

'I thought the station said its cameras were down,' Reshma said, staring at what was quite obviously CCTV camera footage.

Dube nodded. 'Uh huh. But they don't have the *only* cameras,' he said.

Both men had matching grins that made Reshma realise they were definitely in this for the job satisfaction, not the workplace politics. She grinned back.

'What am I looking at?' she asked.

'This is footage from outside the Burger King at the north entrance,' Scott said, showing Reshma a date and a time stamp at the bottom of the screen. 'It's only black and white, but you can see here,' he carried on, pointing with his pen, 'there's some kind of commotion at the door. Which then moves on to ... here,' he said, moving to the second screen, where two men, one wearing jeans and a bulky sweater, the other with jeans and a kind of sports jacket, both wearing caps, could be seen pulling forcefully at a woman.

The men were both of slight build, although it was hard to determine given their baggy clothes. One was carrying a backpack, the other one was holding an umbrella and a plastic bag. The woman was in jeans and a patterned top. She was medium height, medium build – at least as far as Reshma could tell from the angle of the camera – and had blonde braids that went down past her shoulders. All of the subjects were dark-skinned, which was about as much as the camera tone allowed her to see.

The men in caps had surrounded the woman, who was visible trying to escape their grip. In the background, Reshma could see a couple of people looking up from their phones, but nobody did anything. Typical. One of the men leaned in and spoke to the woman. Reshma thought she could see him holding something against her torso, maybe a knife. The entire scene gave her a bad feeling that ran up her spine and out along her collarbones. She was increasingly anxious about what she was going to see next.

'Here is where it gets really interesting,' Scott said, tapping the third screen.

'See, your reports said the men and the woman headed ...' he looked down at a set of handwritten notes on his desk, 'they headed towards De Villiers Street side, but nobody saw her leave the building. Which was how you got to go into the tunnels, right?' he asked.

Reshma nodded. 'There's a lot of traffic at Park. A lot of buses coming in from the continent. Women from other African countries,' she explained. 'We've had problems before, men advertising jobs, bringing women in, fetching them at the station, then they take away their passports ...' She let the story trail off, fairly certain the Scott and Dube could guess what happened next in those situations.

'So, we checked the footage on the other side of Park,' Dube said. 'And we watched for like thirty minutes from the time the woman and those two men left the Burger King. Except, they disappear. Just like your witnesses say. They don't come out this side, they don't come out the back entrance. There's nothing on the Rissik Street bridge either – that camera was working. It's like they disappeared into thin air. Except this morning, Scott had a bright idea. Maybe his neurons got shaken up by the sound of gunfire,' Dube said, laughing.

Reshma was still anxious after watching the woman being forced to go with the men on camera, and didn't get the joke.

Staring at the screens, looking at the woman trying in vain to get away, she wondered if she had let herself get distracted by the big prize of working on the cash heists, and if in doing so, she had left this woman – whoever she was – to some unspeakable fate. She felt cold, and a little sick.

'Relax, Captain,' Scott said, noticing her discomfort. 'Yesterday did make me think – but in a different way. It was about those guys, the ones dressed up in overalls, right? I kept thinking about what we do see and what we don't see.'

'And we don't notice people in uniforms; we don't notice a whole bunch of people when their clothes change.' He went back to the third screen and rewound the footage a bit.

'Hang on a sec. Here it is,' he said, as he hit pause.

The footage on this screen was in colour. Reshma could see tables and gazebos and people spilling out across a brick concourse that she recognised as the south entrance to Park. She had gone past there when she had first tried to get access to the tunnels, only to discover more hidden places, all locked up or blocked off.

'What am I looking at?' she said, peering at the screen and trying not to sound impatient.

'Okay. You see these women here,' Scott said, circling a pair of women who were standing in front of the book stand. Both were wearing black hats, long white shirts, and black skirts that went to at least mid-calf. One of the women had a black bag or backpack slung over her shoulder.

Reshma wasn't sure what she was supposed to be looking for, but Scott carried on talking. 'And see this woman here,' he said, pointing to another figure a few metres away, who was looking at a table that had what looked like belts or jewellery displayed on it. The woman had a short dark bob – probably a wig – and was wearing a dress. She was carrying a plastic bag in one hand, and a red umbrella in the other.

Reshma stared for a few more seconds before she saw it. The umbrella. 'The umbrella. And the bags,' she said out loud, turning back to Scott and Dube to see if she was right.

Dube nodded. 'It's hard to be sure, because of the colour difference,' he said. 'But it looks like the backpack and the rolled-up plastic bag the two males are carrying here,' he said, going back to the first black and white screen, where the woman was apparently being abducted, 'are the same as what these females are carrying here. So, when people saw the woman being pulled into a side corridor, we think that they just went into a corridor to change – maybe they already had the skirts, the tops, under their jackets. And when you think that, it's easier or at least it's plausible to think that what looks like two males in this clip are actually a bunch of women. They just took off their caps, rolled up their jeans or pulled them off, and bundled them into their bags. And the same for the women they were supposedly "taking". She just puts this uniform on over her jeans, puts on a hat and tucks in her braids and you don't notice her any more.'

'But why?' Reshma asked, turning to look at Scott and Dube.

Scott pointed to the fourth screen.

'This is from one of the ATMs a block away. It's not great footage – they're designed to see who's drawing money – but check here,' he said.

The time stamp on the screen was less than five minutes after the women had been browsing books and belts. It showed the three women suddenly together again, moving towards a fenced-off stone building. They approached a black metal gate in front of a wooden door and paused there for a few moments before moving off, heading east.

'That's the end of the footage I'm afraid,' Dube said. But his voice made it clear that he knew more.

'What is that? The gate that they went to? Do we know where they went afterwards?' Reshma asked.

Dube clicked on his mouse and the CCTV footage disappeared, replaced by a screen showing Google Maps.

'That,' he said, tapping on the screen, 'is the side door of the Church of Saint Mary the Virgin. The main entrance is around the corner, on Wanderers Street. St Mary's is an Anglican church. It just celebrated its ninetieth anniversary. The black and white uniforms are for a church group called the Mothers' Union. They often pray at the church, so nobody in the area would notice anything strange about women dressed like this.'

Dube pointed to the map again. 'That is where your missing woman went.'

Reshma went online to get a phone number for Saint Mary the Virgin, and called to ask what time services were, and when she could speak to whoever was in charge. After God, of course.

WOMEN ON YOUR PHONE

Ian stared at photographs of dead women on his computer screen. It had been easy enough to download the photographs from the kids' cracked mobile, and now he was zooming in on the body parts of the unidentified woman who had washed up on the banks of the Jukskei River.

There was nothing remarkable about the woman's face, or at least the half of her face that Ian could see above a bundle of string and what appeared to be an old chicken bone. But when he pulled up photos of her arm and hand, he could make out what looked like a mark around her wrist. Although of course it could also just have been a piece of rubbish that had wrapped around the limb in the river. He clicked through the photos, and checked if there were any images showing the victim's other arm, but the rest of her was masked by garbage.

He kept the photo of the river woman's wrist on his preview screen and scrolled through Myburgh's photos until he found similar photos of the dead woman at the dam. Ian's pulse quickened slightly. Even with the differences in photography, the marks looked remarkably similar.

After a little googling, he discovered the waterways were connected to each other. The Jukskei was one of the tributaries that fed into the Crocodile River before it entered the Hartbeespoort Dam. Ian wasn't sure the water levels were high enough to carry a human body all the way along the Jukskei's course – not based on what it had looked like in Alex earlier that morning, in any event – but perhaps the connection was significant. Particularly in a city that had so little water.

He was still focused on the screen when his phone beeped. It was a message from the cellphone kiosk at the small shopping centre down the road. Ian had used them a few times before, and they'd promised to replace the broken screen on the kids' phone within an hour and a half. That had been eighty minutes ago. Ian grinned at their efficiency and scooped up his wallet before heading out the door. He sent Reshma a note saying that he would be out for the next two hours or so. As an afterthought, he sent a second message asking if he should get anything for supper, or if she planned on working through the evening.

It took Reshma over an hour to reply, by which time Ian had already returned the slightly renewed phone to its appreciative co-owners, and made another round of hellos and goodbyes to MaRejoice and her granny. Ian tried to push aside the brief moment of anxiety he felt before unlocking his screen and reading Reshma's message. Then he tried to modify the almost embarrassing rush of relief he experienced when he saw that she was already on her way home, and suggested a late lunch. He couldn't tell if that meant good or bad things for her case, but he definitely felt like it was better for him. For them.

Ian exited at Empire Road and went past the campus shopping centre to pick up ingredients for a meal. By the time he got home, Reshma's car was neatly tucked into its space on the driveway, and she was in the kitchen drinking tea and checking her Facebook page, grimacing as she scrolled and clicked through page after page.

Ian let her torture herself with social media while he started

preparing the food – a plant-based chicken substitute, fresh vegeta-
bles, and noodles. He mixed dark treacle sugar with soy sauce as he
told Reshma about the two dead women. 'They were both found in
or around water, and both have these, like, marks on their wrists,' he
said. 'The one woman, the one in the dam, her body was found all the
way back in March. The woman in Alex, her body was only found last
week. But if you look here,' he said, reaching for his laptop to open the
pictures he'd been comparing earlier, 'you can see that the marks look
almost the same. Right? Do you think I'm crazy?' he asked, looking
back at Reshma.

She stayed quiet but took the computer from him and clicked
through the different photographs. When she reached the photographs of the woman in the Jukskei, she paused.

'You say the one in the Jukskei, she was found by kids?' she asked.
'That's horrible, man.'

Ian nodded. 'The kids were the ones who took those photos,' he
said, pointing at the screen.

Reshma spent another minute staring at the two different images
of the women's hands and wrists before she spoke. Something about
the photographs had made her go quiet.

'Do you have any photos of her other hand?' Reshma asked. Ian
shook his head.

'So, let's say the marks are the same – and it's hard to tell from
these pictures. I have to play devil's advocate,' she said. 'What would
you do next?'

Ian had already given this some thought on his drive. 'Go see the
bodies at the morgue,' he said. 'The one from the dam, she's unidentified, unclaimed,' he suggested. 'And the one from the Jukskei, she's in

Hillbrow. Maybe if we went to see both of them, we could try and work out who the woman is they found at the dam?'

Reshma rested her chin on her hand while Ian dished up. She waited until he had set her bowl in front of her before speaking again.

'I'll tell you what. I'll think about if I'm willing to go to the lab with you and help you visit your dead women. If you come with me to church,' she said.

The question was so out of context that Ian couldn't work out if Reshma was teasing him or being serious. Sensing his confusion, she gave him a lopsided smile.

'You haven't found a new religion, have you?' he asked, suddenly worried that he'd missed something even bigger than the chasm between their two careers.

Reshma laughed. 'No, silly. But I need to go and visit a church in town, near Park Station,' she said, before explaining about the footage Scott and Dube had found, and what they had seen on the CCTV cameras.

'I can't go back and investigate a missing woman who's not actually missing. Not after I handed the whole scene and story over to another task team. But I want to know why she went in there. Why she changed her clothes, her hair. Who was she hiding from? Because one thing that I could get from the reports on the day was that the woman, the main one, they all said she was scared. I want to know what she was scared of, and why she needed to run to that church. Maybe I'm like you,' she said, bending to blow on her food. 'Maybe I just need to know for my own peace of mind.'

Ian thought that she had a point, and it was more than a fair deal. 'Okay. I'm up for a trip to church. When are we going?' he asked.

'Tonight,' Reshma said, the grin back on her face.

*

The roads around Park Station were never entirely quiet, not even on a Sunday evening, but Ian managed to find a parking spot right outside Darragh House next to the cathedral. The female security guard at the church door gave them a brief look, but didn't stop them from entering.

Inside, the church was warmly lit and spacious – high-volume vaulted ceilings on top of white pillars, dark wood on the floor and the pews, and an impressively large organ. Reshma said the last service had finished some hours ago, but there were still one or two people seated quietly in the pews, lost in thought or prayer, and there was a woman moving quietly around in front of the pulpit, cleaning up flowers and papers and whatever else had been left behind during the early evening service.

Near the pulpit were three pull-up banners. One was for the Mothers' Union, with a logo of the church and the elegant blue MU logo of the association, a photograph underneath of a group of smiling women wearing the same white-shirt, black-skirted uniform Reshma had described. There was another banner for the Albinism Society of South Africa, and a third urging congregants to say no to xenophobia. At the bottom of this banner was the familiar MU logo and another one, an image of a red umbrella, with the words 'Mermaid Bureau' beneath it. The organisation was unfamiliar to Ian, and he pointed it out to Reshma. She stopped in mid-stride, and mouthed the words at him, a question mark implied by her frown, before moving on.

173

Ian followed Reshma into a corridor lined with smooth beige lino-leum. The area was wide enough to double as a hall, and there were a few tables, covered in white cloths, that bore the remnants of trays of snacks.

On the wall was a notice board covered with posters and hand-made signs, and a printed sign with an arrow, pointing left, which said 'OFFICE'.

Reshma followed it.

'You sure someone will be here?' Ian asked, two steps behind her. 'I mean, it's already after six.'

'I called ahead,' she said.

At the end of the corridor was a brick wall and a sign on a door that marked the church's office. The door was open, and a middle-aged woman sat behind a desk, looking at a computer screen and slowly moving a mouse over a giant church calendar that was doubling as a mousepad.

Reshma tapped politely on the door, and the woman looked up. She smiled although she plainly had no idea who Reshma and Ian were.

'Can I help you?' she asked.

'Are you Mrs de Bruyn?' Reshma asked, courteous, also smiling. The older woman nodded. 'I'm Captain Patel. Reshma. I spoke to you earlier today.'

The woman's smile stayed on her face, but her eyes became more guarded. 'Yes, of course, Captain. How can I help? Please take a seat,' she said, waving towards two wooden chairs in front of her desk. She did not ask Ian's name, and neither Ian nor Reshma volunteered it. They sat down, and Reshma started speaking almost straight away. 'How come you're here so late – is this normal for a Sunday?' she asked, trying to keep up the lightness of their first greeting.

Mrs de Bruyn gave another smile. 'No. Not every Sunday. But today we had a special guest speaker coming in, to give the kids a ... motivational lecture, you know? A lot of students around here, it's not always easy to stay unaffected by the troubles of the world around you,' she said.

Ian caught himself nodding, as if that was his role: to agree, to nod, to find parking. He didn't mind. It gave him the opportunity to observe, without being observed much himself.

Reshma began to explain her interest in the suspected abduction at Park Station. She said that there had been a witness – Reshma specifically avoided mentioning the CCTV footage – who thought they had seen the woman in question enter St Mary's.

Ian watched as Reshma spoke. His eyes moved around the room, taking in the scripture quote on the wall – John 8:7 – and the neat piles of paper on the desk between them and the administrator. He saw Mrs de Bruyn's face harden a little, then settle into fixed impassivity. Which suggested that whatever Reshma was talking about resonated with something the other woman already knew, but which she didn't necessarily want to discuss.

Mrs de Bruyn waited for Reshma to finish, and paused before giving her reply. 'We get so many people in here, Captain Patel. I would love to help you, but I'm really not sure that I could,' she said. 'Perhaps you could write a notice, asking anyone who saw this attempted ... abduction you say, asking anyone who saw anything, to contact you. I would be very happy to put it on our notice board. A lot of our parishioners read the messages on the board, because we have listings for jobs, accommodation, bursaries and all of that. But other than that,

I'm not sure what I could do.'

Reshma slumped a little in her chair.

Ian knew it was always easier to get somewhere when people actively participated and wanted to help. Once you had to pull the cop card and force people to talk, the conversations were always going to be more tense and less productive.

'Sure. Of course. I understand,' Reshma said, but the disappointment was evident in her voice. She took a small breath and started speaking again. 'Look, I should tell you something. I'm not interested in their papers. I'm not checking for migrant status or whatever. I just want to know that the woman is safe,' she continued. 'Because I saw footage of two men trying to take a woman against her will, and she looked scared. And I don't know who she is, or who they are, but I will not stop trying to find out, because all I want to know is if that woman, whoever she is, is alright. That, Mrs de Bruyn, is who I work for. People like that scared woman at Park Station. And against whatever, whoever, is behind the things that made her afraid.'

Her words lingered in the air. The deliberate mention of at least some of the camera footage, that there was documentation of a possible crime, and that the police had it. He wondered if it would be enough to tip Mrs de Bruyn's hand – either convince her that it was safe to open up a little to Reshma, or that it wasn't worth fobbing off a police officer.

At that moment, Ian looked back at Mrs de Bruyn's efficient desk and noticed a sheet of paper with a red umbrella on it.

'What is the Mermaid Bureau?' he asked, forgetting that he was supposed to be quiet.

Both women turned towards him, as if he had just said something preposterous, or very important. Ian couldn't make out which it was.

Mrs de Bruyn looked from Ian to Reshma and back again, and sighed. She leaned forward, picked up the piece of paper with the logo, and turned it face-down.

'The Mermaid Bureau is ... it is an African organisation that was established to help sex workers, Detective ...' she let the question linger in the air until Ian replied.

'Mr Jack. Just Mr,' he said, without trying to explain or justify his role further.

Mrs de Bruyn arched an eyebrow in response, but continued. 'We see many vulnerable women, *Mr* Jack. Women who have been taken advantage of. Women who have trusted too much, and who cannot get themselves out of a bad situation. Sometimes these are woman who have come from other provinces, other countries, who think they are coming here for a job, for love ... They may need our help to get away from a bad problem, and we do not judge them,' she said.

'You help women who are being trafficked?' Reshma asked.

The older woman looked at her and eventually inclined her head in concession. 'Them, and others. Yes. Not everybody who is trapped is being sold or moved from one person to another. Not every woman who is being used even knows that she is trapped, sometimes,' she said, sounding a lot more serious and less like the pleasant-faced church official she had been only minutes before.

'We do fundraising for some of these women, or try to integrate them back into our church – through the Mothers' Union. You saw the banner in the chapel?' she asked, looking back at Ian, who nodded in response.

Mrs de Bruyn sat more upright. 'Captain Patel, I can't tell you details of how we work or what we do to help these women. They are very vulnerable, and not everybody who works with the state – not everybody who works with the police – always knows what is best for them. Maybe we don't even know what is best for them, but we try not to judge, and we make sure that we don't expose them to risk or harm. Please know that if we introduce them to the police, it will expose these women to harm. Both the women who have been helped, and the women who are the helpers. But if you are worried about the woman from Park Station, I can promise you that she is safe, and that she will remain safe as long as she stays within our care and support. Will you take my word for this?' she asked.

Reshma seemed surprised by the woman's candour, and also her resolve. 'Yes, of course. I ...' she stammered slightly. 'I mean, I understand what you are saying, and where you are coming from. If I might ask one thing before I go. Not for now, but maybe for the future. This organisation, your bureau, it might help some women, but it certainly can't help all of them. I'm happy to leave the women alone and try go after the ones who do this to them. But I can't do that without help. Without names. Without information. So, if any of your women, any of them, have tip-offs, ideas about where my colleagues and I should be looking ... would you think about letting me know?'

Mrs de Bruyn agreed almost immediately. 'I will think about it, at least,' she said. 'Perhaps we can learn to trust each other with certain things,' she said, still cautious, but her smile less guarded. 'But it will take time,' she cautioned.

Reshma agreed, and they all shook hands.

They exited through the grand chapel again, where all the pews were now finally empty, with only the flowers left to provide living tribute to the glorious space. The woman they had seen earlier was finishing cleaning up at the back. As they passed her Ian smiled, and the woman immediately looked away, almost shrinking from his gaze. It made him feel terrible for a moment, terribly male. The woman had her left arm in a sling, her forearm and hand wrapped in a white crepe bandage, and he felt deeply ashamed imagining what had been done to her to make her terrified of every strange man she saw.

Ian was happy to leave the church. Being there made him consider his own flaws too much for comfort. Outside, the streets were cold enough that people moved without lingering at the few shops that were still open, or huddled in cubicles that sold cellphones, jewellery, toiletries and groceries.

On the drive home Reshma got a call from Super to tell her that a woman's body had been found at a boating resort on the Vaal River, a few hundred metres downstream from Three Rivers.

According to Sobukwe, the victim's eyes had been gouged out.

MEDICO-LEGAL

Reshma never liked the mortuary.

The medico-legal laboratory squatted on the border of Hillbrow and Braamfontein, just above the historical Old Fort that half-heartedly tried to keep one suburb from slipping accidentally into the other. The mortuary and pathology building dated back to the 1920s and had once housed the city's 'non-European' hospital, right next to the police barracks, on Hospital Hill. Now it was painted an unfortunate combination of pale blue and orange, and studded with outside air-conditioning units. Inside it was yellow and smelled of bulk-purchased industrial antiseptic, which never quite managed to disguise that it was a place where dead things lived.

All Reshma had to go on was the photographs Ian had shown her the night before. The ones with the woman's hand, and the painted nails. The same colour as the polish she remembered seeing on the nail of the severed finger that had been pointing at her from the floor of the tunnel underneath Park Station. She hadn't mentioned it to Ian, had wanted to keep the possible connection to herself, keep some part of her cases to herself.

Like many others, the body of the woman who had been found in the Jukskei had made its way to Hillbrow, making the journey from corpse to cadaver in a white and blue van. Reshma had arranged to meet with one of the laboratory's forensic pathologists to find out what information they had obtained from the autopsy, if they had done one; or, to view the body herself, if they had not.

As it turned out, the autopsy on the dead woman had not yet been done – a delay, the helpful pathologist, Martina Wild, explained, not due to the lab being overburdened for once, but because they were still trying to determine the woman's identity.

'We took prints off the hand that was there, but I don't think we'll get anything,' Wild said.

Reshma had told the pathologist about the finger from Park Station when she'd called and asked to see the body.

Now she stared at the dead woman's other arm, where the left hand was conspicuously absent. 'Was that done before or after she died?' she asked.

The pathologist walked around to look at the grisly stump. She picked up the limb with gloved hands.

'I'd say before, but I can't really be sure. I'd need to take a closer look at the blood vessels, tissue damage. Problem with a body being in the water, even for a short while, is it really messes with some of what's left behind.'

'Was the body damaged from the water? I mean, is that why you think you won't get any results from the fingerprints?' Reshma asked.

The other woman shook her head. 'Nope. I just don't think she's from here. South Africa, I mean. Could be Zimbabwe, Mozambique. Angola maybe. Maybe even further away, but probably not South African,' she said.

'How do you know?' Reshma asked.

'Lot of bodies come here,' Wild said, not cruelly, just matter-of-fact.

'I can't be exact about where she came from. I just see enough bodies to know that she probably didn't come from here, originally at least.'

The Joburg mortuary facility received over three thousand bodies a year, which meant that at any given moment there were four or five bodies on gurneys, with a much longer waiting list.

Under South African law, anything considered a death that was not the result of natural causes was supposed to go to a state medico-legal facility. This included suicides, accidental deaths, and of course homicides. The forensic pathology services was supposed to investigate each death, which would allow them to determine the identity of the deceased, the cause and approximate time of death, and to work out if that death had been caused by something someone else had done, or – and this part always intrigued and repulsed Reshma – something someone had *not* done. The law described this as an act of commission or an act of omission. The difference between feeding poison to an unwanted spouse, or starving a hospital patient to death. Reshma had closely followed the enquiries into the Life Esidimeni tragedy, where at least 144 state psychiatric patients had died due to neglect.

There was nothing concrete to link the woman from the Jukskei to the body that had been pulled out of the Hartbeespoort Dam, or the newly discovered body of the woman in the Vaal River. And yet Reshma couldn't help but wonder if Ian was right, that there was something in the discovery of what was now three unidentified women's bodies in or near water. And the tantalising possibility that this body in particular might be linked to the bloody scene underneath Park Station.

Ryk and Mark were scheduled to visit the medico-legal centre in Sasolburg, which was closest to Three Rivers and the Vaal, and was where the third body had been sent. Depending on their results, she would decide if it was worth also visiting the other body – or maybe the first, the one Ian was so keen to investigate, which was being held at the medico-legal facility in Ga-Rankuwa north-east of the Hartbeespoort Dam.

Dr Wild had started preparing the Jukskei woman for autopsy before Reshma had arrived. She explained that she'd conducted a visual examination, and there was no externally obvious cause of death – excluding the mutilated limb. 'There are some burn marks on her arm. Maybe cigarette burns. A few other areas that look like they could be bruised – it's hard to tell, given the victim's skin colour, and lividity. She didn't have the best life before she died,' Wild said, 'but I can't see anything that might have killed her specifically.'

The pathologist had already made incisions across the dead woman's chest and torso. 'I wouldn't normally do such a detailed autopsy right now, giving that we're pressed for resources. But if you say it might be linked to another crime, then I reckon you might need to know more about this woman,' she said.

The Jukskei woman's feet were both intact – the blue plastic that had been covering them in the photos Ian had shown her had been removed, together with the woman's clothes. The pathologist pointed to a pair of boxes on one of the tables against the wall.

'Everything we found on her is there,' she said. 'Clothes, and the trash bag around her feet. We checked it out, but there wasn't much inside except scummy water,' she explained.

Reshma walked around to look at the woman's other hand, the remaining one. The nails were still red, but up close Reshma noticed the edges were chipped. She couldn't tell whether it was an old paint job, or if the woman had been fighting for her life before she died. It was a story with a sad ending either way.

The wrist had a visible raised scar line – Reshma could feel a slight kick of adrenaline when she saw this, because she knew this might link the body in the Jukskei to the body from the dam. It was impossible to check for a matching mark on the other wrist, because of the location of the mutilation.

'Is this like some kind of tattoo? You ever seen this mark before?' Reshma asked about the scar line.

The pathologist was quiet for a moment. There were three other cubicles next to where they were standing with the woman's body, and Reshma could hear the sounds of different conversations coming from each room – pass me this, how was your weekend, I can't believe she used my coffee mug.

The corpse from the Jukskei lay between them, still half-draped in the white plastic she had come in.

'You could call it a tattoo,' the pathologist said at last. 'It's definitely deliberate. Not like a normal scar – I don't think it's from being tied up, if that's what you're asking. It's more like it was cut into her skin. I've seen some of them before,' she said. 'It's more prominent on black skins. The marks, I mean. The scars show up differently. You get some indented marks that go into the skin – like, the scar goes under the surface, if that makes sense? You know, if you traced a stick on wet beach sand?' she said, illustrating the movement with her hands.

Reshma nodded.

'Then you get other marks that are raised, where the scarring forms keloid or hypertrophic scars. That's what you have here. It looks deliberate, I would say. Like whoever made the mark intended for it to look this way,' the pathologist said.

'You seen a wrist scar like this before?' Reshma asked.

The pathologist shook her head. 'Not like this, specifically, no.'

'And nothing on the feet, the ankles, I mean?' Reshma asked. She could plainly see the dead woman's two feet poking out from beneath the cloth, toenails painted the same ruby colour.

The other woman shook her head again.

'No other marks, no other tattoos. Maybe one birthmark on the back, underneath the right shoulder blade – a small mole. We don't really have much to go on here. There was no ID on the body. No missing person's report. Not in Johannesburg, at any rate. She's missing some of her back teeth, but we can't see any other dental work. We did a Lodox X-ray,' she said. 'It didn't show up any other traumatic wounds. I mean, aside from what you can see.'

The pathologist was friendly, but obviously impatient.

'Look, I need to get started with her, now that she's out the fridge. You want to stay and watch? I can't get you a final report until next week, earliest. But if you stay now, I can try and tell you what I think might have been the cause of death, if we find anything,' she said.

The cadaver lay between them, her face towards the ceiling. Reshma noticed a gap between the woman's dead lips where she could just see the teeth. It made the mottled face seem uncomfortably lifelike.

'I'm happy to wait around. I won't get in your way,' she said, as another laboratory worker in a blue gown, white boots, hair-net and face mask joined them. Reshma nodded in greeting, her own outfit a close match with the technician's, except she didn't have an additional plastic apron or plastic visor.

Reshma stepped back and tried to watch, but not too closely. While they were busy opening up the cadaver's chest cavity, she asked if she might look through the boxes holding the woman's possessions and clothing. Dr Wild said it would be fine as long as Reshma kept her gloves on.

The boxes held little to mark the end of a woman's life. A pair of denims, and a tank top, both of which had been cut off the corpse, neither one with a clothing label she recognised, but also nothing recognisably foreign. There was a see-through plastic bag marked with the SAPS logo and a bar code, containing the bedraggled hairpiece that had somehow managed to stay attached to the woman even after death, but which had been removed for the autopsy. Reshma thought it might match the other clump of hair they had found underground. Another bag held a tiny vanity mirror – one of those round mirrors with a plastic backing, like you'd find in a make-up compact. The mirror was cracked right across the middle.

'Where was the mirror found?' Reshma turned to ask.

'It was jammed into her jean pocket,' the pathologist said without looking up. She continued peeling back layers of skin and flesh, and Reshma turned her attention back to the boxes.

The blue plastic bag, shoved into another plastic evidence bag, was most likely just rubbish, Reshma thought. A standard-issue refuse bag – the kind people used for recycling, or garden waste. She couldn't remember which one. There was a slightly frayed cord curled around the bottom of the blue bag, and she pushed around until she could see it better.

'This was the bag that was around her feet? Is that right?' she asked.

Dr Wild lifted her head and nodded.

'Was it loose – I mean, was it just wrapped around her, or was it tied on? What's this rope for?' Reshma said.

The pathologist stopped whatever she was doing on the gurney and thought for a second.

'The bag was tied – although it could also have just been from water action. The rope wasn't knotted, not properly. Sorry. It's been quite a busy week,' she said, distracted even as she started removing internal organs and placing them on another waiting gurney.

Reshma looked away and stared back into the box of nothing.

'Well, the good news or bad news is, I don't think she drowned,' the pathologist said, after another few minutes. 'There's nothing so far in her airways, or the state of her lungs, that seem to suggest that. I mean, this is just provisional, these are my thoughts as I work.'

The bad news, the pathologist added a short while later, was that she still couldn't see any obvious cause of death.

'Heart looks normal. Organs, too. We can take tissue samples. I mean, we *will* take tissue samples, but that might take a while. The only thing I'm seeing so far is damage to the larynx, on the vocal folds. Which might indicate strangulation. But there's no other evidence she was strangled. To be honest,' the pathologist said, 'the vocal fold damage might be old. I'm sorry, I guess nothing I'm saying right now is helping. Maybe you could go looking for a missing person who had an extremely hoarse voice?'

Reshma left with a promise from the pathologist to follow up with a preliminary written report before the end of the week, and a rush job trying to match the severed finger to the woman's body – rush job meaning, at least a month before DNA analysis would be done, if Reshma was lucky. The pathologist offered to take a look and make a visual assessment in the meantime.

'I'm not a machine, but at least I can give you a pretty good idea of whether you can exclude it as a match,' the other woman said.

Reshma thought about calling Ian on her way back to the offices in Modderfontein. She felt slightly guilty about not mentioning the nail polish on the severed finger when she'd seen the photograph the night before, but she was already feeling the pressure of not just one but maybe two investigations getting away from her, and she didn't need Ian stepping in to try and save the day.

Instead she left a message for Ryk and Mark, asking them to call once they'd been able to see the body from the Vaal. But she knew this might take another day or more. She would just have to be patient. The dead bodies weren't going anywhere, she reasoned.

When she reached the task team offices, Scott and Dube were staring intently at their screens with headphones on. She waved a greeting, but they only glanced up and immediately went back to whatever it was they were looking at.

Three other men Reshma didn't recognise were in the boardroom, having some kind of meeting. The door was closed, and Reshma couldn't make out what they were saying. None of them even looked in her direction.

Sobukwe was standing in the doorway of his office, his face an unreadable mask. 'I need to talk with you,' he said, before going back to sit behind his desk.

At first Reshma thought that Sobukwe was going to give her an update on Claassen's status. But as soon as she sat down, she realised that the reason he had summoned her was to chastise her for taking the morning off to follow up on a wild goose chase.

'I know you care about what happens to these ... these women,' Sobukwe said, implying quite clearly that he did not. 'It's not that I'm without sympathy, Captain Patel. But I called you here because I need you to focus. You kept it together when you were under fire. Don't lose it now because you see a dead woman in a spruit, and develop a conscience. She will still be dead tomorrow; you can help her then.'

Reshma nodded without speaking.

'What I need you for right now is to focus on the men from the attack on Saturday. We need to start figuring out who else is involved. I'm one man down with Claassen out of action. He won't even be able to help us at a desk for a few weeks. But I need your focus here, your energy here. Is that understood?' he asked. 'I've told Ryk and Mark to go back to the house in Three Rivers. They'll take a forensic team with them this time, no more hush-hush. The Meyerton SAPS are going to go to the Bargain Build and see if anyone remembers who bought a bootload of overalls. I need you to find out more information about the men that we apprehended – the ones we arrested, and the ones you killed. Find out who they all are, if they have records, who they used to work with. The usual shit. Clear?'

Reshma nodded again and said that she understood.

'Start with the ones we arrested,' Sobukwe continued. As soon as you have info on them, I'm going to go in and do some interviews. I'm taking Dube with me, so it will be just you and Scott. You okay with that?' he asked.

Reshma said that she was. The room was quiet. Sobukwe looked at her as if she was a particularly dim-witted child. After a few seconds, she realised that she had missed her cue to leave his office and get to work. 'Of course, sir. Right away,' she said, and stumbled out.

She was grateful that Scott and Dube didn't look up again.

Back at her desk, Reshma started with the names of the men who had been arrested – she could still hear Sobukwe describing the others, the dead, as men she had killed. She couldn't tell if it had been said with pride and respect, or with derision. She wondered if she had somehow misread Sobukwe's instruction to shoot to kill. She shook her head to clear the thought. There would be time enough to worry about that later. First, she needed to prove that she was as adept with paperwork as she was with pulling her trigger.

Reshma had already done some of the groundwork the morning before – she'd contacted the SAPS office in Meyerton, who were holding the men, and asked for copies of the dockets. She saw that they had arrived earlier that morning, while she was at the mortuary, she realised with slight embarrassment. Perhaps Sobukwe had been right to call her out. It wasn't really the time for wild goose chases.

Although three of the men had been injured, only one had been hurt seriously enough to remain in hospital – he had suffered multiple blunt-force injury, which made Reshma suspect he was the one who had been hit by Claassen's car. The other two injuries were both bullet wounds, but relatively clean. Both men had been returned to the holding cells at the police station until they could be taken to court and charged – something Reshma saw from the notes was scheduled to happen that very day.

She called the Meyerton office and checked to see whether the arraignment had happened. She was put on hold while they went to look for one of the officers involved in the case.

She scanned through the dockets while she waited, noting the given names and ages of the men. She would have to wait for their fingerprints to go through the Automated Fingerprint Identification System (AFIS) to see if there were any positive matches, but, in the meantime, the names were a start. In one of the dockets, she also noted an entry about the dispatch call that had been made, announcing the crime in progress, and listing which officers had been sent to attend to the heist as it was happening. The call had gone out to the station in Meyerton, and the Sedibeng Flying Squad, both with instructions for responding officers to wear full tactical gear. For a moment, Reshma thought back to the naivete with which she and Claassen had put on their vests. She hoped Claassen wouldn't be paying for her own bravado for too long.

Her thoughts were interrupted by a woman's voice coming on the line, an officer whose name she couldn't catch, saying that the arraignment had gone ahead, and that all the men had appeared before court and entered 'not guilty' pleas. Reshma rolled her eyes at this, even though it was to be expected, and there was nobody in visual range to see her facial sarcasm.

She was about to thank the woman and sign off when something else on the dockets caught her eye.

'Excuse me, do you have one more moment?' she asked the officer on the other end of the phone. 'I'm sorry to bother you with this, but I noted on the docket you have a call-out time for when your response unit received a call for help. How do you log the call time, is it manual? Or do you have a phone system?' Reshma asked, a hollow feeling in her abdomen.

The policewoman on the other side of the line said she would ask someone. A minute later she came back on the phone and said that it was an automated system, linked to the switchboard.

Reshma was quiet for a second.

'Look, I'm sorry if I'm asking a stupid question again, but could you check if the time on your phone system is correct? Or is it maybe out by a few minutes?' Reshma asked, hoping the woman on the other end wouldn't think she was crazy, or difficult, and hang up.

A minute later, the woman came back on the phone again. 'We checked everything. The time looks right. Is there something wrong?' she asked.

Reshma quickly assured the other woman that everything was A-okay. She thanked her again for her time and said how much she appreciated the assistance before hanging up.

Then Reshma dug out her own phone from her handbag and stared at the phone entry on the docket again, because something was very wrong indeed.

The day before, while writing out her own statement – which would eventually be added to these dockets – Reshma had gone back over her own phone calls from Saturday, carefully noting the time she had called Scott and Dube, and when they had called Sobukwe for help. She had clearly remembered Sobukwe saying that he would call the Meyerton SAPS office and get them to send back-up. But, on the docket from the station, Sobukwe's phone call to them was logged ten minutes after Reshma had contacted her commander.

Which meant either the Meyerton police station's switchboard had some kind of recording glitch in it – perhaps it only recorded when the cars were sent out, not when the original call was received. Or it meant that Sobukwe had waited ten minutes before calling for help. Which made no sense to Reshma, unless for some reason he was trying to get his team members killed.

She was trying to decide which course of action to take when she saw Sobukwe standing up in his office and grabbing his coat. He moved swiftly to the three men who were still yammering on in the boardroom, and opened the door to speak them. The men all stood up with an almost military efficiency. Reshma noticed that each of them was wearing a gun, disguised seconds later when they also seized their coats and exited in Sobukwe's wake.

The General did not say goodbye, nor did he say where he was going.

Scott and Dube watched his retreat in silence, and waited until they heard a car pull off before they started speaking to Reshma again.

Reshma was considering whether or not to fill them in on Sobukwe's timing anomaly when her phone buzzed. It was a message from Ryk, who had ignored Super's instructions and gone off to the medico-legal mortuary in Sasolburg while Mark handled the forensic team at the creepy Three Rivers house.

Reshma called him back almost immediately. 'Good timing,' she said, before asking him to fill her in on what he had seen.

Ryk told her that the forensic officers were only starting preliminary work on the Vaal body. 'They're obviously going to look at the eyes, see if they match the one they found at the attack scene,' he said. 'And wait, there's more,' he said, his voice dropping slightly. 'They've found traces of blood all over that house,' he whispered. 'Mark says it looked like a scene from a horror movie when they sprayed the luminol. Something bad happened in the bathroom. And outside, in the back courtyard.'

'Did you see anything else on the body?' Reshma asked, not wanting to make Ryk feel like she wasn't paying attention to the obviously shocking revelation about the house, but wanting to know more about the dead woman. She didn't want to prompt anything, but rather waited to see what information he could provide.

'Oh. Ja,' Ryk carried on, evidently no less enthusiastic about the cadaver. 'They say at this stage they don't think it's a drowning – they think she was killed before she went in the water. But they still need to do some tests or checks for that.'

'Do they know what might have killed her?' Reshma asked, trying hard not to pre-empt the answer she was looking for. 'Did they see any injuries anywhere? Anything on her body? Hands? Feet? Anything?'

'Now that you mention it, they did say there were some marks on her arms,' Ryk said. 'No, wait. Not hands, her wrists. Sorry, I'm just mixing things up here. Too many things on the go this morning,' he said, apologising, even while Reshma's skin went cold, waiting to hear what he was going to say next. 'There were these lines around her wrists. Like old scars. They were kind of weird, now that I think about it. Like the woman was wearing bracelets. Or handcuffs.'

SERIAL

'**D**o you think it's some kind of serial killer?' Reshma asked Ian, over a large first helping of vegetable curry.

'I mean, it's two, maybe even three women. All found in water. All of them with this ... scar thing on their wrist. Two of them were mutilated. There's got to be something there,' she said.

Ian had spent a fairly productive day designing research templates and questionnaires for a community survey his organisation was planning in three former townships, but found that his sense of slight satisfaction was somewhat dulled by the news of Reshma's day. Not, if he was honest with himself, that he had any particular fondness for mortuaries. But it just felt like Reshma's work was much more *real* than his. The fact that she had initially withheld information about the missing finger also riled him, and made him feel that she wasn't trusting him with everything. If she had hidden that, what else might she be keeping secret?

It took a glass of wine for Reshma to unwind enough to tell Ian about what had happened with Sobukwe, which made Ian first defensive on her behalf, and then outright angry when Reshma shared that her boss had called for back-up only long after she and her partner had gone charging into a heavily armed cash heist in progress.

Ian was about to rant about the General when Reshma interrupted him.

'Just pause that thought. I need you on my team, but I don't need you mad, okay?' she said, reaching over to touch his hand. Ian could see from her face that she was also angry, but that she was holding the emotions in. 'I have a plan,' she said. 'Okay, not exactly a plan, but I've had some thoughts,' she said.

Ian waited for her to share them.

'So, right now, I can't go back to the medico-legal laboratory. You remember I said it was two, *maybe*, three women?' she asked.

Ian nodded.

'Well, someone needs to go and see that body from the Hartbeespoort Dam that your friend Myburgh found. You know as well as I do the stakes are higher now. I can't go just on the basis of a cellphone photo taken by someone who was a member of the police when Eugene de Kock was still killing people at Vlakplaas,' Reshma said.

Ian winced at the statement, even though he knew she was right. Myburgh had always been like an uncle to him. He knew the man had probably committed violence in his day, but in his heart, he still wanted to believe that Myburgh was a good cop – that he would never have fucked up anyone because of their race, but because they had done something wrong.

Except of course, thirty years ago, what was defined as 'wrong' wasn't always about justice.

When Reshma asked him if he would go to the mortuary in Ga-Rankuwa in her place, he was only too happy to agree.

*

Ga-Rankuwa sat an hour north of Atteridgeville. On the map, it was precisely contained by the border between Gauteng and North West provinces. It had been built sometime in the mid-1960s to accommodate victims of forced removals from elsewhere in the then-Transvaal, and during the later years of apartheid, had seen protests, shootings and even an attempted coup.

The mortuary was in a brick complex that backed onto the Ga-Rankuwa police station, and the Ga-Rankuwa magistrate's court. There was the usual bustle of police vans and cars and people, none of whom looked particularly cheerful.

The entrance to the mortuary was five hundred metres down Kgotleng Street. Ian walked in feeling like an imposter.

Reshma had tried to contact the facility the day before, eventually managing to get the cellphone number of one of the pathologists – who had not yet replied to Reshma's WhatsApp messages, or her one phone call. This had gone straight to voicemail, but at least confirmed that the number belonged to the right person. What she had managed to do, though, was get another of her colleagues to find a case number. Ian was hoping that either Reshma's attempts, or his ability to bluff, would be enough to get him in past reception.

The receptionist, indeed, proved helpful and pleasant, both of which surprised Ian, given the circumstances. After being made to wait for less than thirty minutes, he was shown into a small waiting room with internal curtains – which Ian belatedly identified as a viewing room – and told that the pathologist would be along to see him shortly.

Fifteen minutes later a slender man in chinos and a striped shirt walked in, carrying a small bundle of beige-covered files. He introduced himself as Dr Ramokgopa and immediately informed Ian that he had very limited time, as he had a full schedule for that day. Ian nodded, and decided to skip over the puffery he'd planned to justify his snooping, and stick mainly to the truth. Briefly, he told the pathologist that he had been working on an investigation that involved the body of the woman found in Hartbeespoort Dam, and that the same body had now become a matter of interest for a police investigation a colleague of his was conducting into missing women.

'We think there may be a connection between this woman, and another body in Johannesburg,' Ian said, sticking to the truth, but not giving away all of it. He asked if it would be possible to see the body, or the pathologist's report, to determine if there were any matching features.

'Hmm,' was the other man's response. Ian wasn't sure if it meant the pathologist was considering Ian's request, or critiquing his story.

Ramokgopa put down the files and hmmed again. 'I am sorry to tell you, Mr Jack, that the body of the woman you mention, it was sent off for burial,' he said, at last.

The news made Ian pause. He had been told by Myburgh that the body hadn't been claimed. Foolishly, he had assumed this meant the body would still be at the mortuary.

'Did anyone come and claim the body?' Ian asked, trying to piece together the new information.

The pathologist shook his head. 'No. Not as far as I am aware. I believe it was a burial paid for by the state,' he said.

Which, Ian knew, meant a pauper's grave, a cardboard coffin in a cemetery somewhere.

'When was she buried?' Ian asked.

The pathologist thought for a moment.

'We had our last batch of bodies released three weeks ago, so probably then. I would have to check exactly,' he said. 'It could have been before then. The body had been here for several months.'

Ian paused and reframed his thoughts. 'Is there an inquest report that you could share with us?' he asked. 'I mean, cause of death, or any other identifying features? It's still an ongoing investigation,' Ian said, hoping to remind the pathologist that even though the body was gone, the justice processes would still continue.

The other man nodded. 'Certainly. Wasn't much, though – I remember because when the body came in, we don't get a lot of foreigners like that. But I believe that it was fairly cut and dried. Or not dry, so to speak.'

'What do you mean?' Ian asked.

'She died from drowning. Probably couldn't swim. Sometimes you get these other Africans, they come to the water, they do rituals or baptisms. It happens,' he said. 'I'll see if I can get you a copy of the report.'

Ian nodded that he would like that.

The pathologist left and came back a few minutes later with a very thin beige folder stamped with official lines and badges and case numbers on the front.

'Yes, just as I remembered. Death by drowning,' he said, placing the slim folder on a table between him and Ian.

'May I look?' Ian asked.

The other man pushed the file towards him. 'Sure, you can take photos of the entries if you like,' he said.

There was a photograph of the dead woman's face in the file, but not of anything else – her torso, limbs, nothing. Ian thought perhaps the pathologist might have removed them before sharing the file, to comply with some formal sense of propriety. He didn't raise the issue in case it was an issue.

'May I take a photo of her face?' he asked, pointing at the picture. The pathologist nodded, but remained quiet otherwise.

Ian tried to read the notes in the medical report and make sense of the sparse information that reduced corpses to body parts and processes. He saw clearly that it confirmed suspected death by drowning, although it didn't explain why. There were no other toxicology reports, and nothing about the victim's lungs or heart or stomach, or other internal organs.

'You didn't do an autopsy on her?' he asked, looking up.

The pathologist took the file back from Ian, glanced at its contents, and shook his head.

'We don't cut up every body that comes through here, Mr Jack. We're not barbarians. And we don't have the resources. Whoever did the post-mortem had enough information, including where the body was found, to determine cause of death through observation and examination,' he said, with a small shrug.

Ian nodded. He didn't have enough knowledge or expertise to challenge what the pathologist was telling him. He also reminded himself, silently, that just because he didn't want it to be a random drowning wasn't enough to make this death a crime.

'Were there any other marks on her?' Ian asked. 'I mean, in case we identify her? Maybe someone at the estate comes forward with some information one day. Any identifying marks, anything found on her body?'

The pathologist paused to look down again at the file in his hands.

'No marks here that I can see,' he said. 'Personal possessions on the drowning victim included a mobile SIM card receipt, a small vanity mirror and a broken comb,' he said, looking back up again at Ian. 'Whatever it is you're looking for, Mr Jack, I don't think you'll find it here.'

Ramokgopa took the file of the woman dredged from the dam, and pointedly placed it on top of the other folders. He picked up the pile and stood. 'I have to leave now. There are other cases that demand my attention. I'm sorry I couldn't be of more assistance,' the pathologist said. 'We, uh, also need you to clear this room, please,' he added. 'There's a family coming in to view the body of an elderly woman who may or may not be their grandmother.'

Ian gathered his phone, wallet and keys, and made a quick exit, stopping to thank the woman at reception on the way out. He didn't stop until he reached his car – which had heated up to oven-like temperatures, even in the winter sun. He got inside and sat, leaving the door open, wondering if he should call Reshma or wait until later to tell her the bad news.

He opened up his phone, scrolling back through his WhatsApp to find the photographs that Myburgh had sent him of the woman's body as she lay beside the dam. He moved, back and forth, zooming in and changing angles to be sure. There were definitely marks around her wrists. He couldn't understand why the pathologist's report wouldn't have even noted them. It was too late now. The chance of him – or, Reshma, he should say – getting permission to exhume the woman's body were less than zero. And, even if they did, there was an even better chance that the body would have decomposed to the point that there wouldn't be any flesh left to examine.

Ian scrolled back through his photos to the picture he had taken of the photograph in the pathologist's file. The dead woman's face. Her hair no longer splayed, but instead forming an amorphous lump around her head. Deadlocks.

He realised that his only chance of confirming whether or not there had been marks on the woman's wrists might be to ask the gardener who found her at the estate, which meant having to go through Myburgh again – something Ian was reluctant to do, because he also had nothing to report or update about the still-missing Zebulon September.

As if on some secret signal, his phone started vibrating in his hands at that exact moment, the screen lighting up with the name of the caller: MaRejoice.

When Ian answered, the sangoma commented that he had been fast to pick up. Ian knew that she liked to tease him about having some kind of sixth sense about her, and about other experiences they had shared. Even though he didn't – couldn't – deny the many strange things he had seen in the past two years, he didn't see himself as part of them. He was just an occasional gunman for those who walked the worlds of ancestors and spirits, and he was happy with the role, as he repeatedly told MaRejoice.

When he mentioned that he was in Ga-Rankuwa, he could hear the sangoma draw in her breath with a hiss.

'You are going to think this is very strange, Ian,' she said, her entire voice and attitude suddenly changed from teasing to serious. 'I have found your missing person,' she said. 'I asked some family, some of my sons who have contacts and family up there, by Tshwane,' she said. 'But maybe you also need to start believing in your ancestors, because the man you are looking for, Zebulon? He's in Ga-Rankuwa even now.'

Fifteen minutes later, Ian had stopped off at a shop to buy a cold Fanta and a packet of chutney-flavoured chips, on his way to a bakery in Unit 4 where Zebulon September was working.

MaRejoice had explained that she had not initially tracked down Zebulon but rather his boyfriend, Zakes, who was, indeed, undergoing ukuthwasa – his initiation. The Zee-Zee cuteness of their matching names was what had led another woman, who knew Zakes's teacher in Hebron, to confuse which young man MaRejoice was looking for, although the comedy of errors was soon resolved when MaRejoice finally made contact with her North West counterpart.

She said that while Zakes was completing ukuthwasa in Hebron, Zebulon was apprenticing with a cake baker in Ga-Rankuwa who specialised in wedding and fancy cakes.

'Bring me back something sweet, as a thank you,' she said. 'And not just a cupcake, wena. Something proper.'

The bakery – Evelyn's Bread and Cakes – was on a corner in between the Community Health Centre and a funeral parlour. Ian noted with some relief that the health centre seemed busier than the funeral place.

The outside of the cake shop was painted pink, white and gold, and decorated like the icing on a cake, an effect that was enhanced by lace curtains in the window. The sign on the door said that they sold wholesale and directly to the public, and Ian walked in to a cool white and pink room that smelled of vanilla and sugar, with trays of koeksisters and lamingtons and cupcakes and iced biscuits temptingly displayed, all ready to be taken home. There was a plain white counter with a gold-edged pink cloth attached, but nobody standing behind it.

Ian called out, once softly, then again, a little louder, and a few seconds later, a young man in his mid-twenties walked through.

Zebulon September was dressed in jeans and a T-shirt and had a plastic apron on over his clothing, which reminded Ian briefly of the mortuary. The association faded when Zebulon smiled.

'Hello, can I help you?' the young man said, obviously unaware of who Ian was, or why he was there.

For a moment Ian debated whether he should buy MaRejoice a box of cupcakes before or after he questioned Zebulon. In the end, he went for the 'after' option – better to get the hard stuff out the way. He could support MaRejoice's sugar habit elsewhere, if things with Zebulon turned sour.

The moment Ian opened his mouth, he knew Zebulon had made him. To the other man's credit, he stood his ground behind the bakery counter and didn't flinch when answering to his name.

'I'm not here to cause any shit. Can you trust me on this?' Ian said, keeping his body language neutral, his arms and hands down and low. Nothing that would make him appear threatening.

Zebulon nodded, but didn't say anything. The welcoming smile was gone. 'Talk,' he said after a moment, crossing his arms on the countertop in front of him. Ian noticed a strip of hide – isiphandla – tied around one of his wrists.

Ian tried, quickly, to explain about Myburgh, about the disciplinary hearing, about the job, and then went back to Myburgh again.

'He's really worried about you. I know he looks like a bitter old man, but he's got a good heart,' Ian said.

Zebulon stared back, unmoved.

'Your aunt's worried about you, too,' Ian added, hoping to provoke a stronger response, which seemed to work. Zebulon stood upright again, indignant. And then he slumped, his elbows landing back on the counter and his head dropping between his hands. 'Ah shit, man,' he said, and tapped the sides of his head.

Ian waited, and after a few more seconds, Zebulon looked up again, his expression somewhere between embarrassment and concern.

Ian was already starting to join the threads together. 'Thandeka knows?' he said, looking at Zebulon, asking whether the teenager helping Sylvie knew about Zebulon's deception.

The other man nodded.

'But you don't want to tell Sylvie, because you think she won't support you having a boyfriend?' he asked.

'No, she knows about Zakes,' Zebulon said, almost with a smile. 'But ... she just wouldn't like me doing ... this, you know,' he said waving his hand at the pink room, the cakes and confectionery around him.

'Myburgh, he put so much effort into finding me that job. Paid for my training, everything. And it meant a lot to her, that he did that. She wouldn't let me just leave. But it was horrible. You have been there?' he asked.

Ian nodded.

'It's all beautiful on the outside, but inside, it's rotten,' Zebulon said.

Ian was about to ask Zebulon what he meant when the other man continued. 'Plus, it was impossible, living in that tiny cubicle they called a room. I could never see Zakes. Can you imagine me, trying to get my *boyfriend* permission to come and visit the land of Lah-di-da,' he said, with a bitter laugh.

But Ian still couldn't help feeling like the story was a little too pat

– Zebulon leaving the security industry to pursue his dreams as a baker.

'What about telling your aunt you were becoming a sangoma?' Ian asked.

Zebulon was unapologetic. 'I borrowed Zakes's story. He knows. He knew. It was just easier, because I knew Auntie wouldn't argue with it. She goes to church and everything, but her mother – my grandmother – she used to have dreams, and everyone knows when you get *those* dreams, you have to follow them or bad things might happen. And then, at the same time, Ma Evelyn – she's the boss here – she needed help, because she was starting up a wedding-cake business. And so here I am,' he said, looking slightly sheepish. 'I was going to tell her. Soon,' he said. 'I just hadn't got around to it yet.'

Ian had no interest in reprimanding the young man for walking out on a job propping up wealthy people in a housing estate, especially not while he lived in a dingy servant's room cut off from his family and partner. What he did want to know was if Zebulon knew anything about the woman in the dam, and about the women who had come in through the boom.

'What do you know about this?' he asked. He pulled out his phone and showed Zebulon the photo he'd taken of the picture of the dead woman's face at the mortuary. Then he scrolled to show Zebulon a screenshot he had taken of the other women at the security boom.

'Is there any connection between the woman in the water, and these women?' Ian asked.

The moment Ian asked about the women, Zebulon's face changed again. 'I don't want to talk about it here. Let's go to the back,' he said. 'Ma Evelyn is out, delivering a cake to someone who just had a baby.

We can talk by ourselves.'

He went to the door to the street, and turned the handle once, so that it locked. Then he walked back past the counter and held open a curtained doorway. Ian stepped through into a small seating area with a table, four chairs, a kettle and toaster on a drawer unit on the side.

'You want some tea?' Zebulon asked, moving to switch on the kettle.

Ian shook his head. 'I just had something to drink, thanks.'

Zebulon was quiet while he made himself a mug of rooibos, adding two heaped teaspoons of sugar. No milk. He sat down, but then jumped up again to grab a jar of rusks off the kitchenette counter.

'We make these ourselves. You sure you don't want one?' Zebulon asked, opening the jar and taking out a thick-cut hard biscuit.

Ian declined, already regretting having wasted his appetite on bad shop crisps.

Zebulon talked in between dunking his rusk. 'The women in the car, they come for ... parties,' he said.

Ian stared blankly for a moment.

'Parties. Are they waitresses?' he asked.

Zebulon stared back at him, waiting to see how long it would take Ian to get his meaning.

When the penny finally dropped, Ian blushed. 'Right. Parties,' he said, both surprised and also not surprised that a pristine and pseudo-European place like La Gondola would have what appeared to be fairly pedestrian sex workers visiting the estate.

'Are there a lot of ... parties like this?' he asked.

Zebulon shook his head. 'Mr Kotze, he's the one that organises it. He told me to let the women in, the first time. Before Easter. I've seen them two times before, when I've been on shift. Maybe they've come other times, but I don't know.'

Ian didn't know who Mr Kotze was, but he noted the name to follow up later. 'Did this guy pay you to let the women in?' he asked.

Zebulon paused with his tea-cup halfway up to his mouth. 'Of course,' he said, without blinking. 'You think I mustn't take the money, even if it's from the Broederbond?' he asked.

Ian ignored the last comment. 'Where did the women go?' he asked. 'Did they go to one of the houses? Where were the parties?'

'No, they went to the new development, on the west side of the estate,' Zebulon said. 'It's still under construction, so you can only access it through the boom at La Gondola. Or if you have a boat,' he said. 'It's not even proper houses there. Just one or two show houses so they can sell it in phases. But they haven't sold enough yet.'

'So, this Kotze guy, he uses them for his parties?' Ian asked.

Zebulon nodded. 'He just organises them. I don't think he goes. I mean, he just stays home with his wife and fishes and shit,' Zebulon said.

Ian frowned. 'What are the parties for? Who goes to them?' he asked.

Zebulon drank more tea and took another bite of his rusk. 'Group of guys. I don't look properly at any of them if they come through. Kotze doesn't even have to pay me for that. I'm not stupid,' he said.

'What guys?' Ian asked, again.

Zebulon put his cup down and looked Ian in in the eyes. 'Some black guys. Sometimes a Coloured guy, an Indian guy, a white guy. They change. It's not always the same guys. Like I said, I don't look. And when they come, Mr Kotze always goes and makes sure the camera recordings are deleted. I saw him do it,' he said.

'And ... why exactly do they come here for *parties*?' Ian asked.

Zebulon shifted in his chair a little.

'These guys, they don't do anything before a job – no women, no sex, no booze, no meat even. They want to be like monks, they even boast about it,' he said. 'The sangomas won't bless them if they don't keep pure. So, afterwards, they always have like this ... party. Women, alcohol, whatever they want.'

'By "job" you mean ...' Ian asked, leaving the question lingering.

Zebulon scowled a little. 'I don't know exactly. Robbers. Something like that. Some of the guys have guns when they come in. I don't ask questions. They don't look like nice people. Even if I wasn't worried about Mr Kotze, I wouldn't want to deal with these men. They are worse than tsotsis,' he said.

'Does Myburgh know about this?' Ian asked.

Zebulon looked down at the table. 'No, I don't think Mr Myburgh knew about this. He's busy, you know. Busy in his house, busy on the golf course. There's this old woman he goes out with sometimes. She stays in town. Kotze told me I mustn't worry about Myburgh,' he said, finally looking up, his expression suggesting he was slightly ashamed of his behaviour.

Ian pushed his own thoughts of Myburgh aside for the moment. He would worry about the old man later. 'Did these men, the robbers, Kotze, anyone: did they ever harm any of the women? That night, I mean, that day, the camera footage showed that there were three women in the car when they went in, and only two women when they came out.'

The information seemed to surprise Zebulon. 'No. I know those women. I've even seen them, after. I saw two of them in Saulsville, and one in Laudium. The one woman is on Instagram. She posts pictures of herself in nice dresses. No, those men – they are shits, but they never hurt these women. I mean, I don't know *exactly* what they do, but I have a general idea. I went there once, afterwards, there were condoms, beer bottles, whiskey bottles. But I didn't see any blood. And the mostly nice women, the ones with nice dresses and their own cars, they won't come back if the guys are bad. Sometimes they even have white women out there. They always seemed happy to come, like chatty, not nervous. But they also get drunk with the guys, you know? I think one time, there was a girl who was vomiting out the window. I had to clean it up. Sometimes they get sick,' he said.

Ian thought back over the night-time footage and wondered if he'd overlooked something as obvious as a passenger passed out on the back seat. He added another mental note, to go over the footage again.

'I'll even give you the name of one of them. Gabrielle, Gabriella something. I'll give you her Instagram name. You can check yourself,' Zebulon said.

'And the woman who was dead in the dam? You didn't say anything about her,' Ian carried on, trying not to lose track of the questions he needed to ask.

Zebulon shook his head emphatically. 'I don't know her. But I saw her. The body, I mean. When Jonas pulled her out, when she was lying there. We all went to go and look. She looked like ... she looked like some water creature, she had all this water weed, that hyacinth, it was wrapped around her arms, her legs. You know, I showed Zakes,' he said. 'I took a picture, on my phone. And when I sent it to him, he called me, worried. He said that she was ... what did he call her?'

He looked around the room, trying to find an object to match the unfamiliar word he was looking for. His eyes stopped on a carton of orange juice, and he mouthed the word silently before speaking aloud again.

'*Njuzu.* I don't know if that is how to say it. It's not a word from here. Zakes says it's a Shona word. Like from Zimbabwe. A mermaid. He said she came from the water, from somewhere else, and that it was a very bad sign. Zakes is always like that, taking spirit things very seriously,' he said, with a chuckle.

Ian listened with an increasing sense of the surreal. It was the second time he had heard one of the dead women described as a mermaid. 'Do you still have the photo you took? Of the dead woman, I mean?' he asked, with a new sense of urgency. But Zebulon shook his head and said he had deleted it.

'It's not the kind of thing you keep,' he said.

'Did you see anything else, anything around her wrists?' Ian asked. 'Did you notice any scars, or anything like that?'

When Zebulon shook his head and said he hadn't looked too closely, Ian couldn't help feeling deflated again.

'So, is that why you left? Because of the dead woman? Or because of those guys, the ones who came for the parties?' Ian asked, wondering if, now that they had spoken a little, Zebulon might be a bit more open about his real reasons for walking out on his job.

Zebulon's face went hard. 'Not her. Not them,' he said. 'The guy they work for.'

He paused, and waited, ten, maybe fifteen seconds.

'They work for the man who killed my parents.'

*

The name Jan Hendrik Snyman didn't appear on the website for Commercial Dam Pty Ltd – the company responsible for the La Gondola development, and which was also full or part owner of a number of other waterside estates. But when Ian looked up the firm's details on the Companies and Intellectual Property Commission service, he saw it there in black and white under the list of directors.

Ian had first heard Snyman's name at the Truth and Reconciliation Commission hearings that had taken place between 1996 and 1997. Ian's father had been called to give testimony more than once, but he had refused point-blank to talk about it to either his wife or his teenage son. Ian had worked out that if he read the newspapers on the days his father went to the hearings, he could sometimes get a glimpse of what they were talking about.

Jan Snyman had been granted amnesty for, among other things, the murder of union activist Tallboy Moeti and his wife in Mamelodi in 1991. Snyman, together with other members of a covert unit operating under the approval of then-Law and Order Minister Adriaan Vlok, had arrested and beaten Moeti in the hopes of getting him to turn informer. Moeti had refused and had wound up in hospital, initially under police guard, until the charges against him were dropped and his release was secured by the union's lawyers. Ironically, Moeti, reported not just to be a communist, but a sociable man, had befriended two white police officers while he was recuperating. One of those men was a Colonel named Kobus Myburgh. The other was Sergeant Shaun 'Cousin' Jack, Ian's father.

Two months after he had been released, Moeti's house was

petrol-bombed by a mob who believed that Moeti was a spy. In Snyman's testimony, he revealed how his unit had exploited Moeti's friendship with officers Myburgh and Jack, using this to deliberately plant false rumours in the community about Moeti's true loyalties. The Moetis – Tallboy and his wife, Francinah – were survived by an unnamed infant son and Francinah's sister, Sylvie September, who was staying in a back room at their house, and who had run inside the burning home to rescue her nephew. She had sustained serious burns across her body.

Snyman and the members of his unit had never been charged with the crime, but during the amnesty hearings, the former commander had had to come clean about all of his actions, if he had any hope of getting amnesty from prosecution for his more serious transgressions, which had included killing and disposing of the bodies of at least two other unionists in and around the Vlakplaas area. He had identified the locations of the bodies, which had been exhumed and returned to their family members nearly two decades later by the Missing Persons Task Team, working under a heroic woman by the name of Madeleine Fullard.

Post amnesty, Jan Snyman had re-invented himself as an entrepreneur, and still operated in the same area. Ian wondered what it must feel like to have an apartheid cop like Snyman walk into your store, or drive through the booms of the estate you where you were working as a security guard.

Ian checked his computer screen and scanned the names of the other company directors – there were twelve in total. He googled the first four, adding the search terms 'SAPS' and 'police' – Myburgh had said most of the owners were ex-cops. Three of them came back with matches. He suspected if he tried a little harder, the others would too.

Ian wondered if it was possible that somehow Myburgh didn't know who was at the top of the directors' list. Or, worse, that he did, and had chosen to ignore it.

There was one name that wasn't on the company list, which Zebulon had mentioned: Kotze. Ian found it a few minutes later, under a section on the La Gondola Body Corporate, which was listed on a Hartbeespoort community news website. Brian Kotze.

Under the pretence of following up, Ian sent Myburgh a text saying he would call the next day with an update.

Five minutes later, Ian's phone rang. It was Myburgh, who found it easier to talk than to type.

'What the fuck are you up to, Cousin?' he asked. 'I sent you to look for that kid. And now I got phone calls about you sticking your nose into that drowned woman? I'm not paying for you to run private investigations on the side. And I told you, I didn't want the rest of the fucking estate involved,' the old man said, obviously angry, and a little flustered. 'Now I have the Body Corporate calling me, asking me what I'm doing.'

Ian didn't have the energy to placate Myburgh right at that moment, but he also didn't want to tip his hand just yet. 'I was just tying up loose strings, Oom. You know me. I'm sorry if it made any trouble,' he said, trying to draw out the old man.

He was wondering how Myburgh had found out about his trip to the Ga-Rankuwa mortuary – and why someone was worried enough about the woman's death to inhibit any investigation into the matter. Someone at the facility, possibly even the officious doctor he'd met, had been convinced to skip the autopsy, smooth over the post-mortem, and send the dead woman to a pauper's grave before anyone would have the chance to look too closely into her death. Anyone who cared about justice, that was.

'You got any other news, except for finding out that a drowned woman drowned?' Myburgh asked, his voice still aggressive.

Ian spoke in what he hoped was a calm and measured voice – not condescending, because that would only piss off Myburgh even more. 'I met your guy's auntie last week. It seems he's gone off to train as a sangoma. You know, they have an initiation,' Ian said, hoping Zebulon's lie was plausible enough to obscure the truth until he could get to the bottom of things.

Myburgh was silent for a moment. Then: 'A *sangoma*?' he asked, making sure he had heard Ian clearly.

Ian repeated himself. 'I asked the sangoma who I worked with. You remember from ... from before. Anyway, I won't be able to speak to him until he's finished, apparently. His aunt doesn't know where he is. So my best guess is, he's not coming back to La Gondola,' Ian said.

Myburgh was quiet again. 'Yes, well. I suppose I should have guessed. But ... it's stupid you know, throwing away a job, for ... whatever it is,' he said, still grumpy, but now with the wind largely taken out of his sails.

'I'm sorry, Oom. I guess you tried your best,' Ian said, not meaning it at all. 'Look, I'll give you a final report in person if you like. We can close this off, and you can finalise everything with the Body Corporate,' he said, before slipping in the question he'd wanted to ask all along, banking on the fact that Myburgh still didn't know there was no real connection between the dead woman and the women in the car.

'You said it was a guy at the Body Corporate who pulled that video for you, right?'

Myburgh mumbled on the other side. 'Ja. Kotze. Bit of a piece of work. Ex-cop, not quite as good as he thinks he is,' Myburgh said.

Kotze. The same person who had been paying Zebulon to let sex workers sneak in via the estate entrance. And the same person who had miraculously 'found' the incriminating footage of the women in their car. And, more importantly, had specifically brought it to Myburgh's attention, instead of deleting it as he usually did.

Ian wondered why the Body Corporate man had made such a deliberate effort to expose footage that, based on what Zebulon said, the rest of the company's directors were trying to hide. Perhaps it was to get rid of Zebulon. Or, Ian thought, perhaps it was for some other purpose entirely.

Ian didn't tell Myburgh any of this. He said goodbye, and then he went to pour himself a large whiskey while he waited for Reshma to get home.

THREE BODIES

D r Wild from the medico-legal laboratory in Hillbrow had called Reshma at lunchtime to say that, in her opinion, the finger they had found under Park Station was a good potential match for the mutilated body found on the banks of the Jukskei.

'The nail polish, the shape of the nail bed – they look compatible,' she said.

Ryk and Mark said the Sasolburg mortuary was still waiting for DNA testing on the eyeball found on the cash-heist thug – which could take a few weeks, and that was if they were lucky – but that blood typing from both samples suggested that it, too, could be a match.

It was now evening, and Reshma was staring at photographs of the third body, looking at what were clearly the same wrist markings as on the other two bodies, whatever the Ga-Rankuwa report had said. Or not said. She was scrolling through Myburgh's images on Ian's laptop, trying to make out any obvious mutilation of the body, as in the other two cases.

In the photographs, it was hard to distinguish what might have just been water damage from any deliberate maiming. There were places on the scalp where the skin looked like it was coming away from the flesh and bone, but similar slippage was visible on the body's hands, a common 'de-gloving' effect that happened to bodies submerged for long periods of time.

Not for the first time that evening, Reshma cursed under her breath, at whichever bureaucrat had decided either not to bother with properly investigating the dam woman's death – or, worse, who had specifically chosen to obscure the details of her death. Whatever had really happened to the woman in the water was as good as lost forever.

There was a large map of Johannesburg on the kitchen table in front of Reshma, dug out from the spare room where Ian had stored it after the move. Taking a leaf out of Sobukwe's office, there were red pins for where the women had been found, and black pins for where their body parts, or pieces, had been found. Yellow marked cash heists that had taken place on either side of the deaths, chronologically speaking. For the woman in the Hartbeespoort Dam, they had to use the airtime receipt in her pocket as a guide to a possible timeline. And there it was. A cash-in-transit heist in Soshanguve, four days after the dead woman had purchased airtime for her missing phone. Reshma knew it might just be coincidence. But when viewed together with the other deaths, it was starting to look like part of a pattern.

The Park Station crime was less easy to pin down because there were two possible events. One was a botched job ten days before Reshma had gone on her hunt underground. There, a gang of robbers had attempted to hit a money van making a delivery to an ATM at a shopping mall on the East Rand. The robbers had duffed up their ambush, and the security guards – four outside the van, two with heavy-calibre rifles – had been able to fire first, killing one of the robbers in the process. A video of a guard drawing his handgun and shooting an already-injured robber at the foot of an escalator had gone viral. The security footage hadn't captured much else, but eyewitnesses had said at least two, maybe three, cars had made a getaway, which suggested that a larger crew was behind the attempt. A description of some of the crew had also provided a possible match for one of the bodies Reshma had discovered underneath Park Station – the man in the brown leather jacket.

A week after that, a successful robbery had taken place near Nasrec. A cash van had been made to come to a standstill after being rammed by a BMW. The guards had been forced out of the van, and the attackers had removed an undisclosed amount of money from the back before setting the money van and the BMW alight.

The Nasrec robbery had later been linked to the botched mall attempt. But it hadn't initially been connected with the crew Sobukwe had been investigating – the gang she had helped bust near Meyerton. Reshma now thought there was a good chance that all the attacks were linked.

None of which explained the dead women or the mutilated bodies – unless it was for some kind of muti purpose. She knew many of the robbers had close links with sangomas and other mysterious figures, who promised to bless them ahead of their crimes. It also didn't explain why the women's corpses had been found in or beside bodies of water.

'Maybe the water is to hide evidence?' she said to Ian, puzzling over the locations and their connection to each other.

The pathologist in Hillbrow hadn't known of any other recent bodies that had been found in rivers or dams or spruits. Dr Wild had also said that such deaths were less common in Johannesburg, which had few natural bodies of water. 'We get more swimming pool deaths than anything,' she had said. 'Summer time we get some drownings, with floods. But that's about it.'

Reshma was now reading about the water in Johannesburg on a local history and heritage website. 'Did you know the Westdene Dam was connected to the Braamfontein Spruit?' she said to Ian. 'It starts in the Brixton Ridge. There's a stream that feeds the dam. And then the water joins the Braamfontein Spruit. It's mostly underground in this part. But apparently in Craighall Park, there's a waterfall,' she said, with a hint of wonder. 'And then, get this,' she said, tapping the map in front of her. 'The Braamfontein Spruit? It joins up with the Jukskei, and that feeds into the Hartbeespoort Dam.'

Reshma sat back in her chair.

'And it *still* makes no sense to me,' she said. 'I still have more questions than answers. Do you think I'm looking at this all wrong – trying to make it fit, because of this unit? It could still be some kind of serial killer,' she said, looking at Ian, sitting across from her at the kitchen table.

'Ritual killing, maybe,' he said. 'These women were killed for something specific.'

'We don't even know how they died, though,' Reshma said, frustrated, as she gazed at the screen, and back again at the map. 'I mean, all we could probably guess right now is that none of them died because of drowning. Even the one the state says did.'

Reshma hadn't discussed the women's bodies with anyone on her unit other than Ryk and Mark – who, even then, only knew part of the story, as did Sobukwe. And none of them knew about the woman at Hartbeespoort.

Plus, she was still sitting on the information about Sobukwe's delay tactics. She hadn't told Scott or Dube, and she had been putting off calling Claassen, who was still in hospital, to see how he was coping. She told herself she was just waiting for the right moment. Which, Reshma acknowledged, also meant giving herself some more time to see whether or not she thought she could trust the rest of the team with the information about their boss – and whether they would take Sobukwe's side over hers. The heist task team was proving to be a much lonelier place than Reshma had anticipated.

'If they're ritual killings, shouldn't we, you know, speak to Ma-Rejoice. Again?' Reshma asked, looking at Ian hopefully.

He frowned at her. 'Sure, I can ask her. But you can't treat her like she's some ... zoo keeper for strange things you don't believe in until you need them,' he said.

Reshma knew Ian was right, but she didn't agree with the rebuke entirely. 'It's not that I don't believe her, Ian. I just don't ... see things the way she does. I can't. I know you can. Or, at least, you can see it a little bit more. But for me, it's hard to see it at all. I don't like it when you judge me for it,' she said. 'I'm trying to see the world the best way I can. Right now, it's a pretty dark place. I'm not looking for fairy tales. I just want some justice.'

She turned her attention back to the map in front of her, and after a few minutes, she could hear Ian on the phone. Calling MaRejoice on her behalf.

He apologised for calling so late, even though it was only a little after seven at night. A few moments later, he came over to Reshma.

'I think I need to put her on speaker phone for a minute,' he said. 'You need to hear this.'

He placed the phone on the table, near the corner of the map.

Reshma greeted MaRejoice warmly, but with a slight sense of embarrassment she hadn't actually been the one to make the call herself. 'I'm sorry I haven't been to see you. It's just been ... busy at work,' she said, invoking the time-honoured Joburg excuse.

Luckily, MaRejoice was too busy herself to see the need to engage in petty point-scoring. 'You want to talk about if these women are being killed for muti? You want to know if izangoma are there?' the sangoma asked. 'Then talk, Captain Patel. Tell me what you know, I will try and help.'

Reshma spent a few minutes explaining about the unit she was working with, and the cash-in-transit heists she was looking into.

'One of the men we arrested on Saturday had human body parts with him – a human eyeball,' she said. 'And a few days before that I found a human finger underneath Park Station, near a hiding place that we think one of the gangs had used to store marked money, and old weapons. There are three bodies. Maybe more. All women. All foreigners, we think. None of them was reported missing. And two of them were mutilated. The third one we don't know, because they didn't keep her records. I don't know if it's something you can help us with?' Reshma asked.

MaRejoice was quiet for a few moments. 'There is one man, he is up in or near Musina. Somewhere, I don't know where. I hear, sometimes, people talk about the criminals going to see him. They say he is very strong, very powerful. But it can also just be false advertising. Maybe there are some others here, but I don't know them because they would know to stay out of my way. We don't practise on the same sides of the river,' she said.

For a moment Reshma wondered if MaRejoice meant a literal river, before recalling an earlier discussion about spiritual territories, and metaphysical rivers.

'So they do use sangomas?' she asked.

MaRejoice gave an unpleasant cackle. 'Oh, of course. Even me, I have been asked to help a few times. But I put a buzzing in the ears of people who come to ask me. So they go somewhere else, find someone who can promise them the strength of a lion, or who can make them invisible with a belt, or who can make the bullets melt away from their bodies,' she said.

'Do people actually believe that those things will work?' Reshma asked, incredulous.

MaRejoice went quiet again. 'Captain, you've seen it on the top of a mountain. You *know* it works. These tsotsis, maybe they don't go to the nice, polite izangoma. But of course they go to the ones whose magic works,' she said. 'Otherwise, these men, they would not get much repeat business.'

Without seeing the objects, MaRejoice couldn't give a definitive answer on the mutilations that had taken place with two of the bodies. But she had some ideas which she was willing to share.

'The eyes, they can be used in a few ways,' the sangoma explained. 'It can be to get sight – to see the way ahead, maybe to see if there is any trouble. But if they were holding it while they were attacking, then maybe it was for something else, maybe to disturb the vision. To make the security guards see ... *wrong*. To impair their vision, to make it harder to fight back,' she said. 'I don't know if any of this makes sense to you. You were there. Did you see anything strange?'

Reshma paused, almost afraid to answer. She wasn't sure if she wanted to tell Ian, or even MaRejoice, about the strange shadow figure she had seen, the one she had fired at and been unable to shoot. Pressurised environments often affected sensory inputs, and being shot at was an extreme example of being under pressure. She hadn't asked Wayde about the shooting yet, either.

'I don't really know,' she said, at last, not quite ready to consider that perhaps the reason her own eyes had tricked her had been due to an external – magical – cause. She thought back to the statue of Ganesh, her fingers brushing over brass. 'Maybe there might have been something like that,' she said, conceding the point without mentioning anything specific.

'You should look for other things, on their bodies. On the ones you arrested.' MaRejoice suggested. 'Maybe small bottles, for muti. Maybe knots – like on a bracelet, like iziphandla, but different. A bracelet, or a belt. They won't just have the eyes. Everyone will have something,' she said.

MaRejoice went on to say that the finger Reshma had found under Park Station might have been used to point out a traitor. 'You say these robbers, they work in gangs. Maybe if they suspected one of them was going to betray them, or rat them out, they could use this finger to detect them,' she said. 'Maybe they were worried something was going wrong,' she carried on, 'and they needed to get rid of any weakness or impurity, or any traitor they had with them.'

Reshma thought about the botched mall job. Could the woman in the Jukskei have been killed just to point out the weak link in a crew, so that they could regroup, and complete the Nasrec job?

'And then what? What would they do to a traitor, if they found one?' Reshma asked, thinking back to the other bodies beneath Park Station. The ones near the tunnel with the cash cache.

'You're the detective, Captain Patel,' MaRejoice replied. 'You don't need me to tell you what they do to people who betray them.'

They talked for a few more minutes, but MaRejoice was unable to help with any specific details about what kinds of izangoma might offer human sacrifice as part of their standard service.

'Even if I did know,' the sangoma said, 'I wouldn't send you in there on your own. These are bad people. They are the ones who love power, and they use people who love money. And those people, they will use whatever they want to get those things.'

MaRejoice said she would come and visit them on the weekend, and that Reshma could show her photographs then. 'And don't forget, you owe me something from the bakery,' she reminded Ian before ending the call.

A minute later, Reshma's phone rang. An unknown number with a Johannesburg prefix. It was a woman's voice on the other side.

'Captain Patel?'

'This is she,' Reshma replied.

'It's Angela de Bruyn. You met me at St Mary's church the other night,' the other woman said.

'Yes, of course. How can I help you, Mrs de Bruyn?' Reshma asked.

It took another few moments for the other woman to thread her thoughts together into a proper sentence. She was clearly flustered, completely different to the calm and controlled woman Reshma had met in the office before.

'Captain Patel, you remember that you said I could call you. For help. If I knew something,' Mrs de Bruyn said. 'Well, I don't know something, but I need your help. We need your help. One of the ... one of the women we were supposed to assist was due to arrive on a bus from

Limpopo, last night. But she never came. We think that she may have been ... taken back by the people who had her in the first place. Can you help us to find her?'

ALL NIGHT PRAYER

They met at a coffee and sheesha shop on the border between Fordsburg and Mayfair. Mrs de Bruyn looked anxious and slightly out of place in her office clothes. With her was the woman who had been helping at the church a few nights before, her bandaged arm hidden by a long-sleeved shirt. She looked equally upset.

As Ian and Reshma approached the table where the women were waiting, a third woman approached them – confident and smiling, wearing bright clothes and armfuls of shiny bracelets, and a stylish set of multi-coloured braids perched high on her head.

'I have a space for you at the back. You can all come through,' she said, gesturing for the two other women to join them.

They followed in single file, through a corridor past the kitchen, and to a courtyard that had two tables and a handful of chairs, and an overflowing ashtray on the side next to a surprisingly robust geranium that was showing off a crop of scarlet flowers.

The woman with the braids sat down first, as if she was one of their party. Which, Ian realised, she was. 'I'm Eve,' she said. 'Welcome to my office,' she laughed.

Mrs de Bruyn greeted Reshma and Ian courteously, and introduced the woman with her as Linda. 'Linda knows Ernestina. The woman who is missing,' she explained. After a brief pause, she added that Linda's sister had also gone missing, several months before. 'She has been missing since the end of last year,' she said, in a low voice. 'Linda thinks she is still in South Africa somewhere, but we don't know where, exactly.'

Eve offered to get coffee or tea for everyone and went back down the corridor towards the kitchen. 'This is Eve's restaurant,' Mrs de Bruyn explained. 'She helps us, gives some of the girls jobs, looks after other things,' she said. 'I thought it was better to meet here, instead of at the church. And Eve can help to translate anything, right Linda?' she asked, looking at the other woman, who had done little more than stare at the floor so far.

The older woman looked at her. 'You can relax now. Nobody here can overhear us. Nobody will harm you,' she said.

Linda took a deep breath and sat up a little, although she still wouldn't look straight at Ian or Reshma.

While they waited for Eve to return, Mrs de Bruyn sketched out what she knew about the missing woman, Ernestina. Ernestina was originally from Malawi, like Linda and her sister, Mrs de Bruyn said.

'We think Ernestina came across the border a few months ago, for work. She may have come on her own, or she may have been transported. We're not entirely sure. But she was in contact with her family, in Mitundu, for a few weeks. And then we think she got convinced or ... persuaded to go with a person near Polokwane. And then she disappeared for a few months. She made contact with one of our helpers in Musina – I'm sorry, I realise this may sound very vague,' she said, 'but I can't tell you all the details, and I don't actually know all the details. Anyway, once she made contact with us, we arranged a bus ticket to get her here. We know she got on the bus in Musina at 10 pm. And we know she made it through Louis Trichardt and Polokwane, because she managed to send us text messages. But then, some place between Modimolle and Bela-Bela, she left. And we don't know why, or where she is. She hasn't answered her phone.'

'When did this happen?' Reshma asked.

'Last night. The bus usually stops at Modimolle between 3 am and 4 am,' Mrs de Bruyn said. 'We don't know if anyone saw anything. We can't ask. We don't want to report it to the police yet, because ...'

'Because you don't know if she has papers?' Reshma asked.

The other woman nodded.

'Nobody has papers when they come from Odi's house,' Eve said, walking back into the courtyard with a tray of cups and two teapots. 'He takes everything from the girls, if he takes the girls. Even if they have a passport, he takes it from them, and he gives them rocks to smoke in return,' she said.

Eve set the tray down and proceeded to pour while she spoke. 'He gives the girls drugs, most of them. And sometimes he will also beat them, but that maybe depends on the girl. Some of them are scared very easily, and he is very scary,' she said.

'If you know where this man is, why haven't you reported him to the police in Musina?' Reshma asked.

Eve looked back at Reshma, her face passive, but her eyes flickered in annoyance. 'Because Odi is paying the police there. And before that, he was in another house – near Louis Trichardt. And before that, he was somewhere else,' she said. 'If you try and complain about him, you get in trouble yourself. The police will not solve this man.'

Mrs de Bruyn chimed in. 'We think this man – Odi – he runs brothels. And a few other businesses. He takes young women, not just foreigners, also the ones who travel from the rural areas, the ones from the small farms in Limpopo, even KwaZulu-Natal, Mpumalanga, North West. And then also women from Zimbabwe, Nigeria, Malawi. He is a predator. He is very good at choosing his prey. And he moves a lot. He's hard to track. We don't have the resources,' she said, her voice giving away a sense of defeat.

Eve handed Mrs de Bruyn a cup of tea. 'What you do is more than others do. Don't diminish yourself, sister,' she said. 'God sees your work. And we do, too.'

Mrs de Bruyn gave a small smile.

'Do you have any photographs of the woman who is missing? What can you tell us about her?' Ian asked, trying to focus the still-nervous energy of the group into something productive.

Linda, sitting to his right, silently pulled a cellphone out of her pocket. She opened the screen and tapped on it a few times before handing the phone over to Ian and Reshma.

'This is Ernestina,' she said. 'We came from the lake, together. We cross the water, together,' she said, her voice and her speech more faltering and less confident than Eve's.

Ian wondered if Linda meant Lake Malawi. His grasp of geography north of the Limpopo River was pretty mediocre. The image on the phone showed a much happier and plumper-looking Linda posing with another woman. They were both in high heels and pretty dresses, glowing with fun. Linda held a champagne glass in her hand, and the other woman – Ernestina, he assumed – a bottle of what looked like sparkling wine. They were sharing a moment of the good life on camera.

Ian couldn't help but notice that happy Linda looked a world apart from the demure, conservatively dressed woman beside him. Current Linda was busy pulling at the edge of her bandage, which he could see poking out from under her sleeve.

Linda started speaking again. 'This picture was ...' she broke off and spoke to Eve in an unfamiliar language. Eve replied in the same.

'The picture was from eight months ago,' Linda said, in English again. 'Before her sister went missing. Before everything went bad.'

Eve noted the questioning looks from Ian and Reshma.

'My ex-husband was from Malawi,' she said. 'I learned to speak some of the language, and I taught him some Shona. Along with a few other things,' she said with a wink.

'And how do you all know each other?' Reshma asked. 'I mean, how do you know ... Angela, and Linda?'

Eve laughed at the question.

'I see Mrs de Bruyn has been too much her usual polite self to discuss us and our lives,' she said. 'I met them,' she said, looking at Mrs de Bruyn, 'when I was a sex worker.'

They had finished the first pots of tea by the time Eve and Angela de Bruyn had finished the explanations. Eve was completely unembarrassed by her former profession. 'Sex work is work, Captain Patel,' she had said, adding that hers had paid to get her children through school in the city, and enabled her to save up enough to start her coffee shop.

Eve's work had also brought her into contact with a number of women who were less fortunate than she had been. Eve was educated, and had also previously been married to a South African man – 'I like getting married,' she said, unapologetic – who had later left her with three small children, but also the paperwork that she required to stay legally in the country. When she had met her third husband – another

South African, and an Anglican – she had met Mrs de Bruyn and discovered the Mermaid Bureau. So she helped out when she could.

'Before I met Angela, "all night prayer" had a completely different meaning,' she said, laughing, miming body movements that conveyed sex acts. But a moment later the laughter faded, and she looked serious again. 'If Ernestina goes back with the same people who took her before, they might beat her. Hurt her even more, to convince her that she should stay where she is. Which is a worry. But ...' she trailed off.

'But the problem is that we don't know if that is what happened to her,' Mrs de Bruyn filled in. 'We just don't know. Our contact in Musina, she says Ernestina is still missing. But maybe they wouldn't take her back there?' she said, obviously worried.

'I know where they took her,' Linda blurted out. 'I have seen. I have seen her,' she said, her soft voice rising, her words running into each other. 'I can see her,' she said, as she began to cry.

She turned to Eve and spoke in her own language again, fast. So fast that Eve had to ask her to slow down so she could understand.

Eventually Linda stopped, slumped, tears streaming down her face.

'What is she saying?' Reshma asked Eve.

'She says they have her in the water,' Eve said. Her lips were pursed tight, as if she was annoyed with the other woman, or frustrated at the story of the missing woman.

Linda looked up and stared straight at Ian and Reshma. 'It is true. You believe me. She is in the water,' she said, as she pulled at the bandage on her arm and started scratching at the inflamed skin beneath. Running all the way around her wrist was a thick scab.

DEPARTMENT OF WOMEN

When Wilson Sobukwe arrived at the headquarters of his cash-in-transit task team, Reshma was in deep conversation with Colonel Noma Phalane. She had already given Scott and Dube the low-down on the links between the dead women, and explained what she suspected was going down in Musina – which was why she had called in her old commander, who was working on abduction and kidnapping cases, and who had both an interest in and the resources to more properly check out a violent pimp and alleged rapist with a side business in human trafficking.

Sobukwe glared at Reshma, Scott and Dube, but was polite to his colleague, greeting Colonel Noma as if nothing was out of the ordinary.

He called Reshma to his office the moment he'd put down his bags. 'What the hell is going on here?' he asked, closing the door as Reshma sat down.

Reshma kept her expression as calm as she could. 'When I found that money, and those guns at Park Station, I followed my instinct, which was to call you,' she said. 'Because I realised that the case deserved more resources than I would be able to give. Notwithstanding what you have done with this unit,' she continued, unable to stop her voice from getting sharper, 'there are matters that are now involved with these cases, which I do not believe you are willing or equipped to handle.'

She stared her commander straight in the face. 'There are women's lives at risk, and I was not prepared to let them die so you could call the police ten minutes, or an hour, or two days late, because ... I don't even know why, all I know is that I care too much about them to let you fuck it up,' she said.

Sobukwe was silent. Reshma had been expecting an angry response, for him to be defensive. But he looked crestfallen, embarrassed.

'Why did you do it?' she asked. 'Why did you let us go in, into that mess, without back-up? Why did you wait so long to call for help? When you promised. You *promised*. I trusted you,' she said.

'I'm sorry,' Sobukwe said, almost in a whisper.

'Sorry? Sorry's not nearly good enough. Claassen got shot because of you,' Reshma said. 'And however many of those guys escaped, because we didn't have enough back-up. You can never be sorry enough. Just tell me why, though. Why did you do that? Do that to us?'

Sobukwe sat down heavily in his chair. 'I can tell you why. It's not a good answer, but it's the truth,' he said. 'I waited until you and Wayde got there. I had to wait until you actually saw the heist in progress. I couldn't call it in before, because ... Captain Patel, you have no idea of how deep the rot goes on these cases. I was worried if I called it in too soon, there might be someone at SAPS in Meyerton, or Vereeniging, someone who was involved or on the inside. I don't know who to trust, and so I don't trust anyone. Same with the security companies. Too many rotten eggs, too many people who talk, or do something for money. People willing to do nothing, for the money. I just wanted to catch these guys.'

Sobukwe paused, and drew his fingernail across a paper on his desk. 'Do you know how many weeks, months, I'd been waiting?

Trying to track this gang? And then you come here, and three days after joining us, you spot them by chance. *By chance.* On the highway? There's no ways that opportunity would have come again. I had to take it. I couldn't afford to risk throwing it away,' he said.

'But you could risk me and Claassen? You were willing to risk our lives, for this?' Reshma asked.

Sobukwe stopped tracing his finger across the paper, and put his hand into his lap. Eventually he nodded. 'I thought you could take care of yourselves, and I was right. But, yes. If it meant a chance at getting to the heart of this gang, then yes.'

Sobukwe paused. 'Don't think I'm heartless, Captain Patel. That's what a commander has to do. He – or she – has to decide what they are willing to sacrifice, in order to advance. Those men, the men in that gang. They are killers. You know this. They have killed many people already. It is our job to stop them. And you did. You did your job. And I did mine.'

Reshma wanted to shout, or swear, but she couldn't think what to say, and she couldn't fault Sobukwe's logic, even though it was fucked up. 'Maybe you're right,' she said. 'Maybe me and Claassen, this is our job. This is what we signed up for. But those women who died, they didn't sign up for this. And our job is also to protect them. If you want to do the right thing, you could start by stopping the territorial pissing contest with Colonel Noma. She's good at what she does, which is why I called her. There are women, children, being abducted in Musina. Drugged, held against their will. One of them tried to escape, but she went missing two nights ago on her way to Johannesburg. If you want to help, why don't you go and ask those men we caught last weekend, go ask them what they do with the women, why they kill them. Figure

out if they can help us find *this* woman, before she winds up dead in
the water like the others.'

OLD MAN

Ian had just finished the interminable meeting that had been rescheduled from the week before and was about to check his work emails when he got a call from reception saying that Myburgh had come to see him.

'I'm still a fucking detective,' Myburgh said to Ian, shuffling up and down on the bricks outside as if he wanted to kill somebody. 'Jussis I wish I still smoked,' he growled.

'You sure you don't want to come inside? I can make you coffee,' Ian said.

Myburgh shook his head. 'I'm not going to come into your office and shit on you. I'm going to do it outside. What the hell are you up to, Cousin? I told you. I told you right at the start, I didn't want to get the fucking Body Corporate involved. I didn't want to get the owners involved. I told you my job – *my* job – was on the line here. I'm not some young fucker like you, all set up for this new South Africa. This is my chance. My chance to grow old somewhere nice, not dying in the fucking suburbs,' the older man said, practically spitting the words out.

'You think you know this shit better than me? I been doing this since before you were even born, Cousin. You think investigating some dead woman proves you're more right than me? Even her friends didn't care about her. They just left her to die,' he said. 'I'm not even the worst.'

237

Ian was so taken aback by Myburgh's outburst that for a few moments he couldn't think of what to say.

'You still don't know?' he asked.

The older man glared back at him. 'Know what?'

'The women in the car. They had nothing to do with the woman in the lake,' he said, almost enjoying exposing the faults in the old man's thinking. 'They all live nearby, Saulsville, Laudium. I spoke to one of them. She says the night you saw them leave La Gondola, she was passed out drunk on the back seat. She has braids. A bright pink top. She was wearing it that day.'

Myburgh hadn't stopped staring at Ian, but his expression had changed, his mouth no longer curled in spite and rage, but open in disbelief.

'And you know what else?' Ian said. 'Your mate, Kotze, he's the one who paid to have them let in. He's been paying Zebulon for months to turn a blind eye when he wanted to get women in and out through the booms. So you better hope that the cops don't come after your Body Corporate friend, if they ever try and find out the identity of the woman who they say drowned at the dam.'

Myburgh had closed his mouth, and his expression tightened again.

Ian blinked when he realised what Myburgh's look meant. 'You never even told them, did you?' he asked. 'You never even told the cops about the women in the car. Even when you thought one of them was the dead woman.'

Myburgh kept quiet.

Ian could feel his anger starting to rise. 'I'll bet you don't even know what the women are doing there. Did you know Kotze brings them in for "parties"? For gang members. All on the new side of the estate. In one of the show houses. They do whatever they like there, and they know you'll just turn a blind eye to all of it. Because nothing's more important than your stupid vanilla-colour house, and your handicap,' Ian said.

Now Myburgh was the one who blinked. When Ian looked again, he could see there were tears gathering in the old man's eyes. Myburgh didn't even try and wipe them away.

'I didn't know,' he said, his voice now low, and slightly hoarse. 'I didn't turn a blind eye, I just didn't know. I thought maybe … I thought … I don't know what I thought. Jesus Christ, Cousin. What am I?'

Myburgh was quiet again for a few seconds. 'Zebulon told you this?' he asked.

Ian nodded.

'You saw him? He's alright?' asked Myburgh.

Ian nodded again.

'Is he … is he really becoming a sangoma?' Myburgh asked at last.

Ian shook his head. And then he told Myburgh the truth.

*

Myburgh didn't say where he was going when he left, but an hour later he contacted Ian with the identity numbers of Snyman, Kotze and the other directors of La Gondola. Ian used the information to search through the company registration website and find out who was connected where.

For Snyman, and a few of the others, amnesty had proved profitable. Snyman alone held interests in five property companies – two of which were at Hartbeespoort, the others in North West and Limpopo – plus a handful of other directorships of companies that were registered but not public, and so Ian couldn't determine the real nature of their business. There were other names too. Sakkie van Rensburg. Barend van der Westhuizen. William Craig. All of them commandos. Colonels. Spies. Beneficiaries of both apartheid and democracy.

Ian felt ill every time he read the names. Many of these men would be in their late sixties, early seventies. They had lived long lives, untroubled by consequences or consciences, while Zebulon's generation grew up without fathers or mothers.

Still, evidence that a bunch of apartheid assassins and death squad members had gotten rich off their inhumanity wasn't, unfortunately, a crime. Not if they'd gotten amnesty for their past actions.

Kotze was evidently not high-enough ranked or favoured to feature as a director on any company list. Ian found him on Google – three reports in a community newspaper in North West, about a police official who had been suspended and then fired for misconduct. The final story mentioned a further charge of corruption against Captain Kotze, but there was no indication as to whether he had been successfully prosecuted.

Kotze's name also came up in the TRC reports, but only briefly. He had applied for amnesty for assault, and possession of stolen property. Kotze had evidently been involved in the detention of a member of the Azanian People's Liberation Army, after which the APLA member had been liberated of his car, his wallet, and the four sheep he was carrying in his bakkie at the time of his arrest. Kotze and two other cops involved in the incident had been refused amnesty by the committee, which found that Kotze's objective was more likely criminal rather than political. But, as in many other cases where amnesty had been refused, Kotze had never been charged or tried for any crime.

This told Ian two things: first, that Kotze wasn't important enough, to anyone. Second, it told him that, in all probability, Kotze was the kind of ex-cop who was skilled in making crime dockets disappear, or making sure that autopsies never happened. Kotze would no doubt be hoping that some day, if he curried favour long enough, he would be included in the ranks of the really Bad Boys. Or, Ian thought, Kotze could be playing an even sneakier double game, taking advantage of Snyman and co's properties right under their noses, without telling them. And, maybe he had decided it was time to increase his share of the pie.

Whatever the men had done in the past, it told Ian about their character. But it didn't prove that they were guilty of anything now. One thing Ian had come to appreciate even more since leaving SAPS was that even if the entire former Vlakplaas commando were busy committing crimes in the present day, without enough of the right kind of evidence, there would be no justice.

Reshma was juggling phone calls and WhatsApps from Colonel Noma and waiting to hear back from a penitent Sobukwe, who had gone down to Vereeniging to speak to the men they had arrested the previous week.

'I don't think any of them are talking,' she said to Ian. 'All we have are ideas, thoughts, feelings. It's so frustrating.'

She held her head between her hands, then rubbed her palms over her eyes. 'You really think there's a link between your Broederbond guys and ... this?' she asked, not for the first time that evening.

Ian was about to answer that he didn't know, not for sure anyway, when his phone rang. It was Myburgh, now back at the dam, and possibly slightly drunk, judging from the blur in his voice.

'Cousin!' the older man shouted over the phone. 'I need to send you a picture. There's a story. You must see. It's on the front of the *Kormorant*,' Myburgh continued, making no sense to Ian.

'What's a kormorant?' Ian asked.

'The *Kormorant*. Newspaper,' Myburgh shouted. 'Hold on a minute.'

Ian could hear Myburgh fumbling around with his phone, buttons beeping as they were pressed, then the call cut out.

A minute later, Myburgh managed to send Ian a slightly blurry photograph of what looked like the front page of a newspaper. The title said 'Kormorant' in big blue and white letters at the top. The headline underneath blared the news that half a million rounds of ammunition had gone missing from SAPS in the North West in the past year.

The story wasn't easy to make out on the photograph, so Ian googled the newspaper and found the story online – a parliamentary Q&A session where the police minister had indicated that millions of rounds of ammunition had simply gone missing from police stations across North West, not just in the most recent reporting year; over two million rounds had disappeared three years before that. In addition, the story noted, nearly seventy service weapons had disappeared from police headquarters in Pretoria.

Ian called Reshma over to look at the story. 'Maybe this is the guns,' he said. 'Now all we need to do is link them to the money.'

Reshma read over his shoulder. 'I'll let Sobukwe and his peers chase the money. You help me try find this missing woman,' she said.

GET UP IN THE MORNING

Reshma and Ian had suggested they use their house as a base, away from the bustle of the coffee shop, where they could regroup, and where Reshma could update Mrs de Bruyn, Eve, and Linda. Ian had asked if he should call Surprise, given her earlier help, but Reshma had been firm in saying no. 'I've already had one partner shot and killed. I can't risk ... I can't risk anything happening to her,' she said. Something in her expression told Ian it was best not to argue.

Eve was the first to arrive. Linda and Mrs de Bruyn appeared ten minutes later. Angela de Bruyn said she had been praying for Ernestina, and she looked anxious, and as if she had not had much sleep. Linda was gaunt and even more subdued than before. Eve clucked over the other woman and looked in Reshma's cupboards for rooibos tea and honey, to which she added some powders that she promised were not drugs, but which she said would help Linda with her nerves.

The women were mid-conversation when MaRejoice rang the doorbell. Reshma had totally forgotten that the sangoma had said she would come and visit, to look at the photos of the maimed women.

'Good timing,' she said, pretending that she had been expecting her all along. She showed MaRejoice into the kitchen and went to fetch another chair from the study so that she could sit with the other

243

women around the table.

Ian had gone to the shops to buy more milk, and Reshma quickly texted him to pick up some koeksisters or cakes for the sangoma.

Reshma's first job was to explain to the gathered women what Colonel Noma and her team were planning in Musina. Noma was going in, and they would spend the weekend at least, maybe longer, undercover, looking for information on this Odi person.

'The local police don't know this is happening. And they don't know anyone from Colonel Noma's team,' Reshma said.

Mrs de Bruyn nodded, but Linda asked Reshma how long she thought it would take for the police to catch Odi.

'They'll get in there as soon as they can,' Reshma said. 'But they need to wait to get the right evidence about this man. Otherwise there is the risk that he won't get prosecuted, that he won't go to jail. They know that there are vulnerable women being kept captive. But they can't take the chance of going in too soon and ruining their chance at making a case.'

Reshma realised that the more she spoke, the more she sounded like General Sobukwe, and she hated herself for it even though she knew that what she was saying was the truth.

Reshma didn't tell the women that she had initially wanted to join her previous crew going on the raid in Musina, but her former boss had vetoed the idea.

'You don't get to pick and choose, even if you find the cases. Or, it seems, they find you. You made your bed, Captain Patel,' Noma had cautioned her, although not in an unfriendly way.

Instead, Noma had delegated the case of the missing Malawian woman to Reshma, since it potentially fell between both units.

Ian arrived back just as Reshma started discussing what they were going to do about looking for Ernestina.

'You should listen to this, Ian,' she said, as he pottered around the counter, boiling the kettle. Although she'd discussed the broad strokes of what Colonel Noma and her team had found, there were additional details that Ian wouldn't know yet.

MaRejoice was sitting politely and listening to the conversation, occasionally staring at the other women, which they didn't seem to either notice or mind, but which distracted Reshma. As soon as Ian offered her more tea, and a syrupy koeksister, the sangoma appeared a little happier.

'So, we found out some more about your friend. But we still don't know where she is,' Reshma said, adding the caveat as quickly as she could, so that Linda and Mrs de Bruyn wouldn't get their hopes up. 'The Greyhound stop in Modimolle is at the Engen Garage on the N1. We got the camera recording from the forecourt for the time when Ernestina was travelling. She got off the bus to use the toilet and go to the shop in the petrol station. But she didn't get back on. The driver said she took her bag with her, and that he thinks he saw her go with someone who was in a dark double cab,' Reshma said.

'Is there any chance that Ernestina might have gone willingly with someone else?' Reshma asked, looking back at Mrs de Bruyn and at Linda. 'I mean, I have to ask. Maybe she didn't want to tell you? Is that possible? Is there anyone else she knows in South Africa? Or do you think she might have decided to ... take a client?'

Linda looked slowly at Mrs de Bruyn, and back at Reshma. 'Maybe,' she said, softly. 'But I don't think ...' her voice trailed off.

Mrs de Bruyn spoke up. 'I haven't met the woman before. I can't tell you what she's like. Despite where we're based, we're not one of the very strict religious organisations. We don't expect the women who come to us for help to become nuns,' she said. 'But still, many women, they hear it's a church, and ... sometimes they have bad associations with that. Not all churches have always been friendly to all people. Is there a chance she changed her mind? Maybe. But I can't assume that is true until I know. And I took responsibility for looking after this woman when she came to us to ask for help, and I said that I would help. Until I know that she is alright, I will not withdraw that offer of help.'

Reshma told Linda and Mrs de Bruyn that she had sat with Colonel Noma the previous afternoon, and that the CCTV footage had shown at least two double cabs passing through the Engen between 3 am and 4 am. But they couldn't make out the occupants – one because the car was too far away; the other because the cab had tinted windows.

'They have licence plate recognition software on the cameras there, so we have the licence plates. But we don't know if they mean anything so far. There are a few blind spots where the cameras don't go. Both of the cabs passed through at least one of the dead spots. So we can't tell if your friend got into either of them. We don't have anything on camera of her after she comes out the toilets, at about quarter past three,' Reshma said.

'Who were the plates registered to? Do you have that info yet?' Ian asked, standing at the side, drinking a mug of coffee.

Reshma looked back down at her notes. 'Noma says that one is registered in a company name. A property developer in Rustenburg. But their offices are closed for the weekend, and we don't have an after-hours number yet. The other was for a farmer outside Brits,' Reshma said. 'Her task team unit is following up on both of them, but we don't have any more information yet.'

'What about the water?' Mrs de Bruyn asked, exchanging a glance with both Eve and Linda. 'Linda said she had a ... feeling about Ernestina being in the water. The other night, you said you had other women, also. Women with that marking,' she said, pointing at Linda's now-covered wrist. 'Isn't that also a clue? Can it help us to find her?' she asked.

Reshma looked at Ian for a moment, and then she shook her head. 'The cases we've been looking into, they involve two rivers, one dam. One in Johannesburg, one to the south, in Sedibeng, one in the north, in Hartbeespoort. But it's not so easy just trying to find a body of water,' she said. 'Especially not once we look outside Johannesburg. You know, Modimolle used to be called Nylstroom, because the old Voortrekkers thought they had found the Nile River. There's a wetland there. There are hundreds of lakes and streams. Plus there are the warm springs in Bela-Bela ... there's no way we're going to find your friend if we're trying to look for a place of water. And at this stage, we don't even know *why* any of these incidents are linked to water,' Reshma said.

MaRejoice seemed to be trying to get Reshma's attention, lifting her eyebrows at her from across the kitchen table.

Whatever MaRejoice wanted to say was interrupted by a question from Ian. 'You said one of the bakkies was registered to a property company. Do you have a name for it? For the company I mean?' he asked.

Reshma consulted her notes again. 'Says here it's called ... Hexriver? Hexriv*ier* Eiendomme,' she said, stumbling slightly over the last word.

Ian's expression changed as soon as he heard the name. She watched him leave the kitchen, to return a few moments later with his laptop in his hands. He opened his computer and unlocked the screen.

'Just hang on a second,' he said, typing in the name of a website. He typed again, entering the name Hexrivier into a search bar.

Three listings come back with a positive match for 'Hexrivier'. One of them was the property company. There was a small blue hand icon on the right of the entry. Ian clicked on it, and then on the tab that said 'Director Details'.

A list of names appeared on the screen in front of Reshma. Afrikaans-sounding names, their ID numbers partly blocked out on the left-hand side.

Two of the names looked familiar to her, but she didn't know why. Ian read them both out loud. Isaac van Rensburg, and Barend Johannes van der Westhuizen.

'These are the same guys who own the La Gondola development. They're all linked, Reshma,' Ian said. 'These are the guys who have your missing person. I'm sure of it,' he said.

'Even if I trust your gut, Ian, it doesn't tell us *where* she is,' Reshma said, staring back at the screen.

MaRejoice held up her hand, and waved it slightly. 'I think I may be able to help you there,' she said.

*

Olwethu Mogaramodi was already a killer when he became isangoma, MaRejoice explained. He served four years of a seven-year sentence for killing his girlfriend. He had dreams inside Sun City prison, and when he came out, he went in search of how to be a free man while making other people pay.

MaRejoice made some joke with Ian, which Reshma did not understand, about using her 'sangoma phone' to track down the man who might have been responsible for at least one of the murders of the three women they had found in water.

'They say he is powerful. But it seems it did not stop him from being stupid,' MaRejoice commented. She explained about the new dark blue bakkie that Olwethu had bought himself, and which his cousin Thokozani had to drive because he, Olwethu, had no licence.

'Never believe what the newspapers write. There are not so many izangoma who will do this ... that kind of work. Human parts,' MaRejoice said. 'Mostly, the ones who do it are either very stupid, or very clever. This man, he thinks he is the clever one, but he is mistaken.'

After Ian and Reshma's query about the mutilated bodies and the cash heists, MaRejoice had made a few enquiries with unnamed clients and friends, and the families of friends, both in Alexandra and further north, around Tshwane. The name of Olwethu Mogaramodi had come back to her because he was boasting about his high-powered friends, and because he was flashing his money. Also because he had tried to charge a potential initiate nearly fifty thousand rand for being his gobela – his teacher and guide. According to MaRejoice, Mogaramodi was making a bad name for himself everywhere he went.

The man had been staying in Brits until the incident with his initiate, which prompted a small group from the community to come knocking at his door, suggesting that he leave. Now he was hanging around either in Soshanguve or Mabopane, with his cousin and the shiny bakkie. The man even had a Facebook page, with a photograph of the car.

'But just because he is stupid, don't think he is a fool,' MaRejoice warned. 'This man knows how to kill, without getting punished. And, worse, he doesn't kill just because it's a job and he gets money. This kind of person, they kill because they like it,' she said.

Reshma thought about what Ian had said, about the apartheid covert unit cops, and thought they sounded like they were a perfect match for this sangoma. 'Are you sure he killed them – the women, I mean?' she asked.

MaRejoice gave her a withering look. 'I'm isangoma, not a police-woman,' she said. 'That is your job. I am telling you what I am hearing. That this man could be involved in the crimes you are investigating. Finding proof of his criminal actions is still up to you,' she said. 'But if you know who he is, maybe you can see where he is, and maybe that helps you to find the woman you are looking for.'

Reshma took down the licence plate of the blue bakkie, and sent it on to Colonel Noma, asking for it to be marked as of interest – which meant that if any SAPS or Metro officers noticed the vehicle, they could report its location, but were not necessarily required to stop it.

Ian sent messages to Myburgh and to Zebulon. He texted the licence plate and details of the car, and asked Myburgh if the registration was on La Gondola's system anywhere. In Zebulon's case, he asked if either he or his partner had heard of Mogaramodi – or his cousin – with a note that if they did come across the men, he and Zakes should call it in, but stay clear of them.

Mrs de Bruyn and Linda sat, obviously impatient. Eve, as usual, looked perfectly relaxed and at home, but there was a spark in her eye that suggested she too was tired of sitting around.

'So, are we just going to wait?' the older woman asked. 'Shouldn't we at least head to where you think this man might be? Near Pretoria?'

Eve spoke up. 'I think she's right. We should go. Not just sit on our butts here. We're not manning phone lines or anything, like the nineteen-eighties. If someone needs us, they can call us on our cellphones,' she said.

The other two women nodded.

As much as Reshma didn't see that there was any benefit in driving aimlessly around Pretoria, she could also see that it was equally pointless sitting in Johannesburg when, in all likelihood, the missing woman was almost certainly somewhere in North West, if she hadn't been taken back to Limpopo.

'Look, I can't say what you can go and do there that's going to help,' Reshma said. 'Mabopane, Soshanguve, those are big places. If you want to drive even further, to Bela-Bela, you can go to the bus stop or the petrol station. I'm not going to stop you. But the only thing advantage is you might be closer to her when we do find her.'

The three women looked at each other, Linda making entreating eyes at Eve who was plainly the nominated driver.

'Then that will be good enough for us,' Eve said. 'If we can be closer to her, when help is needed, that will be enough.'

Reshma made sure that she had each woman's mobile number before they left. They made a plan to go past a tearoom in Lanseria, where Eve knew one of the owners.

Eve commented privately to Reshma that the drive would also help keep the other women occupied. 'They have nowhere to put their feelings right now,' she said, as if the same problem did not really trouble her.

'And you?' Reshma asked.

Eve looked back at her. 'I lost a child once,' she said. 'There is

251

nothing worse than that. And I recovered. Linda, she will also recover. Her sister is dead, but she doesn't want to accept it. We must do the best we can. That is all we can do. Except for you, and your friend. You have to do better than that, because that is why we need you. We are trusting you, Captain Patel.'

Once the three women had left, the house was quiet, with only Ian, Reshma and MaRejoice left.

The sangoma went and got herself a glass of water from the tap. 'I had too much sugar,' she said, with a small smile, before sitting down again.

'Do you think I should have let them go off on their own?' Reshma asked Ian. 'I mean, if there's a … bad sangoma in the area, like MaRejoice says, do you think it's a good idea to let a pair of civilians go off in search of him? I mean, not that I could have done much to stop them. But I don't like the thought of them getting themselves into danger,' she said.

MaRejoice gave Reshma a grin. 'I wouldn't worry about those two, they can look after themselves if needed,' she said.

'You mean Mrs de Bruyn and Eve?' Ian asked, gathering the cups and mugs and plates, and putting them in the sink.

'No,' MaRejoice said, showing her teeth. 'I mean Eve and Linda.' She did not explain the comment further.

Just then, Myburgh called Ian. The licence plate for Mogaramodi's bakkie had come back positive on the estate's security records.

Ian put the call on speaker.

'I checked – I did it without Kotze or any of them seeing me,' said Myburgh. 'That car you are looking for, it came here in March,' he said. 'The same week that woman in the dam got killed.'

Almost as soon as Ian put the phone down, Reshma got a voice note from Dube, bearing information from Sobukwe.

'He's too embarrassed to talk to you himself,' Dube's recorded voice said. 'He says he's only gotten answers out of one guy so far. The rest aren't talking. Nothing. The guy says they were all at that house we went to. And he says there was a sangoma there. Scary guy, in a blue bakkie. He says it was the sangoma who gave them the eyes. And did some other things, he wasn't exactly sure what they were. But he says he never saw the girl, or where the eyes came from.'

Dube was recording another note. Reshma waited.

'They all knew the sangoma killed someone on the river. There was a big thing about it being on water. They didn't know it was a woman,' he said.

Reshma texted back to thank him for the info. She got an emoji thumbs-up in response.

The dots were all connecting, but none of it helped her get closer to pinpointing where the missing Malawian woman – Ernestina – might be.

Taking a chance, she texted Sobukwe directly. 'We're going to head up to North West in the next hour. Anything you have that could pinpoint a location will help us,' she wrote.

Sobukwe was silent.

RAPTOR

It was afternoon by the time Ian, Reshma and MaRejoice reached the house of Myburgh's girlfriend, Mitzy. Myburgh had suggested the place as a rendezvous, as it was close to the dam, but away from the peering eyes of the estate. Mitzy had a small freestanding home in Kosmos on the northern banks of the Hartbeespoort Dam, purchased twenty years before with her late husband, who had died two days after taking his retirement.

Mitzy's home was full of porcelain and bric-a-brac, clustered around brass-framed photographs of her obviously large and extended family. There were also two newer photographs, of Mitzy with a happy-looking Myburgh.

Myburgh flushed when he noticed Ian looking at the pictures, but nothing was said, and nothing needed to be said.

The kitchen set-up had carried over from morning tea. Eve had arrived less than fifteen minutes after Ian and Reshma, with Eve and Linda looking like they were relieved to get out the car. They had dropped Mrs De Bruyn back at the church – in case someone was needed there – but had gone past Lanseria and reached all the way up near Hammanskraal, before turning back.

Mitzy, who ran a small catering and home-bake business, was thick in conversation with Eve, who wanted to learn about the older woman's biscuits and tarts.

Reshma and Ian were waiting for Myburgh to arrive – and, a late addition to their party, Zebulon, who was driving down from Ga-Rankuwa with Zakes and his gobela, who had some unknown issue with Olwethu Mogaramodi, and wanted an opportunity to join in the fray.

Ian thought there were too many people to get anything done effectively. He would have preferred if it had just been him, Reshma, and maybe MaRejoice. While he was watching and listening to everyone talk, he was also trying to work out how to divide the group so that he and Reshma could get to work.

Sobukwe had texted Reshma eventually, to add that the only other information he'd been able to get from the suspects was that there were two white men involved in managing the heist. The men couldn't describe the white men, either because they were afraid of them, or because they thought most old white men looked the same, which Ian thought was a fair comment. One of them did mention that one of the white guys had a boat, which he had used at the Vaal, a big boat that had come on a trailer with North West plates. When Reshma had told him about the potential link with Jan Snyman, she said that Sobukwe had become very interested.

'He told me to be careful, and to watch what I was doing – I think he thinks there's a chance for a big bust here,' she said.

Ian had called Myburgh to ask if Kotze had a boat of some sort, but the older man wasn't sure.

'Most of the guys don't keep their boats here anyway,' he said. 'They keep them at the yacht club, or the aquatic club,' he said. 'They used to be at the north dock, but that's overgrown with hyacinth. You'd need a tractor to get your boat out now.'

Ian went onto Google Maps on his phone to get an idea of the layout of the dam and its surroundings. When he switched onto satellite view, he could see how the invading hyacinth had crawled over nearly a third of the dam. North-east of La Gondola, he could see a flock of white shapes, half-trapped in the green-brown of the water plant.

'This sangoma guy, can he walk on water, or water hyacinth?' Ian asked MaRejoice, half-joking.

MaRejoice appeared to take the question quite seriously. 'I don't think so. Not unless he wants to invite trouble with Badimo,' she said. She did not pause to explain who or what Badimo was. 'This dam here, it is very polluted, yes? The same river by my house, it comes here,' she asked instead.

Ian nodded. 'Eventually, yes. It joins up with the Crocodile River. From what I read, there is pollution in all of them,' he said.

MaRejoice nodded. 'It probably suits him. Like this ... this plant that is growing everywhere. He is a man who thrives when things are full of shit,' she said. 'Also, he needs the water to be unclean. He is unclean, so he cannot work in a place where the water is pure, because then it will be stronger than him.'

Ian frowned at her, not quite understanding her words. The sangoma went on, but what she said didn't make any more sense to him. 'Water is neither good, nor bad. It can be used by some. The incautious ones. But if they are not careful, the water will take back what they have taken,' she said.

MaRejoice looked over at where the other women were sitting and talking. 'When are you going to tell them what you are?' she asked Eve and Linda, as they noticed her staring.

Both women immediately looked away, Linda dropping her eyes to the floor, Eve turning back to Mitzy.

Ian wondered if MaRejoice meant sex workers – and, if that was the case, why she was being so rude about it. He had never known her to be judgemental about those sorts of things.

After her outburst, MaRejoice was quiet until Myburgh pulled up a few minutes later. The old man looked hot and flustered despite the chill that had come with the late afternoon, a sign of a cold front, according to Mitzy.

Ian hadn't paused to think what impact the current events might have on Myburgh's long-term living arrangements at La Gondola, but he did ask Myburgh if he thought anyone had seen him or noticed his snooping.

'I don't think so, I don't think so,' Myburgh blustered. 'Ah, shit. I don't even know, Cousin,' he said, a second later. 'I don't think Kotze suspects me of anything. Funny, me thinking how stupid he was all these years, and him thinking the same of me.'

What Myburgh had learned, aside from the information about the other sangoma's bakkie, was that Jan Snyman had his own house at an estate called Waterside, on the other side of Pecanwood – a smaller development but with a lot of land between the properties, unlike the golf estate where the houses were almost terraced into each other, leaving more space for the greens.

Reshma suggested that the ever-expanding group should stay at Mitzy's and wait for news, and she and Ian and a few others would go out.

'Ian and Mr Myburgh can go to La Gondola, to look around the showhouse on the adjoining land. And me and ... MaRejoice, we can go to Waterside to look for Snyman's house, or maybe his boat,' she said, looking to Ian to back her up.

Reshma's suggestion was met with widespread dissent, with almost everyone except for Ian and MaRejoice disagreeing about where they should go and what they should be doing.

Eventually Reshma spoke up against the babble. 'This is not a democratic election process. None of you are police officers, and with the exception of Ian and Mr Myburgh, none of you have experience with handling criminal suspects. You can't just go into a private housing estate because you're feeling ... anxious and enraged,' she said.

'Neither can you,' Eve said, with her arms crossed over her chest. 'And anyway, how do you think you are just going to drive in there, to these white estates? To tell them what, exactly?' she asked.

'That's easy,' Mitzy piped up. 'We'll just say I'm bringing food for the clubhouse. I go there all the time,' she said, even as Myburgh started spluttering on the other side of the room.

'And what about her?' Eve asked, sensing her new acquaintance had something up her sleeve. 'How is Captain Patel going to go in? As your table decorator?' she said, with obvious sarcasm.

'That's probably not a bad idea,' Mitzy said, shrugging off the barb. 'But actually, I was thinking I could take the three of you,' she said, looking at MaRejoice, Eve and Reshma. 'You could all be waitresses,' she said, this time with a grin. 'I even have matching T-shirts you can wear.'

Despite Reshma's initial objections, after a few minutes it was agreed that Mitzy's suggestion probably made the most sense, and would give Reshma the best chance for a brief recce.

'We won't go in for long,' she explained, after conceding to the group decision. 'Just a drive around, then Mitzy realises she's made a mistake, and we leave. Is everyone agreed on that?' she asked. The other women nodded.

After some additional negotiation, it was agreed that Ian and Linda would go back to La Gondola with Myburgh, who didn't need any special access to get in – Linda went with in case she was needed to identify Ernestina – and that the rest of them would accompany Mitzy and Reshma to spy on Snyman.

As they were leaving, Zebulon arrived, his partner and his gobela on their own mission to track down the nefarious Olwethu's quarters. Once they had shared information with the rest of the group, it was decided that Zebulon would go with Ian's little band, because he knew where the parties had taken place.

*

Dusk on the dam was surprisingly beautiful. The sky transitioned from blue to hazy pinks and pearls that reflected off the water. In the soft light, even the hyacinth looked natural instead of predatory. The air smelled of Saturday evening braaivleis, even though it was now cold enough that Ian was shivering through the hoodie that offered scant protection against the air that whistled past their golf cart.

Myburgh drove while Zebulon gave directions in the fading light. Linda and Ian sat on the back, the woman staring out into the distance.

'It's a beautiful sunset,' Ian said, before realising she wasn't looking at the sky, or at anything, really. She was looking ... past things. Staring into whatever maze her present represented.

The golf cart made them invisible. Nobody even turned to look as they passed. Once they left the brick causeway, the cart navigated the veld and grass better than Ian had expected. They crossed an expansive green before reaching less-manicured veld.

'Hold on,' Myburgh called out, before slowing down so much that Ian wondered if it might not be quicker for them to walk the last bit.

The show houses for Haven Harbour were less than a kilometre from the perimeter of La Gondola. While the canalised estate had approximated a pseudo-Italian theme, Haven Harbour channelled the American East Coast, on an outsized scale. A grey and white clapboard colossus rose up behind a white gravel driveway, square-trimmed hedges framing the windows at the front. The house was lit from beneath, a ring of ground-level floodlights completing the monument effect. Against the dusk sky, the empty house looked somewhere between a Disney set and one for a horror movie. A shriek from an unidentified bird on the dam completed Ian's sense of the latter.

'This is where they had their parties,' Zebulon said, climbing off the cart before Myburgh had even come to a halt.

The house was a disappointment. Every room was neat. There was no evidence of any recent human presence except for that of the cleaners – Ian found what appeared to be a recently used dust cloth left on the side of the bathroom sink.

After thirty minutes spent scouring the property for clues, the four of them met back in the grandiose entrance hall and agreed that whatever might have been there before, all traces had been removed by now.

'We could ask the cleaners if they saw anything,' Zebulon suggested.

'Don't they all go home?' Ian asked, remembering the over-long explanation Myburgh had given him, about who did and didn't sleep over in the estate's tiny domestic quarters.

'No. Some of them, they stay over on weekends,' Zebulon said, matter-of-factly. 'Friday night, Saturday night – they'll sleep over so they can get to their houses early, before the madam and master wake up. Or to clean up after their parties.'

'We should have gone there first,' Ian said, looking at Myburgh and wondering if the old man was too blinkered or too biased to be helpful – and what else Myburgh might have neglected to tell him, or inadvertently covered up.

It took longer to get back to the staff quarters. Myburgh drove cautiously in the dark, and Ian grew grumpy and impatient at the back.

When they arrived at the squat brick block, Zebulon was greeted with warm smiles and hugs. Linda was met with curiosity, not all polite. She reciprocated by shrinking even further back into herself. Myburgh's presence was equally suspect. After a minute, Ian turned to Myburgh and suggested it might be better if he left them for a bit while Ian – who was possibly less threatening than one of the bosses – and Zebulon asked about the women.

Myburgh looked like he might argue, but evidently changed his mind. He left without saying another word.

Zebulon told the few staff that were there – about ten people, a mix of men and women – that Ian had been looking into the death of the woman in the dam, and that they were looking for another missing woman, who was a friend of Linda's. This prompted some discussion, and pointed speculation about Linda's presence.

Zebulon switched to Sepedi. The only word Ian could make out was 'sangoma'. This led to further talk.

'I told them we are worried that another woman is in danger. I said you were looking for that sangoma,' Zebulon explained. 'The one who drives that big double cab,' he said, adding the extra detail about the bakkie for the small audience.

A few people looked at Ian, and back to Zebulon.

'This is stupid,' Ian said. 'No one's going to talk while I'm here. I should have gone with Myburgh.'

But a second later, one of the women raised her hand. She spoke, quietly but clearly, directly to Zebulon. There were a few nods of agreement from the others.

Zebulon turned to Ian. 'Call Myburgh,' he said, his voice low. 'Tell him to come here. And to bring the keys. The keys for the staff rooms. They say they saw a bakkie like that earlier today. With Mr Kotze. But they say he was driving it, which is why they are confused. Mr Kotze was driving it, and another black man. Not isangoma. They said this man, he carried something like a bag into the end room – near the end where I used to stay.'

The woman was talking to Zebulon again, but Ian had stopped listening. He pulled out his phone and scrolled through his recent calls, hitting dial when he reached Myburgh's name. It took an agonising few seconds for the call to go through, but Myburgh answered almost immediately, as if he'd had his own phone in his hand, waiting. As soon as he heard Ian's request, he said he was turning around.

Zebulon turned to Ian again, his face sombre. 'We might have a problem,' he said. 'That woman, and two others, they say Kotze came back again, maybe two hours ago, with a trailer and a boat. And they took their bags and put them on the boat.'

'Where did they take the boat after that?' Ian asked.

Zebulon pointed in the direction of the water. 'They said they were going to the Crocodile River."

Myburgh arrived a minute later with the room keys, obviously energised by the possibility that they were going to find something. Ian hadn't called Reshma yet. He didn't want to update her before he knew that there was something to update, and what it was.

Another minute, and they had at least part of their answer.

The room Kotze and his associate had unlocked was empty, but there was evidence that someone had been in there until very recently. There was a small puddle of urine in the corner. It didn't smell rank like an animal's. It looked like human waste, produced by someone who had been embarrassed by their bodily functions, even in the worst situation. There were what looked like droplets of blood on the uncovered mattress that lay on the small bed fame, and several strands of long dark hair. Something about the position of the mattress made Ian look at it more closely. He pulled his hoodie sleeves over his hands so he could reach under the mattress, where his covered hands encountered something small. When he pulled the object out, he could see it was a mirror compact. On the glass, there was a fingerprint in blood.

MARINA

Reshma had almost refused to wear the pink golf shirt Mitzy had given her, which had a stylised heart logo making up the 'M' of Mitzy's name.

MaRejoice and Eve were wearing the same shirts. Wedged between them on the seats of Mitzy's people-carrier-slash-van were Styrofoam trays of empty meringue cups and a few ring trays of last-minute sandwiches, put together in Mitzy's kitchen and cut into triangles.

'Nobody checks these things,' the older woman had said. When they had arrived at the entrance to Waterside, Mitzy lied sweetly about having to take supplies to the clubhouse. The guards at the gate evidently knew her, and had no reason to doubt her story, or the trays of evidence in the back. As an aside, Mitzy asked if Meneer Snyman was in – she wanted to talk to him about another party, she said. The guards said that Snyman had been there earlier, but that he had left half an hour ago. When Mitzy asked, even more politely, which house was his, so she could leave a price list in his mailbox, the guards once again obliged. Being an old white woman really was the magic password to being trusted by everyone, Reshma realised.

Five minutes later, they were parked in the back section of the parking lot near the clubhouse. Mitzy pointed out directions to the house the guards had mentioned. While Reshma and MaRejoice went to go and look over Snyman's place, Mitzy and Eve would pretend to move food into the clubhouse.

'Take this with you, dear, in case you need it,' she said, handing a printed price list over to Reshma. Mitzy had indeed come prepared.

Reshma thanked her, and pulled on her jacket, covering not only the pink shirt, but also her firearm. She stuck her hand in her jacket pocket and felt the figure of the Ganesh that she had, at the last minute, decided to bring along. Then she and MaRejoice set off along a neat pathway that wound through a manicured lawn that was emerald green even in the middle of winter, and which was bordered by white and pink roses.

Reshma was too tense to enjoy the winter blooms, or the sudden pink of the clouds in the sky. She still wasn't sure if she wasn't on another wild goose chase, stuck with a sangoma, trespassing on a gated estate in Hartbeespoort, while Noma and the others were preparing for a raid in Musina. MaRejoice was unusually quiet, perhaps sensing Reshma's mood. Reshma was grateful for her silence, which gave her room to think.

She had no idea exactly what they were looking for at Snyman's house. Sobukwe had also made it clear to her that Snyman was considered something of a big fish, and that meant she had to be extra careful in how she proceeded. Snyman had money and motive. He was the kind of man who would have good lawyers. If she messed up, it might mean a court case that would draw out for years, leaving Snyman as another apartheid commander who would die, out of jail, never having had to serve time for any of the crimes he had committed.

At the same time, if he was involved somehow in the deaths of the other women, and the abduction of Ernestina, then Reshma would act.

'I understand why some of the robbers believe in ... muti and things,' she said, speaking in a whisper to MaRejoice. 'But these are death squad guys. Apartheid cops. Why would they be part of this? Surely they don't believe in it?'

Even in the dimming light, Reshma could tell MaRejoice was frowning at her again.

'Who knows what they believe,' the sangoma said. 'Anyway, you don't have to believe in amadlozi if you believe in power. These men, these apartheid killers, they have used murder as their source of power for years. Perhaps this is very familiar to them. Even you, you know what it feels like. To have the power to take a life. Except you are on the side of what they say is right. These men were also on the side of the law. Then,' she said.

Reshma grimaced at the comparison. 'Do you not think I'm on the side of ... of right?' she asked, suddenly aware of a deeper, unacknowledged need to be told that the acts she had committed in the last few days were the right ones. She had gone into a fight, excited. She had shot at other people. Taken another life. Maybe more than one. It was her job, and she was good at it, but right now she needed to know that it was more than that, and that what she was doing didn't make her a bad person – or that enjoying parts of it didn't make her a bad person.

'I'm here, with you, am I not?' the other woman asked. 'I didn't come to police you. I came because you – you and Ian – you need support. Sometimes more than you know. And you, I know you doubt. But maybe you need this even more than Ian does. Why else do you keep that gift from your mother in your pocket?'

Reshma reached back to her pocket instinctively, feeling for the reassuring shape of the Ganesh figure through the fabric.

'We are here,' MaRejoice said, pointing at a large thatch-topped house with a wood-burned sign that said 'Snyman' outside.

It looked like every other slightly overblown domestic dream that came as part of the package when you bought a house in a fancy waterside estate. A chimney with a hood shaped almost like a bird. A lightning protector for the thatch. The reassuring solidity of wood on the window frames, and pale cream plaster and paint on the walls.

It didn't look like a murderer's house, Reshma thought. But then again, murderers' houses very rarely did.

She and MaRejoice spent five minutes walking around the perimeter, pretending to be looking for the mailbox that was, quite clearly, next to the same wood-burned sign.

There were lights on inside, showing off a large open-plan lounge, more cream paint, but less fairytale-like than the outside. There were animal heads mounted on the wall. They were well-done, not the cheap taxidermies of warthog arses, but, still, dead once-creatures, staring lifelessly out towards the water's edge. There was a wall of alcohol on the one side. Good brands, from what Reshma could see. No cheap brandy for Jan Snyman. Death and booze.

The glass door to the lounge was slightly open, and MaRejoice gestured towards it, asking if they should go in.

Reshma was tempted, but after a moment's thought, she shook her head. 'This is too important to mess up. Unless you have a ... feeling that Ernestina is in there?' she asked, wondering if the sangoma had a special sixth sense about the missing woman.

MaRejoice shook her head. 'I don't know the woman; I can't just magically feel her presence. I'm not like a lightning rod for people,' she said, shaking her head in annoyance.

When they were back at the relative safety of the parking lot and Mitzy's van, Reshma checked her phone – she had put it on silent while they had scoped out the house.

She had missed three calls from Ian. When she called him back, he filled her in about the empty house, and what they'd learned about Kotze and the bakkie. When he told her about what they'd found in the staff room, her adrenaline spiked.

'Shit, Ian. I've got to get over to you,' she said. 'We've got to find them. Is there a boat we can use?' she asked. Her mind was jumping around from one place to another. She thought she remembered seeing a marina as part of the estate where Snyman lived – surely there would be some kind of boat there she could use, if there wasn't one at La Gondola?

Ian said he was just waiting for Myburgh to find out.

'I'll ask Mitzy how long it will take for us to get out of here and back to La Gondola,' Reshma said. Although the estates were not far apart as the crow flew, the complex arrangement of roads around the estates and waterways meant that, on the road, it could take twenty minutes to go between houses that were less than a kilometre apart.

Mitzy was coming down the ramp from the clubhouse, pushing some kind of trolley, with Eve walking behind her.

Reshma waited until they were at the van before she told them what Ian and Zebulon had discovered. She didn't mention the puddle of urine, but she did tell the women that he had found a compact under the bed, with a bloody finger print.

'You're sure that's what he said?' Eve asked. 'He said they found a mirror?'

Reshma nodded, but dismissed the question. 'We need to get back to La Gondola as soon as possible,' she said. 'Ian's trying to get us a boat.'

Mitzy headed back to the clubhouse, to make enquiries about the estate's boats.

Eve waited until the older woman had left. 'I'm afraid we can't leave just yet,' she said, her face serious. Reshma wondered if the other woman had taken leave of her senses, or just hadn't been paying attention.

Eve looked at MaRejoice. The sangoma looked back at her. 'If you don't tell her, then she won't understand,' the sangoma said, speaking to Eve, but glancing at Reshma.

'Tell me what?' Reshma asked, increasingly confused.

The Zimbabwean woman's shoulders dropped for a moment. Then she took a breath and steadied herself. 'That mirror. The fingerprint. It means she's given up. She knows she's going to die. It's ... it's a message. It's more than a message,' she said, fumbling for the right words. 'Do you ever wonder how these men, how men like this, could get these women to go with them? To obey them so willingly?'

'They give them drugs?' Reshma responded. 'Isn't that what you said, about that man in Musina? That he gives women rocks to smoke. And he gets them addicted, and that's how he keeps them hooked.'

Eve nodded. 'For a lot of women, that is how it works. For some, there are other things. You see ... Ernestina, Linda, they are not ordinary women. They are more like MaRejoice, more like izangoma – except they are not exactly the same. Maybe I could just say, they are women who have power.'

Reshma thought about Linda's reserved demeanour, her almost palpable fear of the world around her. She seemed the very opposite of

269

MaRejoice, who was confident, knowledgeable, assertive.

Eve was obviously thinking along the same lines. 'What you see now, in Linda, that is because these men – the pimp, the sangoma, the same ones – when they took her, they tried to make her their captive. That is why, that is why she has this line around her wrist,' she said, 'like bondage. Like a slave. She is still suffering. Like those other women you found. They were the same. These men had to scar them, to make handcuffs written in their skin, that cannot be broken, to control their power so the women could not fight back. With Linda, they didn't finish. But even that, you can see, is enough to make her very scared. To take away her strength. It will take a long time,' she said.

Reshma knew that there were cases where women had been physically and emotionally abused and tortured by their captors, often with powerful psychiatric effects, sometimes for years after. She wasn't in the right frame of mind to engage with whatever Eve was trying to say about the other women being magical, but she could accept they were traumatised.

'I don't understand what this has to do with the mirror, and why we need to stay here?' she asked.

Eve spoke again. 'The manacles, they are just one part of what the captors do to take control of the woman. There used to be old stories that if you wanted to catch a water spirit, you would have to use mirrors – or shiny metal, before they had mirrors – to trick her into thinking she was staring at the water. They give the woman a mirror, and then part of her is always trapped,' she said. 'You can also trap a spirit with a comb, with her hair. But a mirror is easier.'

'Then why did the other women have mirrors with them?' Reshma asked.

'Because, the mirror with the piece of that woman's spirit – they keep that one for themselves. And they give her back a false mirror. So she keeps looking, she keeps looking for herself in the other mirror, but she never finds herself there. If Ernestina has left her mirror, it means she has given up hope of ever being free. The only way she can be free now is to die.'

'Isn't there any other alternative?' Reshma asked.

Eve grinned at her. 'You have to find the mirror with the piece of the woman trapped inside. And then you have to destroy it, so the spirit can be freed. Or the comb. If there is a comb, you must break it,' she said.

Reshma tried not to look too sceptical. 'That doesn't sound too difficult,' she said.

'And then you have to kill the men who tried to bind the woman and her spirit to them,' Eve said, with a sinister smile.

MaRejoice was nodding at Eve's words.

'Now that part seems a little intense,' Reshma said. 'You say it's the only way?' she asked, still not entirely sure what she was hearing.

'Oh yes. The only way that works,' Eve assured her, putting her own wrists out in front of Reshma, and pulling back the thick bracelets she wore to reveal a pair of thin, identical scars around each wrist.

'We need to go back to this man, this Snyman's house, and find where he is keeping his charms or his amulets, where he is keeping Ernestina's other mirror. And maybe Linda's mirror, too,' she said.

'If what you are saying is true, why would he have them, and not the sangoma?' Reshma asked.

MaRejoice explained that the mirrors would have a great deal of potential power. 'These men, they pay a fortune to the sangoma to give them power. Not to keep the power for himself. No, this is something very valuable. Serious stuff. If this man is the leader, the boss, he will not give these items to anyone else, she said.

At that moment, Mitzy came back with a slight problem. 'It seems Meneer Snyman has just returned to his home,' she said, her cheeks flushed with worry. 'And he wants to find the caterer who was looking for him earlier.'

ROW, ROW

Myburgh left without finding a boat for Ian. 'I have to go and help Mitzy,' he said, as soon as Reshma had texted about Jan Snyman's unexpected return.

Which left Ian and Zebulon trying to get a small fishing boat with a forty-horsepower engine onto the water, and lined up with the estate's small wooden jetty. The pulling and pushing had tugged at parts of Ian's weaker shoulder, and a dull pain was already starting to throb through his arm. To make matters worse, he had soaked himself getting onto the boat. By the time he was seated in the tiny craft, Linda and Zebulon at the back, he was freezing.

Ian wasn't entirely comfortable about having Linda with them, nor could he leave her ashore on her own with the slightly inhospitable staff. He rationalised again that she was the only one who could properly identify Ernestina. That was if they managed to find her. The sun had dipped below the horizon, and stars were battling to come out through the slight smog or fog that dusted the lower evening sky. It wasn't pitch black, but it was easier to see the lights on the other shore of the dam than to see what was on the water.

The Hartbeespoort Dam spread over nearly nineteen square kilometres. Where the Crocodile River entered was somewhere to Ian's south-east, which was where he headed.

He hadn't used a fishing boat for nearly thirty years, not since his father had taken him on a water skiing trip to the Vaal when he was a child.

The engine started easily, and Ian was almost grateful for its slight under-power because it excused the slowness of his movements. Zebulon held a torch out in front of them rather than switch on the boat's floodlight, while Ian tried to navigate away from the shore and roughly towards what he imagined was the right section of water. There was a tiny compass on board, and Ian took a few moments to orient himself. They were only a few metres out, and it was already almost impossible to distinguish where the black water ended and where the land began.

The putt-putt-putt of the engine sounded ridiculously loud to Ian, cutting across the water, but also drowning out all other noise.

'You need to use your other senses,' Linda said, from her bench in the back. Since they had moved onto the water, her posture had shifted. There was something more assertive in the set of her shoulders, and in her face.

'People never use their senses properly,' she said. 'Turn off the engine. Turn off the light. Don't try and use your eyes, and your land senses,' she said. 'Try and think like the water.'

Ian looked at her, not understanding.

'Use your ears,' she said.

'Do you know how to start the engine again, if I switch it off?' Ian asked Zebulon. The other man nodded, although he didn't look entirely confident. Ian was going to have to trust that it was good enough. A few seconds later he killed the engine. Then he asked Zebulon to turn off the light.

For a second, darkness swallowed them entirely.

Then, moment by moment, the details came filtering through. First, sound. Water lapping at the side of the boat. A splash of water – small. A frog, or a fish. The noise of frogs croaking. Ian's eyes adjusted at last, and the stars came back into focus above, smudged along the sky.

Across the water – from somewhere else – he could make out voices. Male voices. More than one. He kept absolutely still as he tried to listen. The water made it hard to know where they were coming from. Were they to his right? Or behind him?

'Aim to your east,' Linda said, from her seat. 'I can hear them. If you paddle, I will guide our direction. We are far, but not too far.'

Ian and Zebulon each took one of the blue-tipped paddles on the boat's floor, and moved to either side of the boat. They half-watched each other as they dipped the oars in the water, trying to match their timing. Zebulon was much smaller than Ian, but he was strong, and more than once Linda made them stop so she could correct their direction.

Ian was sweating from the effort by the time Linda put up her hand and signalled that they should stop.

The water slapped against the side of the boat, and a man talked. The water carried the sound so clearly, it was as if they were a metre away from the boat – instead of more like fifty metres, Ian thought, now that he could see the hulking shape of the canopied speedboat up ahead.

'I swear, I heard an engine earlier,' came one voice. White male.

'Just shut up, Kotze,' said another. 'Let's finish our business, and then we done.' A black man speaking. Olwethu. Or perhaps his cousin.

275

'Where's Snyman?' asked the black man. 'What did he say on the radio?'

There was a pause. 'He's just dealing with something at home. He said you should go ahead without him.'

One of the men made a spitting sound.

The black man spoke again. 'Okay. Fine. We do it now. It's dark. It is time,' he said.

A few seconds later a spotlight came on, coming from the side of the boat, pointed down at something in the water.

Ian hoped they weren't going to use it to check the dam around them, because if they did, they would spot their little fishing boat almost immediately.

He heard Linda make a hissing sound, and when he saw what was in the water, he understood why.

The spotlight was pointed at a woman. She was alive – and somehow holding her arms and shoulders just above the water. It looked like there was something around her, a ring of some sort. The distance made it hard to make out details, and the dark and light played tricks so that the woman's face looked peculiar. Her eyes appeared too large, too dark.

Behind him, he could hear Linda starting to cry.

'Is that Ernestina?' he whispered.

Linda nodded, wiping her face.

The woman in the water made no attempt to get away. She was barely even moving. Which, Ian suspected, was possibly a result of the cold. It was increasingly bitter above the dam's surface. Although, he reminded himself, the water was possibly warmer than the surface in places.

'What if this one doesn't work?' Kotze's voice again. 'You promised the last one would work, and it didn't.'

A third voice, another black male, different to the first. 'The last one did not work because your crew were not honest. Shadow man, he likes himself too much. He is the one who made your work fail. You can ask him if it is true,' the voice said.

There was a pause. 'You know I can't ask him anything. He's dead,' said Kotze. 'Anyway, get on with it.'

Under the light of the hand-held spot, a man with short dreadlocks leaned forward off the boat, towards the woman who was still floating in the water, her face turned up towards him.

The dreadlocked man could be a match for the pictures Ian had seen of Mogaramodi. He held out his hand and another figure behind him – presumably his cousin Thokozani – passed him what looked like a large blue plastic bag.

As Ian and Linda and Zebulon looked on, Olwethu Mogaramodi placed the plastic bag over the woman's face, and began to suffocate her.

BOOM

Reshma stared across the table at a killer.

Ian had told her about Jan Snyman's past, and had shown her the reports from Snyman's testimonies at the TRC. But even if she hadn't been told a thing, she would have known from looking in his eyes. Snyman's eyes were bright blue and utterly terrifying. He would look the same if he was just chatting to you or strangling you to death on a bare piece of veld in the middle of nowhere, so that he didn't get bloodstains on the backseat of his car.

Despite Reshma's insistence that they had not entered Snyman's home, nor done anything more than look through his windows – which was not illegal, even on a private estate – Snyman had insisted on calling the local SAPS and waiting for an officer to arrive before he would allow Reshma and the other women to leave.

After sending her message to Ian, Reshma had texted Sobukwe a quick update and settled in to wait. Mitzy and MaRejoice sat a few metres away against the clubhouse wall, silent, staring at the ground. Eve had somehow managed to give the security guards the slip, but nobody except for Reshma and the women appeared to have noticed. MaRejoice had gestured that she thought Eve was fine, and so Reshma decided not to draw her absence to anyone else's attention.

Snyman sat at a table at the centre of the dining room, his hands empty like an honest man. His hair was mostly white, with some darker flecks at the temples, and towards the nape of his neck. In the past, Reshma thought he might have been considered handsome, except for an almost imperceptible weakness in the line from his nose and mouth to his chin. Reshma couldn't put her finger on it, and yet it made the otherwise ordinary man appear as if something was very slightly wrong.

'I still have friends,' Snyman said to her, calm, impolite. He had no lack of confidence in his own bravura, it seemed.

Reshma was trying to keep a poker face, but she was also twitchy not knowing what was happening with Ian and the others. She kept glancing at her phone, which had remained as black and still as the dam water visible through the large glass sliding doors to the north of the clubhouse.

'Are you expecting a phone call, Captain Patel? Perhaps you have somewhere else you need to be? Something else you need to worry about?' Snyman asked, his measured voice deliberate in its provocation.

Reshma simply let the silence draw out between them. It was bad enough that she was stuck in the clubhouse wearing a pink shirt with a giant scribbled heart on it, bad enough that Ian was busy helping the people who needed her help. She wouldn't give Snyman the upper hand with a knee-jerk response.

She thought carefully about her next words. 'You were, what, a Colonel when you left?' she asked. 'It must be distressing for you. After all you did. All those people you killed, and still you failed. It must be hard to see a brown woman like me with a commission.'

Snyman's head drew back, an almost reptilian gesture. For the first time since they had sat down, his eyes showed some sort of real expression other than annoyance.

'Absolutely not, Captain Patel,' he said. 'I am not a racist. Those media reports, they wanted to demonise me. Make me look like I was some kind of psychopath. That is not true. I killed white men, too, if that was what I was told to do. You don't understand how it was. How it is. I was just a servant. What I did was necessary for the stability and for the safety of the state. If you look, properly, at history, you will see that it is true.'

What made Snyman more terrifying, Reshma realised, was that he obviously believed his own version of the past.

'So why are you still killing black girls now, Mr Snyman?' Reshma asked, landing the hook. 'Are you doing it for the power, or because you need the money? Because something tells me it's not for the state any more,' she said.

Snyman went quiet again, but he remained puffed up. Like a snake waiting to strike, Reshma thought.

The stand-off was disrupted by the sound of some sort of commotion outside the clubhouse doors, which resolved into Myburgh trying to make his way through to Mitzy.

'You leave her alone, you bastards,' he was calling.

'Leave him,' Snyman said, waving for the estate's security guards to stand down.

Snyman looked Myburgh up and down, seeming to pause on every one of Myburgh's shortcomings. The cheap trousers. The stomach that protruded above his belt. The red-flushed face contrasting with his yellow-white hair.

'You're still too stupid to do the job your superiors asked you to do,'

Snyman said, bored, not even bothering to look Myburgh in the eyes.

Myburgh's flush deepened, but he kept quiet, although Reshma could see Mitzy was dying to step in and say something.

Myburgh looked around the room, and noted MaRejoice. If he noticed that Eve was missing, he did not mention it. 'You can't keep them here,' he said at last.

'I might want to press charges. For trespassing,' Snyman said, his voice taunting everyone in the room.

Myburgh looked at Snyman and burst out laughing. 'Is that it? Is that the best you've got? Twenty fucken years killing people for the government, and you want to threaten a few women with a bunch of sandwiches, with trespassing,' he said. Myburgh's face grew redder still as the laughter rode up and down his body.

Snyman went dead still, his lips pursed together. Reshma wondered if the hitman had ever been made fun of before. Who would dare?

At that moment, her phone lit up with a throng of messages that had been fighting to get through. She tried not to show any hint of emotion as she grabbed her phone and looked at the screen. She kept her face expressionless, but couldn't help taking a deep, audible breath.

'Bad news?' Snyman asked, his face and body back under control, a slight smile on his face as he returned to the familiar territory of fear and intimidation.

Reshma looked him straight in the eyes. She paused for five long beats, trying hard not to let any emotion show in her face. 'Yes. It seems you don't have quite as many friends as you think you have,' she said, allowing herself a grin at the end of her sentence.

With perfect dramatic timing, Major General Wilson Sobukwe walked in through the clubhouse doors. The smile he gave Jan Snyman was something that Reshma wouldn't forget in a long time. It was the smile of a predator who knew he had finally caught the prey he'd been after for a long, long time.

Sobukwe was about to introduce himself when, a hundred metres away from the clubhouse, Jan Snyman's house blew up.

In the flickering light of the blaze, Reshma thought she saw the figure of a woman run towards the slick waters of the dam, and dive in.

'Is that something you need to worry about?' MaRejoice asked an ashen-faced Snyman.

SLIPPING

Behind Ian, Linda opened her mouth to scream, but no sound came out.

Fifty metres in front of them, a man was killing a woman who was floating in a circle of light in the middle of the Hartbeespoort Dam. The illumination from the spotlight cut off on the surface so abruptly that it looked like it was being swallowed by the black water.

The woman didn't move, didn't even put up a struggle as the sangoma tied the bag around her face, and put his hands around her throat.

Ian drew his weapon and tried to stand. He felt the boat rock sickeningly underneath him.

To his left, Zebulon let out a whimper. 'I can't swim,' the younger man begged, suddenly afraid where before he had been assured. Ian wished he had asked before they had left dry land. Zebulon's bravado might be disastrous for them all.

'What about you? Can you swim?' Ian asked, glancing back at Linda.

The woman nodded.

Ian tried to keep sight of the scene ahead of him as he moved into a crouch more slowly this time, his firearm out in front of him in ready position. He couldn't risk hitting the woman in the water, so he aimed for what he hoped was one of the figures on the boat. Even if he clipped one of them, it might be enough of a distraction to get them to stop the killing. He wasn't sure what he would do after that.

Just as Ian was about to shoot, somewhere behind him, something big exploded. The boat rocked, either from the boom or from something else. Ian heard splashes of water on the side of the boat. The sudden noise and light and movement made him lose his footing again, and he fumbled with the grip on his gun as he swung his arms trying to regain his balance.

There were shouts from the boat ahead of them. The spotlight swung around, then dipped down, as if whoever had been holding it was experiencing the same loss of equilibrium as Ian. By the time the light shone back on the circle in the water, the woman was gone. The piece of blue plastic that had been covering her face bobbed limply on the surface.

The shouts came louder now. The spotlight swung in wide and erratic circles. It was only a matter of time before they saw Ian and his tiny boat.

He looked behind him and saw that the bench where Linda had been seated was empty. He thought back to the swaying boat, the splash in the water.

'Jesus', he cried, grabbing at Zebulon, barking out quick instructions for him to get the light back on and shine it on the water. Ian was past caring whether the others saw them or not. Right now, there were two women in the water, and he had to decide how he was going to try and help them.

'Shine on the water – follow me if you can', he called to Zebulon. 'And if you lose me, then start the engine and go back to the jetty.'

Ignoring Zebulon's protests, Ian held onto his weapon, and flopped backwards over the side of the boat and into the water.

The cold hit him like a punch as he dropped down into the dam, and then through the icy water. In his haste, he had forgotten to take a breath before he went under, and now his lungs were fighting at him to inhale, anything. All he wanted to do was go up and breathe. Except he wasn't sure which way was up. Everything was dark. His eyes were open, but he could see nothing, except black.

A second later there was a noise, then a glow as Zebulon managed to restart the tiny fishing boat's engine, and get the floodlight going. Ian kicked his body towards the beacon, trusting that he would reach the surface before his lungs won the argument with his brain.

He broke through the water with a gasp. A second later the light found him, and nearly blinded him. Ian swore and swivelled in the water so the light would be behind him. The glare had blinded whatever night vision he'd had before. He could barely make out the second spotlight, ahead. The three other men were searching for their missing woman with increasing desperation, ignoring the other light on the side.

'Keep shining the light,' Ian cried, and he dived down again, this time taking a moment to breathe before going under. He paused and kicked around, trying to make out anything below the surface. It was all murk and darkness. He surfaced again and caught a movement somewhere to his right. A shape, and a splash of water. Something big. Big enough to be a person. Another shape.

'There,' he said, shouting for Zebulon, not caring that the other men might have heard it too.

Ten seconds later, the spotlight from the bigger boat turned towards Zebulon, catching on the reflective white sides of the craft. Zebulon stood in the middle, petrified into immobility. A shot rang out from the larger boat, and Zebulon ducked with almost comic slowness.

Ian didn't stop to think if his weapon would work. He took aim from the water and fired twice in the boat's direction. Incredibly, both shots went off perfectly, the spent cartridges leaping into the water. Ian didn't think he'd hit anything, given where he was shooting from, but he heard one of the men cry out in alarm, if not in pain.

'Go, go,' he shouted at Zebulon. 'Go back to shore. Get Reshma,' he called, as he started swimming away, towards a clump of water hyacinth that he hoped might give him some cover in the chaos.

Zebulon gunned the engine and started to move away. Ian heard three more shots being fired. He even heard the bullets enter the water, close enough for him to know that he was lucky not to have been hit. For a moment, he wished he'd had MaRejoice prepare him some kind of protection for this battle. He tried to keep his own weapon above the surface, to limit the chances of getting the bullets wet or debris into the barrel.

From the other boat, the men were still shouting at each other, making it easier to find them in the dark. The sangoma was shouting at his cousin to get into the water, and find whoever was shooting at them. The spotlight was replaced by torches, flickering over the water like fireflies.

The cousin was shouting something back – it took Ian a second to make out what they were saying. It seemed like there was something in the water. Perhaps it was the woman. Ian wondered if it could be Linda.

The men on the boat carried on arguing among themselves.

Eventually one of them agreed to climb down into the water and swim towards whatever it was they thought they had seen. Ian could hear a splash as the first man entered the water, followed immediately by several colourful curses to do with the water's temperature.

'There, there,' one of the voices on the boat said, drawing a line with his torch, pointing to a patch of water five metres away from where the swimming man bobbed.

The man in the water swam slowly to where the torch was pointing 'She's not here,' he said. 'It's just plants.'

And then the black water grew arms, and a mouth full of teeth, and dragged the man down beneath the surface so fast he barely had time to scream.

Ian nearly screamed himself. There *was* something in the water. For a few terrifying seconds he wondered if it could be a crocodile – surely the river had been named for real crocodiles, once upon a time. There was always a chance that some of the animals had managed to return, and make their home on the Hartbeespoort Dam's banks.

Ian felt utter terror, and suddenly very, very alone. For a moment he was so overwhelmed that he nearly stopped treading water and almost let his body sink to the bottom. Wherever the bottom was. He had no idea how deep the dam was, nor how far he was from the shore.

All he knew was that there was something in the water, and that he had to get out. And his only option was to make his way onto the other boat, where the two men still were.

Ian slipped under the water again and prayed to his ancestors.

He surfaced a few metres closer to the boat, but still not quite close enough to climb on board. He tried very hard not to think about whatever was in the water, and how it might be coming for him next. He concentrated on the distance in front of him, and the other problem: that Kotze and the sangoma were on the boat.

They were still arguing. In between their dispute, Olwethu was calling out his cousin's name, calling on the other man to come back, even though the tone of his voice suggested he knew that Thokozani was long gone beneath the surface.

Ian had just about reached the boat's side when he saw something move in the water again. He huddled closer to the boat, begging the water not to betray his presence, and hoping the craft would hide him. He wondered if his shoulder would take the strain if he tried to drag himself up.

The figure in the water had no such constraints. It pulled itself out of the water, and over the rails, with an almost supernatural grace. Silhouetted against the smudge of sky, Ian thought it looked like a woman. For a second, he had a strong sensation of déjà vu. He thought the figure was wearing a pink top, but it was hard to see because the top was wet, the woman was wet, and it was dark except for the torches of the two men on board. The figure sloshed its way along the boat towards Olwethu and Kotze.

Kotze was the one who spoke first. 'What do you want?' he asked, his voice rude and arrogant, even as Olwethu started pleading for his life.

Ian didn't get to hear their responses because whatever happened next was drowned out by the sound of Kotze screaming.

A second later, there were two loud splashes, then a third.

When he swam around and looked up, the top of the boat was empty. He could hear frantic splashing in the water beside him, not far away, and then silence.

For a moment, he took some minor comfort in the thought that with two new bodies in the water, whatever creature had taken Thokozani might just as easily take one of them instead.

Then he felt a hand on his calf, and he was pulled under.

The second time Ian almost tried to breathe water was somehow easier than the first. Like he had given himself over, no longer playing out the trauma of 'not this, again'. His mind just started shutting down instead, forcing everything into slow motion.

He could hardly see anything, but he could feel. Arms, legs, hands. Something human. Something not human. Part of his brain insisted that it was a panicked Linda, dragging him down beneath the water, driven mad by her own fear of drowning.

Except Linda didn't have a head with a crown of bone and skin like a lizard. And Linda didn't have a mouth with rows of teeth, and black dead eyes.

Ian knew he couldn't see underwater; it was too dark. Perhaps this was what his mind was conjuring up for him. A monster, wearing Linda's clothes. Not just one monster, two. Three. Dark eyes and sharp teeth and strange faces.

He opened his mouth and prepared to take what would be his last breath.

And the creatures, the things of his imagination and his nightmare, took pity on him and pushed him to the surface. His head broke the water surface like a champagne cork. He breathed in for the first time in what felt like forever, and let out a scream of absolute relief and terror.

He felt hands take him, lift him, impossibly, from the water and onto the boat. And then he was alone, sodden, on the floor of the craft.

The night's darkness stretched into the water's darkness, and the only sound around him was of the water, splashing. He imagined that he could hear the screams of dead men from under the surface.

And then Ian breathed out, and closed his eyes, and saw nothing more.

BREAK

In the end, there were details that were confusing, but which didn't seem to matter.

Like how Eve had managed to swim from Waterside all the way to a boat in the middle of the dam. Or how she had gotten Ian and Linda and Ernestina out of the water and to safety. She joked about once having helped Kirsty Coventry train for the Olympics.

What was important was that Linda and Ernestina were safe, and, judging from Mrs de Bruyn's updates, in good health and good spirits. They had promised to all meet for coffee at Eve's restaurant once the two were settled into their new apartment.

Eve's water heroics also served as an alibi for her allegedly setting fire to the expensive brandy in Jan Snyman's bar, which had somehow caused a gas canister attached to the kitchen stove to explode, setting the thatched roof alight. Everyone agreed that it was not possible for Eve to have had enough time to set fire to Snyman's house *and* reach the boats in time to save everyone else. Since the other women were literally in the same room of the clubhouse as Snyman at the time his house went boom, the arson suspect remained unknown and at large, although Reshma had heard the investigators comment that a large collection of women's trinkets – mirrors, combs, and even some jewellery and clothing – had been found in one of Snyman's cupboards, all damaged beyond repair from the fire.

By the time Zebulon and Reshma had managed to get to Ian, they could find nothing of the other men. It was assumed that they had drowned, but only one of them – Kotze – washed up on the dam's shore, and even then, only in parts. The post-mortem noted a number of claw-like marks on the flesh, but these were attributed to carrion birds, or possibly an otter.

The fire at Snyman's house had destroyed almost all the evidence that might have implicated the former apartheid hitman in the recent spate of cash heists. Luckily, Zebulon's boyfriend, Zakes, and his gobela had discovered a stash of incriminating items, including photographs and recordings of phone calls, stored in a back room of a home rented by Olwethu Mogaramodi's cousin, where the sangoma had lain low after his retreat from Brits. Thanks in part to this haul, Sobukwe was able to link Snyman directly to a firearm and a stash of ammunition, both of which were traced back to a much earlier heist in Rustenburg two years earlier.

Two days after the fire, Colonel Noma and her team, assisted by Scott and Dube, raided a brothel in Musina. In the basement, they found four teenage captives, and a large stockpile of nyaope, which the owner was using to flood the townships near the borders. The man known as Odi initially escaped, but was picked up less than twenty-four hours later by a female police officer during a standard stop-and-go on the N1 highway. While Odi's arrest was cause for celebration, it also brought less-happy news for Linda; it was confirmed that her missing sister had been one of the women the trafficker had sold on, and she was presumed to be dead.

Three months later, shortly after Wayde Claassen return to active duty with the Special Priority Crimes Unit, Reshma saw a front-page story in the *Mail & Guardian* about a tender fraud involving the company that was managing the railway services sites – which had led to toxic acid minewater seeping into a poorly repaired sewer main, and which had eventually bubbled up above ground near one of the all-night fast food places. For months after that, people made jokes about the colour of the fried chicken at Park Station.

MaRejoice and Eve invited themselves for tea at Ian and Reshma's home, obviously now thick as thieves. Reshma didn't ask about what MaRejoice had said regarding water spirits, and Ian didn't talk openly about the things he had seen in the water. They shared strong tea with biscuits that Eve had made, using Mitzy's recipe.

But Ian, who was still haunted by dreams of women with black eyes and crowns made of bone, quietly asked MaRejoice if she knew anything about mermaids.

'I've never seen a mermaid,' she said, a spark in her eye. 'But if I ever did, I wouldn't want to know any more about her. Some magic, you don't want to look at directly. Or even over your shoulder. You just know that it is there, but you don't always want it to know that *you* are there. Do you understand?' she asked.

Ian thought that he did but, later, when he caught Eve glancing at herself in one of the mirrors, he wondered if he understood anything at all. When Eve noticed him looking at her, she winked.

ACKNOWLEDGEMENTS

It is nearly a decade since I sat in a small Maboneng apartment with Gogo Nokulinda Mkhize (aka Noksangoma) and we discussed mermaids trapped in the Hartbeespoort Dam. The idea stayed with me, not because it seemed implausible but because it had the feeling of truth (this might not be your truth, but that doesn't mean it isn't so).

Years later, when I asked Gogo *why* people would hold water spirits against their will, and why they might be mutilating and murdering these beings, she said, bluntly: 'battle magic'. At which point the plot for *Three Bodies* took an unexpected turn into the world of cash-in-transit heists.

This book would not have been possible without the help, input, guidance and knowledge of a number of remarkable women. Journalist Anneliese Burgess's gripping book *Heist!* provided an excellent, well-researched portal into the brutal world of cash-in-transit heists and gangs and the police who try to stop them. Anneliese and crime reporter extraordinaire Mandy Wiener both gave me valuable input on the nuts and bolts of my text, as did a number of police officers, who corrected my language, my assumptions and my crime scenes. It has become quite popular to criticise the SAPS for what they are not doing. But honestly, I have only awe and respect for these men and women who put their lives on the line for us every single day.

I am grateful once again for the wisdom of Gogo Malepena, Malehloenya Tsoaeli, for reading my manuscript and suggesting corrections and solutions that reflected thought and depth while allowing me to keep true to the whodunnit that I had threaded. Thokozani, Gogo.

I would also like thank my publisher Andrea Nattrass and my superb editor Helen Moffett. It always feels like I have won the jackpot working with both of you.

This is a work of fiction embroidered over a map of Gauteng, and I have liberally appropriated real buildings and organisations and turned them into places of imagination. There are a few real characters that make an appearance: I half-apologise to Louise Ferreira for turning her cat, Stoffel, into the bestest K9 ever; and, while Lucci's is long-gone from Brixton and Westdene, for the record his oven-baked pizzas and calzones were the stuff of legend.